PRAISE FOR RACH

"*The Consequence of Loving Colton* is a must-read friends-to-lovers story that's as passionate and sexy as it is hilarious!"

—Melissa Foster, *New York Times* bestselling author

"Just when you think Van Dyken can't possibly get any better, she goes and delivers *The Consequence of Loving Colton.* Full of longing and breathless moments, this is what romance is about."

—Lauren Layne, *USA Today* bestselling author

"The tension between Milo and Colton made this story impossible to put down. Quick, sexy, witty—easily one of my favorite books from Rachel Van Dyken."

—R. S. Grey, *USA Today* bestselling author, on *The Consequence of Loving Colton*

"Hot, funny, and will leave you wishing you could get marked by one of the immortals!"

—Molly McAdams, *New York Times* bestselling author, on *The Dark Ones*

"Laugh-out-loud fun! Rachel Van Dyken is on my auto-buy list."

—Jill Shalvis, *New York Times* bestselling author, on *The Wager*

"*The Dare* is a laugh-out-loud read that I could not put down. Brilliant. Just brilliant."

—Cathryn Fox, *New York Times* bestselling author

THE MATCHMAKER'S REPLACEMENT

A WINGMEN INC. NOVEL

ALSO BY #1 *NEW YORK TIMES* BESTSELLING AUTHOR RACHEL VAN DYKEN:

The Consequence Series

The Consequence of Loving Colton

The Consequence of Revenge

The Consequence of Seduction

The Consequence of Rejection

The Wingmen Inc. Series

The Matchmaker's Playbook

The Bet Series

The Bet

The Wager

The Dare

The Ruin Series

Ruin

Toxic

Fearless

Shame

The Elite Series

Elite

Elect

Entice

Elicit

Bang Bang

Enforce

Ember

Elude

Empire

The Seaside Series

Tear

Pull

Shatter

Forever

Fall

Eternal

Strung

Capture

The Renwick House Series

The Ugly Duckling Debutante

The Seduction of Sebastian St. James

The Redemption of Lord Rawlings

An Unlikely Alliance

The Devil Duke Takes a Bride

The London Fairy Tale Series

Upon A Midnight Dream

Whispered Music

The Wolf's Pursuit

When Ash Falls

The Seasons of Paleo Series

Savage Winter

Feral Spring

The Wallflower Series (with Leah Sanders)

Waltzing with the Wallflower

Beguiling Bridget

Taming Wilde

The Dark Ones Saga

The Dark Ones

Untouchable Darkness

Stand-Alones

Hurt: A Collection (with Kristin Vayden and Elyse Faber)

RIP

Compromising Kessen

Every Girl Does It

The Parting Gift (with Leah Sanders)

Divine Uprising

THE MATCHMAKER'S REPLACEMENT

A WINGMEN INC. NOVEL

RACHEL VAN DYKEN

This is a work of fiction. Names, characters, organizations, places, events, and incidents are either products of the author's imagination or are used fictitiously.

Published by Skyscape, New York

www.apub.com

ISBN-13: 9781503936270
ISBN-10: 1503936279

Cover design by Shasti O'Leary Soudant

Printed in the United States of America

To my son. You're never getting married! HA-HA!
No, but seriously . . .

Prologue
Lex

Freshman year 2012
University of Washington campus
Zeta Psi Christmas party, 1:00 a.m.

A thick haze of smoke blanketed the living room. Whoever thought it was a good idea to get a smoke machine, toss it into a room full of sweaty dudes, and flip it on should burn in hell.

"Where are all the girls?" I asked my friend Ian. He was thinking of pledging Zeta Psi the following year, but as a star athlete he wasn't sure if he had the time. We'd been invited to what was being called on campus "the party of the year." "It's a freakin' sausage fest!" I said with disgust.

Ian frowned. "Maybe they're coming later?"

"Nobody likes that . . . the coming later part. Coming should always happen sooner rather than later, all things considered." I slapped him on the back. "But those are things you find out when you become a man . . ."

"You're such an ass, Lex." He shoved me hard into the blinding smoke. It burned my eyes and made me immediately want to take out my contacts. If I kept walking through that smoke, chances were I was going to accidently kiss a dude, and I wasn't into those types of parties. "Let's just go."

"Fine."

Ian set his beer on a nearby table and followed me as we weaved our way through the crowd. Just then a trumpet sounded as a hundred girls burst through the door wearing red and green Christmas bikinis.

"Woohoo!" they screamed. Sorority girls always screamed, but this time I didn't mind since said screaming was paired with lots of bouncing in tiny fabric. I smirked as Ian choked out "God bless us, every one" under his breath and started making his way toward the girls.

"Hold up, Tiny Tim." I grabbed him by the shirt and pulled him back. "We don't go to them, they come to us. Remember the rules?" I'd never in my life had to exert myself to get a girl, and I wasn't about to start just because Ian was afraid all the good ones would be taken.

"We've been holding our dicks for the past three hours, and you want to wait longer?"

I rolled my eyes. "It's science." Which is why I specified in our private playbook, also known as *How to Get Laid 101*, that we never approach a girl.

"What's science?"

"Sex." I nodded to a few girls who already looked bored with the guys who had bombarded them and were now making their way toward us. One was wearing a red thong with a tiny Santa skirt to match and nothing but a red lacy bra on top and a cute-as-hell Santa hat perched at an angle on her head. The other was dressed like a naughty reindeer, with little cuffs on her wrists and bells around her neck.

"Hey." Naughty Reindeer performed a little wiggle and wave. "Wanna ring my bell?"

It was on the tip of my tongue to say yes because, hello, she wanted me to ring her bell, and I would be an idiot if I didn't take her upstairs, or down the hall, or even to the pantry to see how many bells I could make chime. But I wanted more of a challenge.

Maybe it was the computer genius in me that needed a complicated formula or something that would at least pose more difficulty than opening my mouth and asking if she wanted to be on top, bottom, or a mixture of both.

"Ian." I elbowed him. "Why don't you go take these lovely young ladies for a drink while I . . . grab something out of the car?" It was a lame excuse, but as one of the stars of the UW football team, Ian could easily take care of himself. Besides, he liked to spread the love, though it was more of a challenge when he had to please two girls at once.

"Right . . . something out of the . . . car." The one we didn't drive. Clearly he got the hint, since he swept both girls under his bulky arms and walked off, a smug smile plastered across his face.

I rolled my eyes as both girls giggled and clung to him like he was Russell freaking Wilson, which, if he kept his stats up, could easily be his reality.

I quickly scanned the room. The rest of the girls looked the same. In a sea of red and green, all I saw were easy chicks ready to spread their legs for muscles and a killer smile—both of which I had in spades. They didn't nickname me Lex Luthor because I was a button-down-wearing gentleman who said "please" and "thank you" in the bedroom.

I was the villain.

The Dark Side.

The dirty.

The bad boy the girl brought home to piss off her father, though the joke was almost always on the girl, considering I was a Mensa member—I just didn't look it. To most girls I was the dark, brooding, motorcycle-driving loser just waiting to flunk out of college. Little did they know: I had more brain cells in my pinky finger, more money in my bank account, than they could possibly imagine—or add using all ten fingers.

Frowning, I moved through the thick crowd of hormones and nearly collided with a short girl, dressed in an elf costume, who had a cute little white mask covering part of her face. Two big emerald green eyes scrutinized me.

"Sorry." My gaze fell to her cleavage, which was . . . refreshingly . . . perfect. Not too much on show, leaving just enough to the imagination. I liked it. Plus she smelled like peppermint.

And I was a damn sucker for mint.

Or maybe it was just tits.

I licked my lips as her green eyes blinked up at me with a mix of shock and then confusion, as though she wasn't sure if I was friend or foe.

Hah, I was both—a little bit of both, anyway. But for tonight? I'd be the best friend she ever had. Her pink tongue snuck out, wetting her lips, and my cock twitched with envy. As if she sensed the direction of my thoughts, a bright red blush stained her cheeks. With a sigh she huffed out a breath. Damn, more peppermint. She could handle my candy cane any day of the week.

There was something oddly familiar about her, though, like we'd met before—but that was the oldest line in the book. And the truth? Had we met before, I'd still be buried balls deep in her. She was gorgeous.

"Lex." I held out my hand, immediately breaking one of my playbook rules. A dude should never offer his hand first. It seemed too polite, and girls immediately assumed you were in the market for a relationship. Ian and I had created the rules the minute we realized there was a serious need to strategically navigate the college world of sex and women in a mutually satisfying way where no strings were attached. I never approached, I never offered my name, and I sure as hell didn't shake a girl's hand when I could be flicking her nipple with my tongue.

Her eyebrows furrowed and then she slowly, methodically reached out and shook my hand firmly. "Gabrielle, but my friends call me Gabi."

Gabi? I grew up with a Gabi. But no chance in hell the scrawny and awkward Gabi that Ian and I used to torture was the vision of sex standing in front of me. Besides, she would be on her last year of high school and probably hadn't even grown into her stubby little legs yet.

"And your boyfriend, what does he call you?" I pressed my body closer to hers.

"Sara." Her lips twitched.

"Huh?"

She laughed, and that damn sound went to all the wrong places. It was an automatic physical reaction; being near her was driving me insane, and I had no freaking idea why. "He was dating me and Sara at the same time and got confused when he kissed me goodnight."

"Damn." I shook my head and smirked. "Did you knee him in the junk?"

"And bit his tongue," she said, smiling like a feral cat. "I'm violent like that."

"Feminism." I nodded. "I give to the cause . . . swear." I put my hand over my heart. "And I hope he walks funny for a year."

"Eh." She gave a casual shrug. "It's not like he had much for me to hit anyway."

"Can we be best friends?" I blurted out with a laugh.

She joined in the laughter just as someone pushed her from behind, sending her flying into my arms. Her delicate fingers pressed into my biceps while her breasts slid against my chest.

My breath hitched as she lifted her face toward me.

And I did it.

I lost my mind, forgetting all about my rules of play, and just went for broke, softly kissing her like I'd known her for years instead of four minutes and thirty-six seconds. Her candy-cane tongue met mine with enough aggression to momentarily surprise me as her fingers ran down my buzzed hair, making my skull and the rest of my body sizzle with awareness.

Groaning, I lifted her into the air as she deepened the kiss. What the hell? How did I get this damn lucky? We pulled apart for air, and her cheeks were still so freaking red I had to laugh.

"You're adorable," I admitted. "Hot. But adorable. How is that possible?"

"Well, if I was Sara, I'd say it's because I'm awesome in bed."

"Oh yeah?"

"Yeah, but since I'm just me, it's probably because I'm too innocent to know how awesome I really am."

"Innocent is okay," I said, feeling protective of the cute girl in my arms who responded so readily to my touch.

She frowned and then slid out of my embrace, her feet touching the ground just as the lights flickered and turned down.

"I don't want to be innocent anymore," she whispered in my ear.

Holy shit.

I quickly glanced around the darkened room as the sound of techno pumped through the cheap speakers, crackling every few seconds.

"Well"—I grabbed her hips and leaned down, my lips caressing the outline of her ear—I think you've found the right guy."

"Me too."

I grabbed her hand and led her toward the stairs. On the outside, I was calm; on the inside, I was high-fiving myself while my dick was doing cartwheels.

My grip tightened on her hand as I dragged her up the stairs, my feet floating as she ran behind me. The sound of her laughter, the look of her flushed cheeks, was too much to handle.

We made it to the bedroom in ten seconds.

The door was closed. I opened it, slammed it shut again, and pressed her against it. My lips found her neck as she twisted the door-knob, sending us into the room in a fit of frenzied hands.

"What the hell?" Ian's voice shouted behind me.

Gabrielle and I pulled apart.

"Oh shit," I said around a breathless laugh. "Sorry, man, didn't know you were in this room."

"Gabs!" Ian shouted. "What the HELL are you doing?" Ian was half naked with two nearly naked girls, and he looked more pissed than I'd ever seen him in my entire time knowing him. He never got angry.

I took a cautious step back and held up my hands. "Ian? What's wrong, man?"

"Gabs!" Ian shouted again. "Do you know who that is?"

He was pointing at me like I was a criminal.

"Ian, stay out of it!" She raised her voice, placing her hands on her hips. "Just . . . go!"

"Go?" he repeated, then louder: "GO?" He stomped over to her. "Why are you at this party? I told you to stay home, to do homework. You promised after Mark—"

"Mark?" I repeated, my mind fuzzily coming to terms with the fact that this was Gabi, the Gabi I grew up with, the very same one who'd called Ian last week in tears over her ex-boyfriend cheating on her. "Oh shit!" I took a step back. Was she even eighteen?

She rolled her eyes. "I'm eighteen."

Thank God!

"Doesn't matter." Ian looked like he was ready to puke. "You can't be here, Gabs. I'm your best friend." He shared a look with me, a look that said more than I needed to know. This was Gabs, the girl who was at every one of Ian's birthday parties when he was little, who never missed one of his football games. The same Gabs I used to throw rocks at before moving across town.

The Gabi I had sworn up and down to Ian I'd never touch, not even for a million dollars. Then again, we were eleven when I made that promise.

She wasn't just off-limits.

She was untouchable. The one object between Ian and me that could destroy our friendship, create a chasm so deep and wide that I'd never be able to come back from it.

"It's cool." I quickly held up my hands. "Nothing happened."

"Nothing happened?" Gabi whipped her head around and glared.

I knew I had two choices: play the gentleman, let her know that I wasn't a horrible guy, that I was just trying to be protective of the girl who was basically my best friend's only family; or lie and make her think I was a horrible person. A girl like her—hell, most girls—wanted the gentleman, wanted to believe all men were good and just needed a chance. She was giving me those eyes, the eyes you give the mean dog at the shelter just as you reach out your hand to pet him.

I could nuzzle.

Or bite like hell.

And a girl like Gabi needed the bite . . . if I was to keep the waters peaceful between Ian and me. I sighed. I needed my best friend, sometimes more than I think he needed me. Hell, I needed him like he needed Gabi, damn it.

I had no choice.

"Shit." I burst out laughing. "I'll just go downstairs and find another one. It's not like there aren't a million others just like her." I winked, then grabbed her by the ass and pulled her against me and said gruffly, "It was real, but I have other tits calling my name."

I nearly puked as I made my way out of the room and down the stairs, not even looking at the people around me as I left the party and the only girl who had ever tempted me . . . to want more.

Chapter One
Lex

Four years later
Senior year

"Right. There." I could feel her breasts pressed up against my back as she pointed to the book that just happened to be at least two feet above her. "The one with the blue spine."

Smirking, I read the title aloud: "A Thousand and One Ways to Please Your Man?"

"That's the one." Was it my imagination or did her voice get husky? Her hands snaked around my waist. "Oh sorry, I thought I saw another book that looked . . . exciting. My mistake." She pulled her hands away from my crotch and the empty shelf near it.

With a snicker I pulled the book down, still not turning around. "You know, I'm a really good study partner."

"I've heard," she purred.

Of course she had. My reputation was legendary. By day I was a typical computer nerd, spending most my time in the labs teaching my own professors how to code. Hell, I even adopted dogs, handed out fliers on Greenpeace, and donated to homeless shelters.

But by night?

"So . . ." Soft, wet lips caressed my right bicep. "What do you say?"

An irritating female voice broke through the lustful tension. "Of course, you know it's a real sex addiction when you actually hang out in the *Kama Sutra* section just so you can pick up girls you won't feel the need to grade in bed—or, God forbid, give a manual to."

"Gabs." I turned around, teeth clenched, fists tight, ready for a fight or ready to cover my dick lest she try to kick it off again. "You gain weight?"

"Hmm, I don't know. Did the free clinic help you get rid of those crabs?"

The girl—whose name escaped me, as most did—grabbed the book out of my hands and quickly scurried away while Gabs gave me a pointed look.

"For your information, she asked me for help." I don't know why the hell I was defending myself to the spawn of Satan. Maybe it was because she looked at me as if I was one bad decision away from going to prison.

Gabi's soft pink lips pressed together in a judgmental line as her green eyes narrowed. "You're late."

"Actually"—I shoved past her—"I was early, saw a damsel in distress, and made myself available. You know how it is. I can't help that I attract estrogen on an hourly basis."

"Yes." Gabs pointed to the stool right next to the bookcase. "So very needy . . . and so very stupid. Was that the best excuse she could come up with? Why not just say, 'Hey, I'm afraid of heights, mind grabbing that book for me?'"

I rolled my eyes. "Gabs, I know you're short so everything from down there looks really, really scary, but that stool's only a foot tall. If she's scared of that, then it leads me to believe she's afraid of all things that equally measure up." I smirked and leaned down, lifting her hair so I could whisper in her ear. "Though who am I kidding? I love it when girls scream in bed."

Gabi shoved against my chest. Hard. "Gross! Go give a disease to someone else." She shuddered and then stomped off, calling over her shoulder, "Let's just get this over with, alright?"

"Fine." At the pace of a handicapped turtle, I followed after her, dreading every freaking step that took me to the table where she'd laid out her pink backpack and highlighters.

Everything had a place.

It was so Gabi that I had to fight not to smile or even laugh. That would make her think I at least liked her as a friend—which I didn't.

She was completely off-limits, meaning the minute I'd walked away from her four years ago, she'd become nothing to me—i.e., androgynous, sexless, a really ugly dude, a brother, a goat.

And girls and guys as friends? Yeah, that worked, like, never. Ergo, the goat theory. If I think of her as an animal or some sort of sexless human, I won't fall prey to her charms and decide to be her friend and then long for more, sleep with her, ruin everything, and end up truly hating her almost as much as myself.

Vicious cycle.

I wanted no part of it.

Gabs sucked on a tip of her hair, which was a gross habit, then started pulling out sheets of paper. "Okay, so I went ahead and plugged in all of the new male applicants and cross-referenced them with the female clients already in the database. They've all been imported into the new program, but with your and Ian's schedules I just don't know how it's going to work."

"Cute. You say that in bed too?"

"Lex," she growled, sliding the papers over to me. Numbers, numbers, and more numbers. They were my addiction—my drug—and I loved them. The first thing I noticed was that she hadn't messed up the data, which meant I had no excuse to fire her from Wingmen Inc. Ian had hired her so she could pay for school. He knew she needed the money, but she was too proud to take it as a gift from either of us—not that I'd ever offer.

So instead he gave her a job.

At *my* company.

Okay fine, we both owned the company, but it still pissed me off. She'd completely ignored all the McDonald's and Starbucks applications I'd left on her kitchen counter. I'd even called in a favor at Microsoft, where I'd interned over the summer, and she'd declined the offer!

Ian and I had one semester of school left.

One semester where I was cursed to put up with her shit, not only because she was Ian's best friend but also because Ian and Blake had hooked up a few weeks earlier, and he'd been unable to keep up his schedule.

I groaned as the numbers all blurred together. Wingmen Inc. was exactly what it sounded like. A simple service Ian came up with after getting injured during his first season with the Seahawks. We, as wingmen, help girls—the good girls, not the ones who grope me in the freaking bookstore—find their happily ever afters.

We keep them from settling for complete idiots.

And in doing so help them achieve self-confidence.

I know, I know, I really do deserve a Purple Heart. Maybe that's why my nights are filled with so much . . . ass. My soul can only handle so much goodness before I explode with glitter and butterflies, and that shit isn't cool.

It was Ian and Blake's idea to start accepting male clients, and as much as I wanted to say no to the workload, they were right. My major alone was filled with so many dudes who'd never even gone on a date that I knew we'd be doing society a favor.

I'd quickly altered our computer software so that we'd have a database, or dating pool, of available men and women, and then I started scheduling the most desperate cases, something my program also figured out for me.

"Lex?" Gabi snapped her fingers in front of my face. "Are you even listening?"

"No." I pushed her hand away. "I was reading. And as much as I hate to utter these words . . ."

"I'm right?" She beamed, biting down on her lower lip.

With a grunt, I mumbled, "You're right. Which also means we either need to hire someone else or you're going to have to step up your game."

"My game?" Her dark eyebrows drew together as she twirled her long dark-brown hair in her fingers. "Um, that wasn't part of the deal."

"The deal's changed." I stood, crumpled up the paper, and tossed it in the trash. "If I take on more clients, I'm going to fail my classes." Okay, that was a lie, but I didn't want to book my days with clients back to back only to be too tired for extracurricular activities. "So that means you're going to have to take some of the dudes."

"No!" Gabi jumped to her feet. "You know I can't do that!"

"I do?" I looked over her head as a blonde chick with huge tits glanced my way and winked.

"Oh no you don't." Gabi jumped onto her chair and grabbed my face with both of her hands. "Look at me."

"I am looking at you," I said in a deliberately bored tone while trying to look through her so I could see Big Tits.

"Lex!" Gabi smacked me on the side of the face. "Focus, stop thinking with your downstairs, let the blood go up."

I burst out laughing. "I think you're confused on what that would actually mean . . . Up is—"

She covered my mouth with her hand, and I noticed that pink highlighter lined her index finger, which smelled like strawberries. Of course it did.

Her green eyes widened. "I can't meet with the male clients and coach them and—"

I rolled my eyes and removed her hand. "Gabi, I'll train you this week. How hard can it be? They're nerds looking for other nerds so they can have baby nerds, who will produce more nerds who will probably one day create enough robots to bring about the apocalypse." I left out that training included testing her seduction skills as well as a few other things I was pretty sure that, given the chance, she would rather die than actually follow through with. One way or another, I was going to get her to quit. At least I dangled hope in front of her so then in the end, when she backed out, it would be all on her, completely her decision. See? I was a total gentleman when I wanted to be.

I started walking away, but Gabi jumped onto my back like a monkey, her feet digging into my sides. "Stop!"

I leaned my head back, smacking her in the jaw.

"Ouch!"

"Sorry!"

"No you're not!"

"How the hell do you know?" We were starting to gain an audience. "Get off of me!"

"Not until you promise I don't have to whore myself out!" she hissed.

An employee looked in our direction. Great.

I lowered my voice while simultaneously trying to loosen her legs from my waist. "You aren't whoring, you're helping. Big difference, Gabi, believe me."

I turned my head just as she leaned down, and her lips brushed against my ear.

I froze.

She froze.

Time stood still.

I took two deep breaths. "This is the job, Gabi. If you can't do it, I'll find someone who can and will." And there it was, the perfect plan. I could fire her for refusing to do her job, and we'd both go our separate ways. Being next to her strawberry-scented skin was already driving me to the edge of my sanity, and I'd always prided myself on being hard to break.

Until Gabi.

"Nope." She pinched my neck. "Ian owns half the company. He'll simply—"

"Will that always be your excuse, then? Your fallback plan? You're always going to have Ian to bail you out when things get hard?"

Her breath hitched.

Gotcha, Sunshine.

"That's what I thought. Look, I'm tired, and I need sex, so if you aren't offering then please get the hell off my back and go home."

She slid down my body. I could feel her perky breasts waving goodbye while my teeth clenched with irritation.

I turned around and grinned wickedly. "You start tomorrow."

Gabi's cheeks turned red. I was betting on her backing out. She should, after all; she was innocent, hardly dated—hell, my grandmother had more sexual experience than Gabi.

A turtle had more experience.

We shared a best friend, and when drunk, our mutual friend explained why he was so protective of our dear, lovely Gabi. Virgin. She was a freaking virgin.

Which basically meant she was going to crash and burn, and I was going to document every damn thing and then tell Ian she had to find somewhere else to work.

Perfect plan?

Hell yes.

"That is, unless"—I winked—"you want to start tonight." I licked my lips and tilted my head. "My record is forty-eight seconds . . . Bet you'd only take twenty."

A book flew by my head.

Guess that was my answer.

"You know . . ." I rocked on my heels. "There's always McDonald's. Let me call in a favor, Gabs. You don't belong with Wingmen Inc."

Her nostrils flared. "I need this job, Lex. It's the only job that pays me enough to be able to—"

My eyebrows shot up. "Able to what, Gabs? Buy more shoes? It's not like you haven't already paid for your tuition."

"Bastard!" she screeched, tossing another book in my direction. I ducked. "Did you hack my school account again?"

"Me?" I shrugged innocently. "Honestly, Gabs, I'm surprised a five-year-old hasn't hacked your account already. You do realize using 'password' as your password is basically like putting a welcome mat in front of your login, right?"

"I hate you."

"Feeling's mutual, Sunshine." I smirked. "Now, go complain to Ian like you always do, and I'll go stand outside while women fall at my feet, like I always do."

She stormed off.

And a piece of me left with her, not that she knew, not that she'd ever know, because every single time we argued, it was like part of my soul cracked.

Hah, maybe that was why I was hating her more and more.

Gabrielle Sava was making me soulless.

Hell, by the end of the semester I was going to be either a demon or a vampire.

The blonde with the big tits winked at me again and waved. I smiled and stared at her plump, shapely body. For tonight? I'd bite.

"Vampire it is," I whispered as I made my way over to her.

Chapter Two
Gabi

I hated him.

HATED him.

Hate, hate, hate. I chanted the words to myself that very next morning as I stomped toward his ridiculously expensive house, next to the ridiculously nice lake, with his ridiculously loud red Mercedes parked out front. Jackass.

I'd be doing society a favor if I set it on fire.

Seriously.

The thing was probably filled with so much bodily fluid and disease that if he got in a car accident he'd infect the entire freeway and start a citywide epidemic.

I shuddered.

I compartmentalized Lex into two boxes.

The first box was Childhood Lex, the friend who used to hang out with Ian and me before he moved across town, never to be seen again. He used to ride with me to school, and when I was sick he gave me my own box of Kleenex—never mind that he stole it from his teacher's desk. The point is, Childhood Lex was a keeper.

Box number two?

Asshole Lex, also known as the version I was walking toward. The Lex I met when I was eighteen, who momentarily stunned me speechless with his godlike beauty, had been a figment of my overactive, sad, hormone-riddled imagination.

On the outside? The perfect man.

With a brooding and sultry smile.

Biceps the size of my head.

Who gave me the distinct feeling that if I ran my hands over his buzzed hair I'd orgasm before he even touched me.

Whatever. I was over it. So over it.

A lot of people had stupid crushes when they were eighteen, right?

Now all I saw when I looked into his stormy blue eyes was syph or the clap, and that was being generous. The dude was a walking STD and seriously tried every nerve I had. He was an ass. Plain and simple, no sugar coating. He was the type of guy who'd tell a chick that she looked fat in a dress or who refused to share the communal breadbasket. See? He couldn't even adhere to typical manners during mealtime! Just thinking about him had me tied up in knots.

Last year, when I went shopping and stupidly invited Ian along—which of course meant Lex *had* to come—I was told in no uncertain terms that if I would just stop drinking chocolate milk in the morning I'd be able to fit into a smaller size.

He'd smiled.

His dimples had deepened.

He'd even crossed his arms as if to say, Look, I did you a favor, pat me on the back.

Instead I had kicked him in the balls and tried to give him a black eye, clocking Ian in the face.

My point? Lex. Was. The. Devil.

I made a point of only hanging out with Lex when absolutely necessary, and even then I almost always had Ian as a buffer. But now that he was playing love nest with my ex-roomie, Blake? Well, I was on my own.

Lex opened the door after my third aggressive knock. Black sweatpants hung low on his hips, a vintage Mariners shirt fell open around his neck, and he was wearing black-framed glasses that made his eyes more appealing than should be legal.

"Sunshine," he said, his smirk deepening as he crossed his burly arms over his chest.

"Dickhead." I smiled sweetly. "New glasses? They look thicker than last time."

"Better to see you with." He leaned forward, his eyes narrowing into tiny slits. "There they are." He reached for one of my boobs.

I slapped his hand away so hard my palm stung.

"Probably not the best way to treat your new male clients." He shook his hand and turned toward the living room, leaving the door wide open. Manners were completely lost on him.

Gritting my teeth, I slammed the door behind me and took off my shoes because I knew if I didn't he'd give me hell.

He was a freak like that.

For as much ass as he got, it was shocking how much Lysol he used around the house. His clothes were never wrinkled; everything was pristine.

Even his breath.

Damn him.

He drank coffee like a Starbucks employee but never had coffee breath.

It was almost painful, staring him in the face, knowing that everything on the outside appeared perfect—but didn't match the inside at all, not even close!

Beauty like Lex's was dangerous and wickedly tempting, like something out of a paranormal romance novel. Sometimes, at night, when

I dreamed of Lex getting hit by a car, I imagined him as a vampire roaming the streets in his favorite black sweats, shirtless, shimmering under the streetlights, just waiting for whores to line up so he could take a few bites.

A pencil flew by my head.

"Yo." Lex's eyebrows shot up. "We have a lot of work to do if we're going to get you ready for the next two clients. Daydream about chicks on your own time."

"I'm not a lesbian."

He bit on his bottom lip, sinking back in his chair as his eyes slowly roamed from my mismatched socks all the way up to my head. "Okay, whatever you say, Gabs."

I will not commit homicide. I will not commit homicide. "You know," I said as I tossed my purse onto the table in front of him, "it's offensive that you assume all lesbians dress like crap." So what? I was wearing a ratty white T-shirt and ripped jeans, and I was pretty sure I still had mascara on from the night before. It was my Lex repellant. He hated sloppiness.

"Offensive." He nodded. "Also true . . ." He used the spare pencil from behind his ear to slide my purse over to the farthest side of the table. "It wouldn't kill you to wear something other than jeans and T-shirts, Gabs." He sighed. "Say it with me: dresssss—"

I grabbed the pencil from his hand, broke it into two pieces, and handed them back to him. "I wear dresses, just not for you. Dresses are your kryptonite, especially short black ones. I refuse to be a part of your 'shower time.'"

He snorted. "You wish."

"Yes. Every night when I go to sleep I pray for Lex to dream of me while he jerks off because yet another girl refused to follow his instructions in bed: 'Damn it, use the manual!'" I said, using my best imitation of Lex's voice. I'd only heard him shout instructions to a girl once, and it had scarred me for life. *What the hell are you doing? Do I look like I'm satisfied? There's a diagram!* Ugh.

Lex rolled his eyes. "Very funny, and the manual is there for a reason. Do you even know how many chicks get confused when I call out sexual positions? It's like, get there faster, you know?"

My feelings were torn between fascination and disgust. "So," I changed the subject. "Let's train, because I have about ten years' worth of Organic Chem homework."

Lex sighed and held out his hand.

"No." I crossed my arms. "I don't need help."

Okay, I needed help, desperately needed help, and Lex wasn't just passably smart but a certified genius, at least when he applied himself. I refused to ask him to go over my homework just because Organic Chem was, to me, like reading a foreign language.

He cleared his throat.

I didn't move.

Finally, he stood, slowly walked over to the end of the table, and fished the chem book from my oversized purse. "What chapter?"

"Lex—"

"If I'm teaching you Organic Chem, at least say Professor Lex."

"Listen very closely, Lex." I went over and jerked my book out of his hands. "I didn't need your help last year when I almost failed biology, and I sure as hell don't need your help now. Let's just get this training done so I can go home and suffer in silence, alright?"

"Fine." He dropped my book against the table and then, without warning, grabbed me by my shoulders and pushed me against the counter that bordered the kitchen. My butt hit the cupboard. "Up until now we've been helping women find their perfect matches. Basically acting like a wingman so that the idiots of this world see the girl who's been standing in front of them all along."

Why was he standing so close? Did we have to be touching? I told my body not to respond to his proximity, but Lex was magnetic, even if every part of him was evil. My brain was having trouble functioning while his large palms were pressed into the tops of my shoulders.

"Okay." I swallowed. "And now that you're allowing guys to become clients of Wingmen Inc., I basically do the same thing. Give them confidence, help them capture the one girl who's always seen them as the friend—or worse, who they've been invisible to."

"What's that like, I wonder?" Lex still didn't release me. "Being invisible . . . Maybe next time a dude ignores you, take notes."

And another insult.

"Lex." I huffed out a breath. "Just get on with it."

"Right." His eyes momentarily locked on mine before he rubbed the bridge of his nose where his glasses were perched. It was not sexy. It wasn't. Really. That. Sexy. "So whenever we take on a new client, we give them a list of questions, meet them in a public place, and then use the power of human emotions like jealousy and curiosity to get the other person interested. That's where you come in. If another girl sees our client as desirable, he becomes desirable."

"That easy?"

"Sort of." Lex leaned forward. "But you can't suck."

"Suck?"

"At anything." His lips hovered near my mouth. He was starting to freak me out. I wanted to run away, but I was pinned.

"Lex, if you kiss me I will bite your tongue off. I swear."

"If I was actually kissing you"—Lex released one of my shoulders and placed a finger against my mouth—"you'd know it. This, my frumpy friend, is training."

His lips descended.

They pressed against mine, then pulled back. "Yeah." He shook his head. "Gabs, you're going to need to open your mouth a bit more. Guys are stupid. They always assume that more tongue means better kissing, when the opposite is true, but you still need to have your lips parted, not locked down like Fort Knox."

"What's happening?" I tried to push away from him.

Lex rolled his eyes. "Gabs, believe me, this is all business. You can even keep your hand on my junk the whole time."

"What!" I roared.

"So you know without a doubt that nothing about you turns me on." He grinned menacingly. "Seriously, I don't mind."

"I do!"

"Hey!" He chuckled. "I was just trying to help."

"Grabbing your penis is *not* the answer, Lex!"

"Weird, because it so often is."

"I hate today."

"Is it the rain?" He frowned.

"It's not—"

"It is."

"Stop that!" I shoved him. "Hurry up and grade my kissing skills so I can go home and study."

"Kissing, hand holding, hugging, cuddling, laughing, winking—just a few things you need to master." He was firing off so many horrible, body-numbing words.

"Just hurry up," I grumbled in a defeated voice as I tried to block out the fact that he was a good-looking ass who offended me with every single breath he took.

"Ah . . ." Lex held up his hand. "One never hurries a kiss."

"What about a passionate kiss?"

"A passionate kiss isn't hurried, it's frenzied. Damn, don't you know anything?"

Heat swamped my cheeks.

"How many guys have you kissed, Gabs?"

"Plenty!" Five. I'd kissed five.

"You blush down your neck when you lie." Lex cupped my chin and then brought his lips down against mine again. "Part."

Sighing against his mouth, I relaxed my lips while his slid across.

He pulled back, wearing a frown of irritation. "A bit more, Gabs. Guys want access."

I kept my eyes open.

So did he.

I didn't want him assuming I was into it, which was probably his exact line of thinking. Only keeping my eyes open was an entirely raw experience, watching him watch me while I felt him.

I shivered.

"Cold?" That stupid smirk was back.

"Frigid." I glared, putting myself down before he had a chance to.

"You read my mind." He nodded seriously. "Now stop being a bitch, and let me teach you how to kiss."

"I know how to kiss!" I don't know what came over me—maybe it was the need to prove myself, or possibly it was just stress over the entire situation. Needing to stay in school and hating that *he* was the answer, I wrapped my arms around his neck and jumped, my hips colliding with his as I mauled his mouth with as much passion as I could conjure up, this time closing my eyes and putting everything I had into it.

With a growl, Lex pushed me back against the countertop. As my butt collided with the edge, his tongue plunged into my mouth and his hands dug into my hair, pulling it free from its ponytail while he changed positions, his lips demanding a punishing kiss from a different angle as he gave my hair a harder tug.

I grasped at his T-shirt, pulling him closer and nearly falling backward into the sink.

And then, just when I was in danger of losing myself to the kiss that would probably be the best kiss of my life, I bit down on his bottom lip.

That move didn't work out the way I'd planned, not at all. In my head it was smart. I'd piss him off, get him to pull back and leave me alone.

It did nothing of the sort.

Nothing of the sort at all.

With a hiss he pulled back, fire blazing in his eyes. For a split second that seemed to go on for an eternity, he hovered and I waited, both of us on the edge of something. He wet his lips, I mimicked the movement, and then, like a snake, he struck. His mouth fused to mine in a ferocious kiss, one that bruised my mouth while imprinting its essence on my soul.

The hard length of his arousal pressed against me, and that was when I knew I needed to either kick him or break free before he was in danger of becoming more than a hated enemy.

I shoved him as hard as I could.

He stumbled back, chest heaving. "Why the hell did you bite me?"

"You said you wouldn't get turned-on!" I fired back, pointing at the front of his sweatpants.

He smirked. "That was before you bit me. All bets are off when teeth are involved, Sunshine."

"Stop calling me that." I jumped off the counter and hurried over to my purse. "So, we done? Do I pass?"

Lex moved to stand behind me, and I could feel his body heat as he leaned forward and whispered in my ear, "You were right. You can kiss."

My eyes widened as I turned to face him. "Was that a compliment?"

"Nope." He drew back. "It was the truth. Truths don't count as compliments." He angled his head and studied me. "You really don't know anything about guys, do you?"

I closed my eyes and pinched the bridge of my nose. "I should buy stock in aspirin, that's how often I get headaches after hanging out with you."

He shrugged, a look of utter unconcern on his face.

"I'm leaving. We can keep training tomorrow, all day if you want. I only have one lab in the morning, but I really need to get this homework done before then. Otherwise, I'll be stressed about it."

"Great." Lex grabbed his cell and smirked down at it.

"So tomorrow?" I asked.

He didn't answer, just kept texting on his phone.

"Lex. The skank can wait. Is tomorrow okay?"

"Yup." He sighed. "Also, I'm sending you the client list via e-mail. You'll need to have it memorized. We'll get blood work done tomorrow and make sure we get you on the pill . . ."

"WHAT?" I roared.

"Hah." He tossed his phone onto the counter. "Kidding, Gabs. Geez, do you really think I'd whore you out?"

"Yes!"

"Don't worry, I'd only do it if we got a really good offer."

"Good-bye, Lex."

"Later, Sunshine."

Chapter Three
Lex

There was no text.

Just my locked screen and an imaginary message I'd been pretending to write so Gabs would get the hell out of my house.

My plan to make her uncomfortable, to get her to back out and run away screaming, had completely backfired and gone up in lust-filled flames.

I had expected her to bail, panic, yell. Hell, I'd half expected to need the cops to come to my rescue. Instead, she'd kissed me back.

Damn it.

Would it take another four years for my lips to forget what it felt like to be locked with hers?

The minute my door slammed, I exhaled a sigh of relief. The kiss unnerved me, in a way that had my black heart mourning the loss of her sultry lips. But that's where it stopped. Believe me, no part of me hoped that Gabs was going to be the one girl to hold my attention long enough for me to utter the word "commitment" while we skipped through the park with a damn picnic basket.

I just wasn't used to girls who kissed like that.

With passion.

I was never the kisser, I was the kissee, meaning I'd been on the receiving end of a fair share of kisses, and none of them had ever affected me with such blinding lust that the only logical thought in my overly complicated brain was sex, sex, and more sex.

Don't get me wrong. I thought about sex all the time, but it was always muddied by formulas, code, ideas, and laundry lists.

Hell, I'm not even ashamed to say that the last girl I slept with helped me damn near solve world hunger. I'd been so effing bored that at one point I'm pretty sure I fell asleep.

And even then she didn't kick me out of bed.

Because she was as selfish as I was. There were always a few of them in the bunch, women who used me just as much as, if not more than, I used them.

Sex was just another formula I excelled at. And orgasm? A simple mathematical equation that I'd mastered, and when a good-looking guy actually knows where to lick, when to pause, how to suck—well, word spreads fast.

It really makes you wonder what all the other dudes are doing in bed if so many women are that unsatisfied.

"Hey." Ian walked into the house we shared, and the door clicked shut behind him. "Was Gabs here?"

Oh, she was here alright. I tilted my head as I examined the table. Yeah, it could probably handle the weight of both of us. She'd stab me with her pencil if she knew the direction of my thoughts.

But she'd bitten me.

It was hot.

Even though it stung like the fires of hell. "Yeah, she was here, we kissed." I reached for my water bottle and brought it to my lips just as what I'd said registered across Ian's face.

"I'm sorry, what?" He gripped the edge of the counter with his fingertips. "You kissed?"

"Training." It was a small lie, a white lie, but whatever. I reached into the folder on the table and slid over the top sheet with all of the new applicants for Wingmen Inc. services. "I don't have enough time to deal with all this shit, and I know you don't want to work with the clients as much because of Blake." I paused for a minute, then pulled off my glasses. "Ian, we're expanding way too fast, and computer software doesn't write itself." Honestly, it was a real pain in my ass that Ian had decided to settle down. He used to juggle three clients in one week, all single females who needed a happily ever after. His success rate was so high it was ridiculous. Whereas I simply got the job done and moved on, he almost always had to have a come-to-Jesus moment where he explained to the girls that theirs was a strictly professional relationship. A few had cried.

None of my clients felt that way about me.

Probably because I wasn't as empathetic as Ian. When I printed out a client's bio and started working with her, it was all business. Get the job done, get out.

Ian glanced over the report and whistled. "Yeah, I think we grossly underestimated how many guys want to be in a relationship."

"I thought it was a fluke at first," I admitted. "Who actually wants to stay committed to one person? At our age?"

Ian glared.

"You don't count in this scenario, since you successfully boned half the campus before your sophomore year. Most of the names on the list are dudes who have never even had a serious girlfriend, let alone more than two sexual partners."

The more I thought about it, the more irritated I became. We started this business thinking it would be mildly successful, not something on its way to becoming Seattle's premiere dating service. Though we only offered Wingmen assistance to our fellow UW students, the dating app was basically like Tinder—only safer and more badass, with a rating and warning system—and we allowed anyone to download it, as long as they were paying customers. We basically did a background check for every member and required that they use real names with real birthdays and, yes, Social Security numbers—you're welcome, world! Our app was the opposite of private. Not only did it alert you if you were in the same area as people on your favorites list, but immediately stats would pop up about the individuals—from their jobs to their ages, hobbies, and what they had done the previous weekend. It seemed that in a world full of people who wanted privacy, the last thing they wanted was privacy when it came to dating.

Women loved it because they were able to actually know the person behind the picture, and we soon discovered that most guys who used the app wanted to settle down and loved the fact that they knew within one minute what the girl's job was and whether she would go to Mass the following day.

"Thanks"—Ian rolled his eyes—"for that glowing compliment." He pulled out a chair and sat. "Do you really think Gabs is the best person to be handling these guys? She hasn't exactly had a lot of boyfriends."

"Exactly." I exhaled, relieved. "Finally you see things my way. I'll go ahead and call her, tell her we don't need her anymore—"

"Whoa, whoa, whoa." Ian stood. "She needs this job. It's the only one that's going to pay her enough for her to be able to afford tuition. You're just going to have to do a hell of a job making sure she's ready." He plopped the playbook we'd created onto the table and pointed.

The hell!

"I have one week," I muttered through clenched teeth. "And today we kissed. Do you even realize how long it takes to turn someone into a relationship guru? Add in the fact that she hates me, and, well . . . I imagine one of us is going to die this week. My money's on her poisoning my coffee."

Ian still didn't look convinced that hiring Gabs was a bad idea.

"I could die."

Too far?

"Stop being dramatic." Ian waved me off. "And the hate is mutual. At least she doesn't have some sort of pathetic crush on you . . . right?" His eyes zeroed in on me as if I was getting cross-examined.

"Right," I repeated, feeling guilty all over again for freshman year. I stood and stretched my hands over my head. We were in dire need of a subject change. The last thing I needed was him breathing down my neck about something I didn't even do! "Is Blake coming over?"

"She has volleyball practice and then she's coming over to watch *Game of Thrones*. You in?"

"Nah." I was in a weird mood after that kiss, which meant my computer and I needed to spend some serious time together. I guessed the only other option would be to drive Gabi so insane she would quit on her own before she had a nervous breakdown. "I'm going to go work."

Ian's shocked expression wasn't helpful. "And by work do you mean you're going to trade your glasses in for your cape and tell some poor woman in downtown Seattle that you can only save the world if she sleeps with you?"

"One time." I rolled my eyes. "On Halloween."

"Still counts. She believed you."

I smirked. "That costume was legit. Of course she believed me."

"You wore that spandex, not the other way around. Well done." Ian shook his head and walked off. "Try to keep those sticky fingers from hacking the government's database. I don't want the FBI making another visit."

"One time!" I shouted after him.

"Weird, that seems to be your MO!" he called back as he flashed me the bird, then disappeared into the living room.

Ignoring him, I took the stairs two at a time and pushed the door open to what Ian jokingly referred to as my Fortress of Solitude.

The lights from my three computer screens flickered in the darkness. I popped my knuckles, did a little stretch, then sat back in my leather chair while visions of taking over the world danced in my head.

Not really.

Okay, at least not all the time, but what the power hackers had at their fingertips was addicting.

I stayed out of everything illegal. The only time I'd ever been flagged was when I'd accidently stumbled upon something that may or may not have pissed off a certain government agency enough to give me a warning and then a job offer.

I declined.

I was only a freshman at the time; the last thing I wanted was to work for suits.

"What shall we do today?" I said, tapping my fingertips against my desk. For some reason, images of Gabs wouldn't quit. First it was Gabs biting her lower lip, then the way she had moaned in my arms while we kissed in the kitchen, which of course naturally turned into an extremely graphic vision of her taking off her shirt and crooking her finger in my direction. Hot damn.

That wasn't what I needed.

I checked the clock; it was only ten in the morning. And just like that I was back to thinking about the playbook. Ian wanted hands-on training for Gabi? Proof that she could do the job? I was just going to have to alter my training a bit. Why make it easier on her by giving her the actual guide that Ian and I had memorized since freshman year? I smiled, even though I felt slightly guilty at the thought that I was screwing her before she even started.

Whatever. It was her fault to begin with.

If she hadn't had homework, we could have gotten all of the training done today. Instead she'd scurried off like a little mouse, leaving me stressed about finding time to train her the rest of the week. Every minute I spent with her drained my superpower, or at least it felt like it. A villain can only handle so much light before he wants to go all freeze-gun on someone's ass. Small doses. I needed her in small, manageable doses.

"Hmmm . . ." I quickly brought up the school Ethernet, and with one swipe of the keys I was typing in Gabi's login, cracking her password, and looking for her class schedule.

I pulled it up in seconds and frowned as I read through her workload, which was almost as intense as mine. Technically she shouldn't be graduating with us, but she'd done summer school along with the UW premed intern program, so she was well on her way to walking in a few months—that is, if she passed the rest of her classes.

Curious, I hacked into her student account and pulled up this semester's grades.

Biology was a B-minus. Shit, talk about teetering on the edge of failing. That was basically like getting a D. It was a core class.

Organic Chem was next.

C-plus.

She really did need to study her ass off if she had any hopes of bringing that grade up.

I could do Organic Chem while sleeping. I played with a thought . . . If I helped her, really I'd be helping me, because she'd be free to get her training over with.

Making my evil plan that much easier: help her with her grades, earn her trust, then get her to quit. Either that or she would just kill me in my sleep.

I needed her gone. She'd been easy to avoid before because I hadn't seen her on a daily basis. The last thing I needed was to be on the wrong end of an unfortunate accident where Ian cut off one of my nuts because I looked at Gabs the wrong way.

Which I was already doing.

Because it was Gabi.

Damn me to hell.

I stared at the blinking cursor.

Technically, my motivation was completely selfish.

I could deal with that.

I quickly grabbed my keys and cell and told my stupid-ass body to stop humming with excitement—this wasn't a booty call.

More like charity work for the mentally unfortunate.

Chapter Four

Gabi

It was only eleven in the morning, and my eyes were burning with unshed tears. I was reading but not understanding anything, making it so I had to go back and reread sections. I literally wanted to bang my head against the very expensive, very heavy book.

I wanted a scone.

Not just any scone, but one with blueberries, one that promised me that regardless of how crappy my day was, there would always be sugar.

My mouth watered.

"Focus, Gabs." I was ten pages in. I had to read eighty. And on top of not understanding anything I was reading, there was that kiss.

And the bite.

And the . . . um, hardness.

"Nooooo!" I wailed, slamming my book shut. I would not go there. I refused to remember the way he felt pressed against me. With a cry, I jammed my fingertips against my temples and counted to three while I did some breathing exercises. I just needed to focus. Coffee. I should make a pot of coffee. Coffee always made things better.

I placed my book and highlighters on the coffee table and stood just as the doorbell rang.

My roommate, Serena, wouldn't get it. She never got the door. Just like she always conveniently forgot about trash day or when rent was due.

"I'm coming!" I called just as I reached the doorknob and jerked.

Lex poked his head through the door. "In that case, should I leave you to it?"

I narrowed my eyes. "You suck."

"And blow," he confirmed. "Just in case you're making a mental checklist of things I do well . . . I can also do this trick with my tongue where—"

"Why are you here, Lex?" My anxiety tripled as he stepped his large body through the doorframe and held up a small brown bag and Starbucks coffee.

"Shit." I stomped my foot. "What did you do, Lex? Seriously. Did you kill Ian? Is that why you're here giving me treats? Or did you put Ex-Lax in a muffin? Or my coffee? Both?" I let out a groan. "The Fates despise me because all I want right now is a pastry. On a scale of one to ten, how much Ex-Lax are we talking?" I eyed the bag, imagining the scone I was craving, my mouth watering almost to the point of drooling. "It might be worth it."

With his free hand Lex reached out and pinched both of my lips together with his fingers, giving me immediate duck face. "First off, it's really hard to put Ex-Lax in baked goods—it throws off the consistency. Second, pastries make your ass big. The pastry is bad enough without me having to poison it." He released my lips and shoved the bag in my face. "You're welcome."

"I'm not thanking you," I grumbled as the scent of blueberry scone floated into the air. It was as if he'd read my mind, and I refused to think about what that might mean. I inhaled deeply. "It's warm."

"Like my heart." He winked.

"I love your jokes." I sighed. "Next you're going to tell me you helped a nice old lady cross the street before saving her cat from a large oak tree, and you were given the keys to the city."

Lex ignored me and kept walking into my living room. He stopped in front of the table, picked up my textbook, and sat on the couch with it in his lap.

"I didn't invite you," I said around a mouthful of scone.

"You've got crumbs on your shirt, and you look like a starved hyena. Chew, Gabs, the food will still be there when you swallow."

I made a face.

"Saw that," he sang as he turned the page and kicked off his shoes, putting his smelly boy socks up on my clean couch. Though who was I kidding? Nothing about him was even remotely smelly or revolting. His socks were probably clean enough for me to lick. "Hurry up and eat so we can study."

"We are not doing anything!" I kept eating the scone—even though it was a pity scone and would probably give me diarrhea, but it was so damn good. "I'm studying, you're leaving! Or are you here for Serena?" He'd had a one-night stand with my roommate, and to this day she still talked about how he'd changed her life with one lick. I was way too much of a prude to ask what that meant, and instead I'd nodded my head and changed the subject to the rent she was always late coughing up.

"You have a C-plus in Organic Chem," Lex said in a bored voice as he licked his finger and turned another page. "I can't have you failing out of school with no job prospects and no money, needing to start a very lucrative career stripping for cash." He looked up from the book and winced. "Not that you'd make a killing or anything. Most strippers appear female—you know, with actual boobs rather than whatever the hell it is you've got going on upstairs."

I refused to cross my arms in embarrassment. "You wouldn't know real boobs if they smacked you in the face, since you only sleep with plastic!"

"Oh, they do." He burst out laughing. "Smack me in the face. Then the girl, then me. It's like a mating dance. I've got some footage on film if you're into that sort of thing, you dirty little girl."

"Just because I'm eating your scone does *not* mean I want to watch your pornographic videos. I will puke up blueberry all over you."

"Wouldn't be the first time you puked on me."

My cheeks heated as the scone went dry in my mouth. The one and only time Lex had ever been nice to me was the previous semester, when I thought I was dying from swine flu. Really it was just a stomach virus, but he'd seen how sick that virus had made Ian, and he'd made himself a permanent resident in my house until I got better.

"I come in peace." Lex let himself into my house, holding a grocery bag up in surrender. He took one look at me and cursed. "Gabs, have you eaten anything?"

He was blurry, and I was so hot. "I don't remember."

"Shit." Strong arms wrapped around me, lifting me into the air.

I started shivering.

"You're burning up."

"Put me down," I whispered, my voice hoarse. I had zero strength and felt like I must be hallucinating if Lex was carrying me up the stairs and not purposely throwing me down them.

He used his foot to push open the bathroom door, set me on the toilet lid, and started the shower, then began peeling off his shirt.

I was too weak to do anything but stare at his six-pack and wonder how it was physically possible for a computer science major to look so hot without his clothes on.

Once he was down to his black boxer briefs, he tugged at my T-shirt. I moaned out a weak no, but he ignored it like he did everything else that came out of my mouth. My teeth chattered as he lifted me into the air and slid my shorts down. I was naked except for my underwear and black Under Armour sports bra.

"Try not to scream," he said under his breath, stepping with me into the shower. The cold water was horrific; I immediately clawed at him and struggled to get free, but he held me firmly in his muscled arms. I was locked in place.

And I felt like hell.

I started sobbing uncontrollably. It had been forever since I'd been that sick, and I just wanted my mom and chicken noodle soup. What I got? A nearly naked Lex and a cold shower.

He sat me down, then ran his hands up and down my arms. "Just bringing the fever down, Gabs, and then I promise you'll have some soup."

"With stars?" I asked, blinking up at him. "Chicken and stars?"

"Yeah." His voice was etched with a heaviness I couldn't quite place, and he cleared his throat. "Nothing but the best for you."

"I'm hallucinating," I admitted.

He smirked. "Oh yeah? How's the hallucination so far?"

"Cold." I shivered as my hands grazed over his firm chest. "And hard."

Our eyes met, and for a very brief second I felt it, a lingering pull as if the invisible thread that had connected us was suddenly on fire, tugging our bodies toward one another. But just as quickly as I felt it, he closed his eyes and backed away. "Let's get you dried off so we can feed you. Skinny does not look good on you."

I frowned. "So now I'm too skinny?"

He flashed me a grin. "What can I say? I'm hard to please."

"I'm sure," I grumbled as he helped me out of the shower.

The next two days were absolute hell, between my fever and Lex.

I felt so smothered that at one point I locked him out of my house.

He called the freaking police.

His reason? He was worried. I highly doubted it.

I shook the memory from my head as a realization struck. "You ass!" Mouth full, I nearly choked on a blueberry. "You hacked the registrar's office, didn't you?"

"Hack is such a dirty word." Lex grinned smugly. "I simply evaded a few passwords in order to gain information that would mutually benefit us both."

I took a sip of the strong-brewed coffee and nearly sighed in relief.

"Is it good?"

"The treats change nothing. You still hacked into my records. I knew you did something wrong. You always bring food when you want to apologize—which is rare, by the way, since, according to you, you never mess up, you simply misstep."

"I love it when a girl knows me inside and out." Lex put his hands behind his head, smile still in place. "And the treats are because I know you forgot to eat breakfast . . . again."

I looked away, unwilling to give him the satisfaction of being right and seeing it in my eyes as I continued to eat my shame muffin. I always forgot to eat when I was nervous about school.

"So . . ." He reached down and tapped the book with one finger. "I know you'll never say it, but you need me. Let's get this sweet hell over with so I can train your sorry ass."

My mouth was still watering from the scone, and my body betrayed my good sense as I trudged over to the couch and gave a pointed look at Lex's feet.

"Fine." He sighed, slowly pulling his feet from the edge of the couch. "Happy now?"

"Am I ever happy when I'm with you?"

"If you are, it's because I put pot in your scone. Surprise," Lex said without looking up from the textbook.

My stomach dropped. "You didn't."

"I didn't." He glanced up, a wicked grin marring his perfect features. "But admit it—that would be hilarious."

I had to stay calm. If I reacted, he'd actually do it. So I shrugged and went for casual. "Sad that the only way you can have your way with me is if I'm high on drugs, Lex. Seriously."

Lex glanced up. "You have a crumb on your left tit. I'd get it, but I don't want to touch any part of you that may respond to my caress. You understand."

I growled out a curse. "Just . . . get on with the whole study session so you can leave and I can drink my body weight in wine."

"That's a shitload of wine—just saying."

"Lex!"

"Organic Chem . . ." He held up the book. "I'm going to help you ace this chapter in less than thirty minutes, but you have to do something for me in return."

"I'm not giving you a blow job."

His eyes narrowed. "Like I'd ever have to use extortion."

We were at an impasse, both of us staring at one another, my gaze more irritated and just pissed off while he looked way too calm. If I blinked, he'd win. I kept my eyes wide, watching, waiting, while his upper lip twitched. Why did all the good-looking ones always have to possess evil powers?

I crossed my arms.

His eyes lingered on my lips before he cleared his throat and looked down at the book, knocking it with his knuckles once before saying, "I help you understand all the complicated stuff, and you're mine to train for the rest of the day."

Panic erupted all over my body—or maybe it was just the pot scone. Spending time with him wasn't just emotionally damaging and draining but physically altering. I never walked away from Lex the same.

But I needed to pass this class, and already I was behind.

"Fine." I lifted my chin, faking a confidence I really didn't feel. "But no more kissing or touching of any kind."

"Can't train you unless you have actual hands-on experience, Gabs, and I'm pretty sure the last dude who touched you was that really weird emo kid who said you smelled like cheese."

"Lex!" I calmed myself down by imagining him getting hit by a party bus full of prostitutes. Something about him dying by his own sin really sat well with me. "His name was Josh, and he was really nice." There, that sounded calm, collected.

"Right." Lex nodded and leaned forward. "Are we really not going to revisit the romantic moment where Josh leaned in to kiss you, then said your hair smelled like feta and burst into tears?"

"It's called turophobia, and it's a real thing, Lex!"

"The fear of cheese"—Lex nodded as a smug expression crept over his face—"can also be diagnosed as a fear of different types of cheeses, which in turn can trickle into xanthophobia, the fear of the color yellow." Lex was talking so fast it was like I'd just typed "phobias" into a search engine.

I huffed. "What's your point?"

"My point!" Lex barked out a loud laugh, his bright white smile making my stomach clench with . . . something. It was an ache, and not a good one but one that reminded me what that mouth felt like, damn him. He leaned in and spoke in a low tone. "My point is that it would be totally understandable if one such as yourself suffered from . . ." He tilted his head. "Phallophobia."

"The fear of the letter *P*?"

He scratched his chin. "Nah, the fear of male genitalia. But don't worry, we'll get you over it. The first time's scary for everyone; we'll rip that Band-Aid right off."

"Swear on Ian's soul if you show me your penis I'm going to whack it with my hand, and not a good whack but one that will take the tiny appendage from one end of the room to the other, where my cat will most likely pee on it and make it so no woman ever touches you again. Eunuch," I said through clenched teeth. "You'll be a eunuch. But hey, if that future sounds like fun, and you feel like taking a walk on the wild side, by all means, unzip, Casanova."

"So . . ." Lex nodded knowingly, as if he had a dirty secret. "You got a sexual cat fantasy? Good to know."

"That's what you took from that whole speech? That I wanted you dressed up as a cat?"

"I'd probably do a song from the musical right before you org—"

I covered his mouth with my hand and shook my head. "Lex . . . I will kill you."

"You say that at least ten times a day. It's lost its effect, Sunshine."

"Let's just"—I moved away from him—"go over the next few pages, make me understand, and work your Lex magic, and then we can talk about sexual phobias."

"Promise?" He licked his lips.

"EXPLAIN THIS!" I pushed the book into his hands. "And I may not kill you."

"Sweet."

"I said may."

"I'm not worried. I'm a genius."

"And yet you still managed to get herpes."

Lex rolled his eyes, picked up the book, and cleared his throat. "Give me twenty minutes, and you'll know this backward and forward."

"Isn't that what you say to girls in bed?"

"Actually, yes . . ." His eyebrows pushed together. "But I typically only need five to ten with them."

It was going to be a long morning and an even longer day.

Chapter Five
Lex

What should have taken twenty minutes took twenty-two, which irritated me because I wasn't typically wrong. Then again, if Gabi hadn't raised her hand every other sentence, I wouldn't have had to stop and tell her to put her damn hand down. Finally, in a fit of frustration, I sat on both her hands, grabbed her by the face, and explained the last two points.

I could tell the exact second the concepts suddenly made sense. Her eyes widened, and then in typical Gabs fashion she grinned so big her eyes nearly disappeared into two tiny slits. She was always like that, smiling with her entire face. If someone gave me a picture only of her eyes and asked if she was happy or sad, I'd be able to tell—not that I would ever admit that out loud to anyone. Hell, it was hard admitting it to myself.

"So." I rubbed my hands together. "Any more questions?"

"How?"

I frowned and looked down at the discussion questions. "You're going to have to be more specific, Sunshine."

Gabs stood and stretched her arms over her head. I purposefully looked away and then muttered under my breath, "You really should wear deodorant."

A pillow smacked me in the nose, making my eyes water.

"How does a computer science major know Organic Chem?"

"Easy." I shrugged. "I was bored in high school so they kept putting me in AP classes, and then when my teachers found out that I spent most of my class time listening to music and drawing stick-figure renditions of my classmates, they told my mom to either enroll me in harder classes my senior year or get me out. I chose harder classes." I smiled wickedly. "I always choose harder . . ."

Gabs ignored me and put her hands on her hips, a move I refused to fall prey to, though most guys couldn't help themselves. When a chick put her hands on her hips, it was basically like a homing beacon for a guy's eyes, a big giant red arrow that said "Look. Right. Here."

I did not look. Someone should probably give me a medal, because her jeans were really nice—baggy but nice.

"Gabs, I'm saying this in the kindest way possible, but if those aren't boyfriend jeans, you need new ones."

She frowned and looked down. They bagged at the knees and hips. What the hell? I teased her about gaining weight, but really it was the opposite. Holy shit! Were my comments making her anorexic? Panic filled my chest and radiated to my arms, legs, fingertips. Without thinking, I jumped to my feet. "We should eat before we work."

Gabs yawned, then grabbed her purse. "I just had a scone, though."

"Typical females at your age and height need at least eighteen hundred and forty-eight calories a day, give or take a few calories. It all depends on physical activity, metabolism, and how much you sit."

"Thank you, Siri. I don't remember ass-dialing you, but as always you're so very helpful."

Fun Lexism: I had a really weird tendency to just throw random facts out into the universe when I was uncomfortable or nervous—which was *usually* never.

Damn Gabi, making me lose my edge on life. For my own sanity I needed Training Day to be over with so I could get back to my little black book full of numbers and needy women who wouldn't care less if I spent the night in their arms and jumped into someone else's a few hours later.

Not that I liked women's arms.

Too clingy.

I wasn't into that.

"Stop bitching. I'm going to feed you twice in one day. You should be worshipping the ground I walk on. Aren't you poor? Eating Top Ramen and mac and cheese?"

I eyed her bare countertops and had half a mind to peek in her cupboards to see if she even had any canned goods. What the hell? I knew she was short on funds, but she could still eat, right?

Her stomach growled.

Gabs immediately blushed, bringing her hand to her stomach. "It's just the pot scone digesting."

I burst out laughing. "Pot on an empty stomach, not the most wise choice. But hey, who am I to judge, mon?"

"You aren't Jamaican."

"Finally! Someone who knows I'm white." I sighed heavily. "Thank God. I've been mistaken for Kanye at least twice today."

"Well, the ego matches, so I can understand how people would be confused."

"Thanks, Sunshine." I messed up her hair and pushed open the screen door. "Now hurry up. It's food time, and then we train." I turned around and walked backward so I could see her expression, which wasn't at all eager or even a little bit excited. In fact, she looked like she was going to start blowing chunks. "Don't worry, we'll treat this as a little pretend date. God knows the last one of those you were on didn't go well . . ."

"I hate how much Ian tells you." She reached for the car door, but I made it before her and opened it.

Time froze.

I freaking hated it when that happened.

When we experienced those moments, the ones that only you and that other person are aware of but refuse to talk about.

Gabs tucked her dark hair behind her ear and ducked into the car, mumbling out a thanks, while I tried to slam it as hard as I could after her. I wasn't pissed, but I sure as hell didn't want her to think I was in love with her either.

Not that opening a car door proclaimed marriage, but in a relationship like ours? It sure as hell felt like a promise ring.

"So, where to?" Gabs asked once I started the car.

"Hell." I smiled brightly. "Where else?"

"I can't believe I'm about to say thank you twice in one day . . ." Gabs looked down at the table. "But thank you."

"What was that?" I cupped my ear. "My inflated ego didn't hear you. Please, stroke it a few more times."

"There will be no stroking."

"Your loss."

"Highly doubt that."

"If you stroked, your doubts would be alleviated, believe me." I pushed the basket of chips closer to her. "Eat a few more."

"Says the guy who calls me fat."

"I ask if you've gained weight. I never mean it in a negative way."

Gabs gave me a dirty look.

"Okay, fine, no more fat jokes." I cleared my throat. "You, um, you do eat, right?"

Her confused expression wasn't helping me crack the code. I'd probably have to investigate later. Fine, I could do that, though I hated hacking into people's personal accounts. But sometimes the benefits outweighed the risks, right?

"I'm fine." She shrugged, then started chewing on her thumbnail. Bullshit she was fine. I didn't care. I didn't want to care.

I changed the subject. "Look, you're going to be helping guys land the girls they've always wanted but have always been too nervous to actually pursue. If the program shows that the prospective couple will have a sixty-percent chance of success or higher, we print out a timeline and help them with each step."

"I know." Gabs rolled her eyes. "I've watched you and Ian juggle school schedules, girls, and the business for the past year."

"So." I chomped down on another chip. I'd been too busy making sure she ate and hardly even touched my own Nachos from Hell, the name of the place I'd taken her to. "Jealousy is really what our business is about. If a girl sees her guy with another attractive girl, something sparks in her. It's basic human chemistry. She becomes jealous and then suddenly sees the guy in a completely different light. For you, that will be step one. Think you can handle it? We already know you can kiss; we just have to make sure you can make someone jealous. It's about confidence and—"

Gabs stood and walked away.

While I was still talking. Hell, that was easy. Just start talking about the business, and she freaks out!

A couple was sitting at the bar. She cut off the girl by squeezing between them and then started hurriedly talking to the guy, her hands all over the place, her face alight with so much excitement I was momentarily stunned.

He handed her a napkin and she jumped up and down and made her way back to me, her cheeks flushed. "I'm so sorry, but I didn't want him to leave!"

"Him?" I pointed to the guy, who was about five foot seven and half bald. "You didn't want *him* to leave? *That* guy?" Was she drunk?

"Yes!" Gabs waved at him and then turned red again as though he made her nervous. What the hell? "He's only, like, the most amazing musician. He opened for Ed Sheeran before he hit it big, and I've been following him on Instagram for the past year! I can't believe he gave me his number!"

"What?" I shouted, nearly inhaling bits of tortilla chip from my throat up into my nose. "He did what?"

"He's in the area for a while, and when I told him what a fan I was of his music and how long I'd been following him, he said he'd love to hang out sometime while he tours the area. Amazing, right?" She was literally jumping around in her seat.

I scratched my head and looked back at the guy.

There was seriously nothing impressive about his slight build or black-rimmed glasses that looked eerily like something I'd wear. Bastard.

He was like me, only nerdier.

And shorter.

And dare I say possessing only half the amount of hair I did?

"Sorry." Gabs grabbed a chip from my plate. It was dripping with cheese, so she leaned under it, licking her fingers as she popped the whole thing into her mouth, including the very hot jalapeno. Her eyes didn't even water. "You were talking about something . . . Go ahead."

"Actually . . ." I pulled out my phone. "I have a date. A real date."

Her face fell a bit before she cracked a smile. "Okay, well, I may stay then and hang with Eugene."

I burst out laughing. "That's his name?"

"What?" She looked hurt. "He's a genius."

So am I! I wanted to yell.

"Plus . . ." She stood. "I thought you said you had a date."

Well, yes, I had . . . but I'd been lying. I just needed to get away from her. Something was shifting, changing. I did not do well with change.

Chameleons should all burn.

Anything that could roll with the punches pissed me off.

Damn lizards.

"Yeah." I stood, joining her. "But remember, we still need to go over some training and have you sign the company consent form before you start this weekend."

I glanced down at her, then fired off an e-mail with the correct forms. "Fill them out ASAP, and I'll text you in the morning."

She nodded and hurried off.

"Hey, Gabs?"

She turned, her dark hair whipping around in perfect slow motion. Maybe *I'd* mistakenly had a pot scone, because my world wasn't feeling the same; it hadn't since that morning.

"Be safe."

She rolled her eyes. "Thanks, Mom."

I clenched my phone so tightly it should have bent, or at least melted inside the palm of my hand.

Instead, I quickly sent out a text to a random chick I'd met last weekend and asked her to meet me at the restaurant bar.

It wasn't jealousy I was experiencing.

It just *felt* like it.

And when Musician Eugene hugged Gabs for the second time right in front of me, it was heartburn, only heartburn, that made my chest feel as though a knife was getting twisted and then caught between my ribs.

Apparently, Sunshine didn't just have kissing down.

She knew exactly how to make a man feel like the superhero and the sidekick, all within the same breath.

Chapter Six

Gabi

Lex was acting weird.

Weirder than normal.

Less mean.

But I knew it was only a smoke screen. Eventually he'd be an ass again and remind me why I hated him in the first place. I'd let him in too many times to count, only to get burned—twice.

Two times I'd fallen for that sexy smile, buzzed head, and six-pack. And twice I'd been singed. I was so done being that girl, the stupid one who thought, "Aw, maybe he likes me . . ." I mean, it wasn't that I wanted him to confess undying love, but anything would be better than the constant game of verbal Battleship we had going on a daily basis.

"So . . ." Eugene pulled back from our hug and patted the barstool next to him. "Tell me, what's your favorite song?"

"Song?" I echoed, as my eyes zeroed in on a tall, lanky Asian girl making her way toward Lex. Her legs went on forever, no exaggeration, and she could probably wrap them around his waist twice with ankle to spare. My eyes narrowed—I couldn't help it—as he pulled her in for a kiss.

I saw tongue.

Whatever, not my problem.

Not my problem at all that he'd called a girl during our so-called date and asked her to meet him. What if I had wanted to hang out?

Please, Gabs, when have you and Lex ever really hung out? Alone? Without your puke in his hair?

"Gabrielle?" Eugene frowned, then ran a hand through his thinning hair. He reminded me of one of those scraggly tomcats you pick up on the street. Damn, he'd never stray, would he? Even as a musician he didn't have much going for him other than his kind smile and straight teeth, especially when you compared him to Lex.

He had nice eyes.

That's what my life had come to.

Sitting at the bar with a man who looked like he'd still be holding my hand when I was eighty-eight years old and couldn't find the chessboard even though it was right in front of me.

Crap, was I even making myself blind in my daydreams now?

"My, um, favorite song . . ." I bought some time by scratching my head and then motioning the bartender over and ordering a beer even though I seriously couldn't afford it. Maybe Eugene would pay for it. ". . . is 'Heartless Romance.'"

Eugene made a face, a very unattractive one that had me thinking about stupid felines again. "That's the most unromantic song I have. It's . . . sad."

"What can I say?" I really tried to focus on him, but Lex was whispering into the girl's long, sleek dark hair as she sat across his lap. His fingers inched up her thigh. I shivered. What would that feel like? To have those huge warm hands on me? Good. It would feel good. And I'd only let it happen for a few seconds, just so I could know what it was like, and then I'd slap him in the face.

Right?

"I, um . . ." Wait, what was I talking about? "I don't do romance." May as well tell Eugene I was a lesbian. Good one, Gabs.

I'm going to die alone.

And name my cat Eugene.

"Oh." All of the excitement in his eyes just disappeared, right along with his smile. He fumbled with his IPA, pulling at the blue-and-white label, and then looked away from me.

I was *that* interesting.

Lex glanced over at us, one eyebrow doing that stupid judgmental arch that made me want to shave it off on an hourly basis.

"So!" I faked enthusiasm, my voice louder than usual. "When's your next concert?"

He did a humble shrug and then smiled broadly, his black-rimmed glasses lifting off his face as his cheeks continued to pinch up with a wide smile. See? Adorable! "Tomorrow night, I'm playing at a club downtown. It's a small set, but it should be good, you know? After all, it's about the music."

"Yes." I nodded seriously. "The music . . . It's all about the—" My jaw dropped open as the girl moved from Lex's lap to the seat next to him and started slinking her dirty little hand up his pant leg. He smiled tightly, and then she cupped him.

In the middle of the freaking restaurant!

"Hey, you okay?" Eugene asked. "You look a bit . . . upset?"

"I'm fantastic!" I may have yelled it. "I just—Is it hot in here?" I tugged frantically at my T-shirt. "You were saying? The music?"

"Yes." He clasped his hands together in front of his face, his fingertips touching his thin lips. "It's so important that the music resonates with the fans, that it reaches deep inside—" He kept talking, but all I heard was "deep" and "inside," and then my eyes locked on Lex's as the girl started massaging him.

His smile was wicked.

I should have given him the finger.

But something shifted as his lips parted.

My chest felt heavy, my legs liquid as I watched her . . . *feel* him and watched him respond as her fingers dug into the front of his pants and rubbed up and down.

She was going to town.

But he was watching me.

The. Entire. Time.

"It's like a caress," Eugene said in a whisper. "The way the music floats into the atmosphere, almost like a sexual experience."

I felt my body lean toward Lex, my eyes hooded, as he licked his lower lip, and then he bit down gently as his head fell back.

The girl kissed his neck.

Moment gone. I quickly looked away and started chugging my beer.

"Don't you think?" Eugene asked.

"Yes." I nodded. "Absolutely."

"I asked if you thought I was a good vampire."

"Oh." My face fell. "Eugene, I'm sorry, you're super interesting. It's just that—"

"No." He stood, a sad smile on his face. "I get it; sometimes I get carried away with music stuff. Look . . ." He pulled a piece of paper out of his pocket and held it out to me. It had his name with a time and location for his next concert. "If you ever think of ditching your ex-boyfriend"—he pointed back at Lex—"or ever decide it's time to get over him for good, you should come to one of my shows. I think you'd like it." He dropped a twenty on the counter and walked away.

The minute the door closed, Lex pushed the girl off his lap and said something, then laughed. Clearly he'd pissed her off because she stomped away.

He winked at me, shrugged, stood, and then sauntered over.

"Prostitute of yours?" I asked sweetly.

"Silly, innocent little Gabs." He shook his head. "It's only prostitution if money exchanges hands."

"And bodily fluids?"

"You tell me, were there any bodily fluids? You were looking hard enough."

"Like a car wreck, it's hard to look away when you've got a girl jerking you off in the middle of a family establishment."

"The off didn't happen. Thought you noticed." The prick actually had the audacity to adjust himself right in front of me.

"Aw." I played a tiny violin with my two fingers. "Poor Lex."

"So . . ." He leaned in. "What happened to Eugene?"

"He had a thing." I nodded confidently, then slammed the piece of paper against Lex's rock-hard chest. "But we're going to hang out later."

"Want me to come so I can provide the free show again?"

I rolled my eyes. "I don't watch porn."

"Me either."

I threw my head back and laughed. "Yeah, okay."

He actually frowned, like I'd hurt his feelings.

I shook it off. "You gonna give me a ride home?"

"That depends. Are you going to annoy the hell out of me the entire way back?"

"No," I lied. I lived to irritate him. It kept the line between us firmly in place. The universe balanced.

He rolled his eyes. "Fine, I'll give you a ride home, only if you promise I get you for an hour tomorrow."

"No."

"Yes." He crossed his arms. "Got all night, Gabs."

"Fine," I grumbled. "But just an hour. I mean, what else could I possibly need to know about the business? Just give me my first client, and I'll knock it out of the park."

Lex tapped his chin. "That confident, huh?"
"Absolutely."
"Fine."
"Fine!"
"Fine." He cracked a smile.
What had I just agreed to?

Chapter Seven
Lex

Later that night, when sleep failed me, I was stuck staring up at the boring white ceiling, wondering why the hell I'd told Ashley to run along when I could have been balls deep inside her.

Gabs.

She was the reason, damn it.

All the bad things in my life easily could be traced back to her, like the time I got a black eye from an elderly lady at Costco because Gabs just had to have the last bag of Pirate's Booty.

The elderly lady cried.

I was arrested.

The Pirate's Booty? Lost.

Or the time I nearly failed midterms because she had a flat tire and Ian was out of town, leaving me as the only option to help her. My professors thought it was just an excuse. Then again, word had gotten around that I had slept with a few of their daughters.

But it wasn't like they hadn't been willing.

With a curse, I kicked off the down comforter and padded over to my computer.

I had one new e-mail.

From Gabs.

"All filled out!" The subject said, with all the forms attached.

With a confident smile, I clicked on the first one, the one with her Social, and very easily answered her security questions for Bank of the Cascades.

Favorite family pet? Scooter. An aging goldfish that her parents replaced whenever it went belly up. He had originally died when she was six, but she hadn't noticed the changeover until she was eighteen. Right. Eighteen.

Mother's maiden name? Hernandez.

And finally . . . best friend. Ian Hunter. Though the details were a bit sketchy, it seemed that the Sava family had basically adopted Ian when he was young. His own parents had barely paid attention to him, and then they died, leaving him a shitload of money. Not that it had mattered; he would rather have had parents.

Instead, he had Gabs.

The one girl he'd told me was off-limits.

"Hah, dodged that bullet," I muttered to myself, ignoring the guilt I felt at saying it.

Her accounts popped up. "Bingo."

I stared.

Then stared harder, my eyes narrowing in on both her savings and her checking account.

Both of which had exactly twenty-five dollars.

That couldn't be right. Could it? I clicked on her account activity and noticed that she'd drained half of her savings to pay for school, which I already knew. But the rest, which was around six hundred dollars, she'd pulled out in cash. That had been a month ago.

There was no way she'd been able to live and pay rent with the remaining fifty dollars.

Licking my lips, I signed out of her account and continued to stare at my screen, irritated that my heart had suddenly decided it existed and felt bad for the girl who really was only my friend by association.

I mean, if Gabs killed someone, I'd most likely get in trouble because I knew her, or probably would be with her—or, in my unlucky case, driving the getaway car. But I wasn't the best friend. I wasn't . . . Ian.

He should be the bastard dealing with this.

In a way, he was.

By giving her a job that she'd been begging me to start her in for the past few days. It wasn't like we hadn't paid her, though. I'd made sure to send her payment for getting our books in order, though it hadn't been a lot and clearly all of it had gone toward school.

I had a busy day coming up. I needed to be sleeping, not thinking about Gabs. Again.

But when I crawled back into bed, all I could focus on was the girl mauling her food like it was better than sex, or eating part of my nacho plate when she didn't think I was looking.

Was she hungry?

Was I suddenly Mother freaking Teresa?

Damn it.

I sent out a text to Ian.

`Lex Luthor: What do girls eat?`

`Superman: Is this some sort of perverse sexual joke? It's two in the morning. Just tell her you're out of food and send her out the door. Easy. Done.`

Lex Luthor: No girls in my bed, bro. I mean, just in general, what do girls eat?

Superman: Food.

I rolled my eyes. Really, Ian?

Lex Luthor: Thanks for narrowing it down, man. Can you ask Blake?

Superman: Be honest, are you drunk right now?

How hard was it to answer one simple question? Hell, it would have been faster to look it up online.

Lex Luthor: Nevermind.

Superman: Cool your balls, dude. Blake says that girls like to eat food too, but she's a tomboy—she'd eat you if I drizzled you in ketchup and she just got back from a three-hour practice. Girls like snacks, you know like that pirate booty shit you nearly went to prison over? If it's worth getting arrested for it's probably worth eating.

Duh. Pirate's Booty!

Lex Luthor: Thanks!

Superman: If you're going to the store, can you get me condoms?

Lex Luthor: Get your own damn condoms!

Superman: Extra large, ribbed, thanks man.

Lex Luthor: What part of no don't you understand?

Superman: Blake needs tampons.

I purposely put my phone on silent and threw on a sweatshirt and my flip-flops, only to see my screen going crazy again with messages.

Superman: She says to get the ones in the black box that look like candy, whatever the hell that means.

Lex Luthor: I'm moving out.

Superman: Oh, and ice cream!

It was no use arguing with Ian. He knew I was full of shit and that I'd probably buy the damn tampons, because as much as I hated buying girly things, I was secure enough in my masculinity to do it and usually ended up getting phone numbers solely based on the fact that I was a good enough guy to get my "sister" her feminine products. That shit almost worked better than babysitting a poodle and taking it for a walk in the park.

The closest store was only a few minutes away. I quickly grabbed Blake's stupid tampons and Ian's condoms, then made my way over to the food section.

The bags of Pirate's Booty were kind of small, not like the Costco bag—that one could have fed an entire elementary school—so I grabbed three bags, some chocolate, and a few cans of Coke Zero because I figured the Pirate's Booty was enough calories, and girls were weird about that stuff. Pretzels sounded good. Almonds, some beef jerky, and a pack of gum because of the beef jerky.

When I went to check out, the guy helping me held up the tampons with a quizzical brow.

"Sister." I coughed.

"Aww!" A girl in line behind me gave me the tilted-head smile, the one universally known to guys as the "I'd totally do you in the backseat of the car if it was socially acceptable to do so" look, while I smiled and started up a conversation.

"You live around here?" I asked innocently.

"Just around the corner."

"I'm pretty close too. College student."

"Aw . . ." There it was again. She looked a bit older than I was, left hand with no ring, and she was buying light beer.

"Having a party tonight?" I teased.

"Me and my dog, Phil, are going *wild*." She leaned forward, pressing her tits together as she licked her lower lip.

"Lucky Phil."

"That will be one hundred and twenty dollars and eleven cents," the checker said. I slid my card and winked at the girl.

"Hey," she called, just as I was given my receipt. "We could always use some company . . ."

"Why don't I give you my number?" I held my hand out to the checker, and he rolled his eyes and handed me a pen. "So next time you and Phil aren't lonely."

"That would be nice." Her voice was airy. I think she was trying to sound sexy, but I almost needed to lean in to hear her.

"Name's Lex." I handed the receipt with my number over to her. "And you are?"

"There's a line," the checker said in a stern voice. "In case anyone cares."

"Alice." She giggled.

"I hope to talk to you soon." I waved and took my groceries out.

A few days ago I probably would have been having a quickie near the toilet paper aisle by now. But . . . I had groceries to deliver, a test to ace, and a girl to train.

I also had a puzzle to figure out.

Where the hell was Gabi's money going?

And why was she suddenly without any of it?

Chapter Eight
Gabi

I was just taking my first sip of morning coffee when the doorbell rang. I waited in vain for Serena to answer it. She was lounging in the living room, on her iPhone, playing Candy Crush or whatever the heck she usually did in the early mornings.

The doorbell rang again.

"You gonna get that?" she asked without looking up from her phone.

I had to grip my coffee cup extra tight to keep from smashing it over her head and getting arrested for purposeful assault.

"Blake!" Serena yelled from the couch. "Door!"

Right, and that was another thing. Our friend Blake had moved closer to campus so that she could spend as much time with Ian as possible. His house was closer, and it made more sense for her with all her volleyball practices. Technically she lived in the dorms, but really I imagined she was with Ian more than anything.

"She moved out," I said through clenched teeth.

Serena still didn't look up.

"Why don't I get that?" I said pointedly, slamming my coffee cup on the counter so hard that hot coffee singed my fingers.

Still nothing.

My stomach growled as I stomped my way over to the door and threw it open.

A giant basket was on the doorstep.

And when I say giant, I mean something you'd see a candy-crazed kid get on Easter, the ones with giant bunnies and enough chocolate to put someone in a diabetic coma.

Only my basket had Pirate's Booty.

I smiled.

My favorite.

Poor Lex had nearly lost a kidney trying to grab me one of the last bags at Costco the second time I'd let him into my life, into my heart, only to find him making out with some chick inside his jail cell. The asshole.

The basket was on my doorstep, without a person attached to it.

It wasn't my birthday.

Or any sort of holiday.

Maybe it was a prank and something would pop out through the cellophane?

My stomach grumbled again as I took in the packages of chocolate and almonds.

I hadn't eaten since last night, and before that the last great meal I'd had was when Ian, Lex, and Blake had come over for family spaghetti night.

The food would go to waste if I left it out in the rain.

When I went to pick it up—or basically slide it into my house, since it was so bulky—I noticed a little red piece of paper on the inside. Curious, I tore open the plastic and grabbed it.

From your friendly neighborhood Spider-Man.

Just kidding. I'm way hotter—EAT!

I dropped the card with a laugh. Seriously? Was this Ian's idea of a joke? Then again, he hadn't been answering my calls, probably because every time we talked I complained about Lex, and he said he refused to take sides in World War III.

My phone buzzed in my pocket.

Asshole Lex: You're mine today, Sunshine.

Gabi: What? No please?

Asshole Lex: I rarely use that word, too demeaning. Don't forget to put on makeup, wouldn't want you scaring dogs and small children. Have a heart, Gabs.

Gabi: Did you put Ian up to this?

Asshole Lex: Why yes, since I can read your mind, I did tell Ian to pay for plastic surgery. You gonna go for the double Ds or straight up to Fs? Taking suggestions?

Gabi: Never mind.

Asshole Lex: Dinner.

Gabi: Huh?

Asshole Lex: Dinner. You're meeting your first client at dinner tonight. I'll watch and grade you. Try wearing something that you didn't buy in the little boy section and, for the love of men everywhere, lipstick. Pad the bra.

Gabi: Last night I had a dream you choked on a girl's tongue and asphyxiated.

Asshole Lex: Not the worst way to die.

Gabi: The girl ended up being a dude.

Asshole Lex: Tits are tits.

Gabi: I'll put that on your gravestone.

He didn't text back. With a growl of frustration, I shoved my phone back into my pocket and tore into the first bag of Pirate's Booty, nearly biting my tongue in excitement as the cheese puffs filled my mouth.

Just when I was on my second, maybe third, handful of pirate goodness, my phone buzzed. Mouth full of Booty, I crunched down, nearly biting my tongue, then licked my fingers and pulled out the phone.

BFF Ian: So Lex is into dudes now?

I rolled my eyes.

Gabi: On a scale of one to ten, ten being so irritating I want to reach inside his chest cavity and squeeze his heart with my cheese covered hands, he's an eleven. And is it really all that shocking? That he can play both sides and still score?

BFF Ian: No. Not surprising. I'd be more surprised if he struck out.

The cheese was starting to leave a metallic dry taste in my mouth. I swallowed and fired back another text as my stomach settled with fullness.

Gabi: Thanks for the food.

BFF Ian: ???

I frowned.

Gabi: The food basket? With a card that said it was from Spider-Man? But hotter?

BFF Ian: Spider-Man's a child. Superman's a man, ergo, man in his name. May as well be Spiderboy, piece of shit!

Gabi: Are we seriously having this conversation right now?

BFF Ian: The comics are better, I'll give Spidey that.

Gabi: So it wasn't you?

BFF Ian: I would never demean myself by pretending to be an inferior superhero whose only claim to fame is being bit by a harmless radioactive spider. Superman was born on another freaking planet . . . I rest my case.

Gabi: It's too early for this.

BFF Ian: Spider-Man's a little bitch.

Gabi: Alright then! Talk to you later, keep your cape on, the world isn't out to get you. Ever think you take the whole Superman nickname a bit too . . . seriously?

BFF Ian: >>>>>

In Ian speak that basically meant we were on a time-out until he deemed me worthy of his forgiveness. I sighed and glanced back down at the basket. Maybe some chocolate wouldn't hurt. I felt like I was hungry all the time, which was stupid. It wasn't like I was homeless.

Just soon-to-be homeless.

My phone rang.

Seriously! Was the entire world up early?

"Lex, I swear I'm going to castrate you if you say one more thing about tits!"

The phone was silent, and then, "*Mija?*"

"Dad!" I choked. "Sorry, Lex has just been—"

"No need to explain." He chuckled. "I've met him."

My dad was the best. He knew me inside and out, which meant the last time Lex came to my house for Cinco de Mayo and I accidently confused him with the piñata, my dad was the one to hand me back the wooden bat and then twist me back toward him. He was a prankster like that.

Lex claims it didn't hurt.

But I used to play softball, so . . .

"What's up, Dad?"

He was quiet, and then, "Mija, we know it was you."

I blinked back tears as my throat swelled with emotion, injustice, and—if I was being completely honest—a lot of anger. "And I tried to be so nonchalant about it."

He laughed. "Yes, well, I recognized your handwriting. What did I tell you about giving us extra money?"

"You said I couldn't drop out of school. You never once said I couldn't help out," I argued.

"Mija, you need to be able to live . . . We are just fine, I told you this."

But I knew they weren't fine, because last time I was home I saw the bills, and the envelopes that went with them, the ones with "Overdue" in angry red letters. Ever since my dad had been laid off a few months before, things had been tight. My mom tried to pick up extra shifts at the hospital, but it wasn't enough. They lived near Seattle, for crying out loud; Bellevue wasn't the cheapest place once the tech boom started, and it made me sick to think that at their age they might have to downsize and move.

My dad was looking for jobs, but it was hard. He was either too qualified or too old, though the hiring managers never actually came right out and said that.

He had his MBA but his company had gone under, and now he had all this education he couldn't really use, not when he was competing with college graduates who would do the same job for less pay and with a more energetic approach.

With a heavy sigh, I focused on keeping in my tears. He'd sense my sadness, and that was the last thing he needed. "Dad, I got another job, so . . . what I'm giving you is my extra. I swear I'm okay!"

"There was food," he said in a quiet voice. "You dropped off money and food, mija."

I smiled through my tears. "Dropping off the makings for your favorite chili is hardly food."

"It was delicious." His voice was warm. It killed me that his pride was hurt because he felt he couldn't provide.

"Mom made it, of course it was."

"Thank you," he whispered. "Come visit soon, bring Ian?"

"Yeah." I licked my dry lips and glanced down at the basket. "Dad, how do you feel about chocolate?"

"Is this a trick question?"

I laughed. "No. I'll drop some by later."

"Love you, *mi corazon*."

"You too, Papa."

When the phone went dead, I wanted to crumple into a heap on the floor and cry. But I had a test to ace, a career to figure out, and a new job to say yes to.

With shaking hands I dialed the number with dread, and the man who picked up said a gruff hello.

"Yeah, this is Gabrielle Sava. I'm calling about the opening at the club?"

Chapter Nine

Lex

"You're late." I didn't glance up as Gabs plopped hurriedly onto the plush leather seat across from me, her sweet perfume floating into the air. Normally, perfume had a negative effect on all my senses, making me feel like I was about to get smothered by someone's crazy aunt or grandma and then get my cheeks pinched until I bled. But everything was always different with Gabs. Always. The Matador had a dark, cave-like feel. Candles were suspended above each table and outlined most of the ceiling, giving the restaurant a very eerie but sensual atmosphere. It was the absolute last place I should take a girl like Gabi, because it made my mind think of things, and thinking of things just got me uncomfortable. And pissed.

"So?" she asked, sliding her hands across the table.

"You painted your nails." They were bright pink, matching the natural pink of her lips that I refused to look at, not that I needed to. Her top lip was fuller than her bottom, and a large, pronounced bow that I'm sure most women would pay thousands for framed the top of her mouth, giving her the perfect pinup pout without her doing a damn thing. I'd had several vivid fantasies about that mouth, though they all ended with my death, mainly because Gabs reminded me of a black widow—mate, then kill. Ergo, me dying by her hand.

"So?" Gabi's voice was strained. It was usually deep, with a soothing effect. "Where is he?"

Finally, I looked up from my drink, careful to keep my emotions indifferent as I took in her cherry-red lips, dark eyeliner, and flat-ironed hair, which was in her face. I hated when her hair was in her face. It made her look too seductive, giving the impression that she was hiding secrets, secrets she'd gladly tell you if you could make it past the barrier of silky smooth hair.

"You wore makeup," I said dumbly. Too much. I liked her natural, vulnerable. Today she wore a mask, one I didn't approve of. My hand twitched for the napkin, ready to smear it off so I could see her—really see her. But doing that would just piss her off. Then again . . .

"Don't." Her eyes narrowed as she gripped my hand with hers. "Don't you dare dip your napkin into the water and try to wipe anything off my face."

"That transparent?" My hand tingled with awareness.

"Yes."

"Well, damn."

"Losing your touch, Lex Luthor?"

"In the comics he rarely loses his touch, simply alters his plans. Evil geniuses are like that. Thought you knew. Where one strategy fails . . ." I leaned forward and with my free hand brushed a bit of lipstick from her mouth with my thumb. Her lips parted as she drew a tiny breath.

It wasn't an invitation, but damn, I wanted it to be.

What the hell were we doing?

I needed to put walls up again—fast. And not because I was afraid she'd see through my bullshit and save me from a lonely existence where I indulged in meaningless sex with too many women. Hell, put her in a firefighter's costume and ring the siren. I just respected Ian too much, and, honestly, I respected her just as much, if not more.

A guy like me didn't typically have a conscience or scruples, and friends were even more of a rarity—especially with the way I grew up. The last thing I could afford to lose was them.

A vision of my childhood came bulldozing into my consciousness. Fighting. My parents were always fighting. Over finances, over the house being messy, over having more kids. Thank God I was an only child, because I wasn't sure I would have survived without punching my dad in the face for the way he probably would have treated a younger sibling.

In hindsight, both parents were equally responsible for my unruly behavior. I'd been so desperate for one of them to put down the research or step away from computer and at least have a normal conversation with me that I was willing to do anything for attention—even the bad kind.

I lost my virginity at thirteen.

Who the hell does that?

A guy who really has no other options for human companionship. My parents were cold individuals who never should have had kids, considering they loved work more than family, and based on everything I'd seen on TV, that wasn't how families worked. TV raised me; my parents simply lived with me.

A guy who girls were naturally drawn to because of his good looks and ability to smooth-talk anyone or anything. At the time, it had been this huge confidence boost. Girls wanted me, I wanted them. Period. I gained acceptance, and it felt good—until it stopped feeling good and just started feeling empty.

Until my parents, after finding me in bed with a girl that same year—in my bedroom, of all places, under their roof—simply ignored me more.

My dad gave me a condom the next day.

Some parents.

My behavior became increasingly self-destructive.

Until Ian.

Even after my family moved across town, Ian never stayed out of touch.

It was Ian who convinced me I should go to science camp that next year. Ian who made me think that there was more to the world than sleeping around.

At least now when I slept with women, I didn't do it because I needed love—I did it because I enjoyed it. And because, for the most part, I knew that it made them feel good, and I knew that look, that empty feeling that sometimes disappeared when you were in someone's arms, even if for just a few minutes.

"*Le-e-exxxx* . . ." Gabs drew out my name, jerking away from my touch and grabbing my half-empty drink and chugging the rest of it down.

I pried the cup from her hands and set it back on the table. "Relax, he's a computer science major. The most important woman in his life is probably still his mom, okay?" My voice was shaking. Damn it! This was why I didn't reflect on the past; it did nothing for me.

Gabs blinked dumbly. "Lex, you do realize that's your major, right?"

"So?"

Her eyes widened. "Is this you fishing for compliments?"

"When have I ever had to fish for anything? Compliments? Women? Fish?"

"Right, I get it." She stared longingly at my cup, and with a smirk I waved down the waiter and ordered drinks for both of us.

"Moscow Mules change lives." I nodded seriously. "Now you know my secret."

She snorted. "I highly doubt knowing something that impersonal about you is going to gain me entry into your Batcave, where you share your plans of world domination over a pillow fight."

Our drinks arrived.

"First"—I slid her drink away—"never confuse a villain with a hero, it's insulting." She reached for the drink, but I held it back. "Second, I refuse to acknowledge Batman as a superhero. So what? He's scared of bats, tough shit! Villains are scared of nothing."

"Joker's scared of Batman."

"The Joker has a permanent smile on his face, he laughs in the face of bats. Batman cowers and then cries and then tries to conquer his fear. Mad props for going after what you're afraid of, but put him up against Magneto, Dark Phoenix, Dr. Doom!" I slammed my hand against the table, while Gabs gave me a blank stare. "What?"

"Sometimes I forget how nerdy you are."

"Physical perfection has a way of doing that." I winked.

"Can I have my drink now?"

"Am I still Batman?"

"No." She slinked her hand around mine and gave her cup a little tug. "You're back to being the creepy, bald Lex Luthor."

"Hair or no hair, I'd still get laid. Also, now that we've reached a shaky peace agreement of sorts, I'm totally down for penciling in that pillow fight."

She pinched my forearm.

"Ouch!" I released her drink.

"Can I stuff my pillow with razors?"

"Girl wants me to bleed before sex?" I nodded. "Only if I'm allowed to keep my world domination plans to myself, you understand, just in case you injure me, drug me, steal the nuke codes, then sell them to Superman."

"Ian wouldn't know the first thing to do with those codes, and you know it." She lifted her drink into the air and winked.

I burst out laughing and clinked my drink against hers. "That's my girl."

Her smile fell.

Shit.

"So." Back to being nervous and shut down, Gabs tucked her hair behind her ears. "Where's the nerd?"

"Open your eyes." I cleared my throat. "He's been sitting at the bar for the past twenty minutes, staring into his chocolate milk, filling it with his tears . . ."

Gabs rolled her eyes.

"Fine." I reached into my briefcase and pulled out his folder. "As you know, each client takes my infamous matchmaker test to see if they're compatible with their object of desire. We match them based on personality, background, majors, likes, dislikes—you get the picture. It's like a really intense Myers-Briggs personality test—on crack. Once a client fills it out, I um"—I coughed—"research the other candidate, and then determine if a match is to be made. We like to see compatibility numbers over sixty percent." I turned the page. "The next section discusses his background, hobbies, interests, where he spends his time."

"And this?" Gabs pointed to the section labeled *Sex*.

"Sexual experience."

"Oh." She frowned. "It's blank?" She glanced up. "Run out of ink?"

"Yes." I nodded at the sad individual sitting at the bar. "Steve's sexual experience was so vast, so detailed, that my printer broke."

She looked at the guy again and scrunched up her nose. "He seems nice. Maybe he's a freak in bed, you never know."

"And by freak you mean he wants to talk about his feelings and goes 'what are you thinking' every five seconds?"

"Hey!" Gabs looked offended. "Nothing wrong with asking direct questions."

"When someone asks 'What are you thinking?' what they're really asking is 'Are you thinking about me?' Narcissism at its worst."

Gabi's face fell as if I'd just told her Santa and the Easter bunny got together and ate Nemo and the dog from *Up*.

I changed the subject. "Introduce yourself. Always keep Wingmen Inc. cards on you." I gave her a stack of Wingmen Inc. cards with Ian's Superman-style insignia on the front and our e-mail information on back. "Remember, this is the first meeting, so he can still say no. Be persuasive, make him feel good about you, this process, how you can help him, your knowledge, and you'll be fine."

"But—" Gabs paled. "I don't know—"

"Off you go." I smirked, ready for the train wreck to happen. She'd be completely lost without the playbook. She wasn't cocky like Ian and me. She lacked the arrogance to make someone feel small one moment, only to make them feel like the most important person in the room the very next.

She'd see she needed me.

And I'd happily come to her rescue.

Because that's what . . . Ian did.

What the hell? Not what I did.

I didn't even want her working for us, damn it! What the hell was happening to me?

I was supposed to be training her.

That's it.

So what happened when the training was over and she was by herself? With all the nerds? What happened when I didn't have any more excuses to drive her insane?

I sipped on my drink and ignored the panic rising in my chest.

Friends.

Enemies.

We were both.

No need to add any more labels to what was already turning out to be the most confusing relationship of my life.

Chapter Ten
Gabi

"Before I forget." Lex crooked his finger. "Lean down, Sunshine."

"I'm not giving you a view of my breasts, I don't care if you're breathing your last breath or the world will end if you don't see nipple. Not happening." I crossed my arms as if to make my point while Lex rolled his eyes and held up a small microphone. "Oh."

"Feel stupid yet?"

"No."

"Just let me fasten it between whatever the hell these are." He pointed to my breasts and then, before I could protest, slid his hands into the front of my dress and attached a small microphone to the middle of my bra. My black dress had a V neck, so it wasn't hard for him to access. His hands were warm, damn him.

"Done?" I asked in a high-pitched, airy voice that so didn't sound like mine.

"Testing." He spoke into my cleavage. "Testing one, two . . ."

"Now you're just playing around."

"Sunshine, if I was playing, your tits would know it"—he lifted his gaze to mine—"and you would too."

I jerked away from him and straightened my dress. He held out an earpiece.

"You've got to be kidding me! This isn't a sting operation!"

Lex gave me a condescending look and shrugged, still holding out the earpiece. "I'm not sending you in blind. Not someone like you."

The comment stung, more than it should, which meant somehow the bastard was slinking his way back into my life. Normally I brushed off every comment that came spilling out of his mouth. So if I was actually taking some of his barbs to heart, I was letting him in. Again. Things had shifted between us, and they needed to stay the hell *stable* before I lost my mind. His gaze was lingering more than usual, as were his hands. I shivered.

"Fine." I grabbed the earpiece and put it in my ear while Lex did the same and then spoke into a tiny microphone in his hand.

I nodded. "I hear you just fine, and no, I'm not going to fluff your towels."

"But they need fluffing, Gabs, help a man out."

"You don't want me fluffing anything, believe me . . ."

"Fine." He leaned back. "Now run along and prove to me you're ready to start taking on clients, and good luck, Gabs. Remember, he still has a choice about whether he wants to hire us, mainly you . . . And remember, when the girl he's obsessed with walks in and he doesn't feel that what you're doing is working, you're not just making yourself look stupid, but Wingmen Inc. No pressure or anything."

He crossed his arms. I seriously wanted to strangle him.

Instead, I turned on my heel and made my way toward my target. This really did feel like a sting operation, especially with Lex in my ear.

How was it possible that even through the earpiece, it felt like his voice was caressing my body? No, Gabs. No.

My mind conjured up the image of us kissing. Mouth watering, I nearly had to clench my thighs together as the feel of his tongue sliding into my mouth became such an electric turn-on that I whimpered.

"Don't be scared . . . look sexy," Lex ordered.

"I'm trying," I said through clenched teeth.

"Sway your hips more."

I tried swaying and nearly collided with the leather chair at the next table.

"Damn, woman, he's going to think you're drunk if you pull that stunt again."

"Sexy, sexy, sexy," I repeated under my breath.

Lex paused and then said, "Your ass looks nice . . ."

"Thanks, Lex." I paused as warmth filled my chest. "That was actually really—"

"I can't even tell you gained ten pounds."

"You're a dick."

"Maybe take it easy on the Pirate's Booty, Gabs."

I paused, my heart galloping in my chest. "How'd you know about—"

"I nearly died in order to get you the last bag, Gabs, I know your obsession."

"Stop doing that!"

"What?"

"Finishing my—"

"Sentences?" he guessed.

I let out a little curse, then flipped him off behind my back.

"Don't encourage me, Gabs. You know what that gesture means, and I'm just desperate enough to bend you over the table and take what I can get."

"So romantic . . . Tell me, would it be next to the chips and guacamole, or would you at least wait until dessert?"

He was quiet and then said in a hoarse voice, "Why eat food when I get you as an option . . ."

I opened my mouth to say something, but I was almost to Steve and he'd just turned around.

"Hey." I nearly choked on my tongue as I sat down next to the guy I was hired to help gain the attention of the love of his life. Her name was Stella, and based on the pictures in the file, they looked like they could be brother and sister. It was a match made in heaven . . . At least it appeared so, since they had an eighty-percent chance of success once they passed the first three months of dating.

"He's a computer science major, Gabs. You're going to have to do better than 'hey,'" Lex interjected.

Steve looked up. He had shaggy brown hair that gave me the impression that he was allergic to scissors. His hair covered one eye, leaving the other peering up at me in curiosity.

Brown. A pretty brown. I could work with that, right?

"You have nice eyes," I said softly. "You should maybe make people aware you have two of them, otherwise they may mistake you for a pirate. Arggg."

Lex let out a groan. "You did not just Jack Sparrow him."

Steve smirked and then laughed out loud. "Yeah, that's what I'm going for, dark and dangerous. Did it work?"

I nodded vigorously. "I'm here, aren't I?"

He looked me up and down, then took a slow, cautious sip of his drink. "You're here with that guy." He pointed at Lex. "So, either this is a bet to see if you can get me to embarrass myself or"—his eyes narrowed—"you could be part of Wingmen Inc."

Smiling, I pulled out the chair next to him. "Mind if I sit?"

"Beautiful and evasive," he said over his glass. "I like it."

"Funny, because that guy over there hates it." I jabbed my thumb in the general direction of Lex.

"When have you *ever* heard me utter those words?" Lex said in an angry tone. "Dude's a jackass. Walk away, Gabs, he was staring at your tits."

I ignored Lex.

"Think he'll kick my ass if I insult him?" Steve asked.

"Hell yes I'll kick his ass, tell him, Gabs. His stomach is concave. If we were the last three people on earth and we had to eat him to survive, we'd starve."

I shrugged. "He's more lover than fighter, more bark than bite."

"I'm not even insulted." Lex sounded like he was yawning. "I have a hell of a bite . . . You just wouldn't know. Poor Gabs. Hey, did you get that vibrator I sent to your house? Put my face on the box and everything."

Too far. I mentally imagined myself punching Lex in the face and forced a smile. Focus on Steve. Steve was the important person, not Lex.

"He looks like he could rip me in two." Steve coughed into his hand. "By blinking."

"Eh." I shrugged. "Can I tell you a secret?"

Steve leaned in.

I cupped my hand and whispered, "In bed, girls call him Shorty."

"Very funny, Gabs," Lex said in my ear.

"Shorty?" Steve repeated. "Because of his . . ." He didn't say the word.

"If he can't say 'penis,' it leads me to believe he doesn't know what it's for, Gabs. Just saying. Object *A* goes into object *B*, and sometimes they produce a *C* . . . Oh, and just in case you were wondering, *C* stands for 'conception.'"

Lex wasn't easy to ignore, but I tried. I slid my hand across the table and patted Steve on the arm. "Let's just say that when girls leave his bed, they always have a smile on their faces, but it's not from pleasure . . . it's from laughter."

"They point and laugh?" Steve's eyes widened.

"I think they would," I said seriously, "if they could actually see the object they were pointing at, but, I mean, who has binoculars just laying around, right?"

"I do," Steve said quickly.

"Of course he does." Lex sighed. "And it's huge, you felt it. Stop trying to insult King Lex."

He'd named his penis.

Why was I not surprised?

"So . . ." I licked my lips. "Stella, huh?"

Steve immediately blushed, his cheeks burning a bright red as he looked down at the counter, then started playing with part of his frayed cuffs. "Yeah, well, I mean I've hinted that I like her, but I don't want to ruin our friendship."

"Ask him what he means by hint," Lex instructed.

I cleared my throat. "So when you say 'hint,' you mean you went in for a kiss or tried to hold her hand? That type of hint?"

"I leaned." Steve nodded seriously.

"Oh dear God," Lex muttered.

"Oh." I kept my expression steeled. "So, you . . . um, leaned toward her?"

Steve nodded vigorously. "You know that movie *Hitch*?"

"Sometimes I blame world hunger on Will Smith, just because I can. I mean, *Hitch*? He gave nerds everywhere the worst advice on the planet . . ." Lex's monologue was hard to keep track of, considering I was supposed to be focusing on Steve.

"Yes." I finally said. "The one with Will Smith?"

"He's a baller." Steve laughed. Though he said "baller" in such a painfully white way that I had to fight to keep myself from cringing, while Lex mocked him.

"Baller, yo, wanna go play some ball in our new kicks and bang some chicks in the back of my Benz? Word to your mother."

My lips twitched into a smile.

"I know, I know." Steve laughed harder. "It's stupid to get dating advice from movies like *Hitch*, but I mean, I went in at least eighty percent for the kiss."

"Doesn't the movie say ninety?" I corrected, wondering why the heck he was taking advice from a ten-year-old Will Smith movie.

"I got to seventy-five and panicked," Steve confessed in a defeated voice.

"Shocker," Lex added.

"So that's it," I said, feeling the need to clarify. "You went in, she shut you down, and you haven't tried since?"

"There haven't been any good romance novel moments, you know? I mean, I tried kissing her in the rain and I nearly face-planted against a cement wall because the sidewalk was slippery. And at the movies, when it got dark, I reached for her hand but she moved it to grab the soda." He sighed. "I'm an idiot."

"No." I shook my head vigorously.

"Yes," Lex said in a bored tone.

"That's what I'm here for." Just as the words came out of my mouth, Stella walked in the door. "Don't look now, but she just walked in. This is all part of the plan, though, okay? Do you trust me?"

"No." He laughed. "But I'm just desperate enough not to care."

"Dude's got more romance in his pinky finger than . . ." Lex's sarcastic voice trailed off. Then he whispered, "Showtime, Sunshine, show me what you got."

I quickly scooted my barstool close to Steve and then whispered in his ear. "Smile, but not too big. I'm going to grab your hand, alright?"

"Okay." He looked ready to puke.

"Try not to blow chunks on me." I giggled while moving my hand up his arm until I was gripping his bicep. "Wow!" I pulled back, then frowned. "You're actually way more built that I thought!"

"Uh, thanks?" Steve looked confused.

"No, seriously." I squeezed his arm again, then moved my hands to his other arm, running them up and down his skin. "You're like . . . buff!"

His chest puffed out.

"He looks like what happens to pretzels when you throw them in water and they get all bloated and shit, but whatever," Lex commented. "Good work. Stella's looking over at you guys. If looks could kill . . ."

With a giggle, I leaned in toward Steve's mouth. "I'm not going to kiss you, but I'm going to make it look like I want to. If she really likes you, she's either going to leave and get super frustrated when you talk to her next, or she's going to stomp over here and stake her claim."

"Moment of truth." Steve swallowed, his Adam's apple bouncing down, then back up.

"Hey," I said in a quiet voice. "If the worst happens, you're still a great catch."

"You're just saying that because you want me as a client."

"No." I shook my head. "I'm saying that because everyone has something to offer the world, and if she doesn't notice what you have, she isn't worthy of keeping it in the first place."

Steve quieted. His eyes zeroed in on my mouth, and suddenly I wasn't sure if he was just playing along or really wanted to kiss me.

"Steve!" A high-pitched voice interrupted our moment. I glanced to the side to see a shaggy-brown-haired girl in a plaid shirt and black leggings put her hands on her hips and nearly jump into his lap. "Out on a weeknight?"

"My Steve's crazy like that." I winked.

"Your Steve?" Her arms crossed.

"Well done, grasshopper, well done," Lex whispered his praise. I winked at him over Stella's head.

"Hey, Steve, it was real, here's my card." I slid him the Wingmen Inc. business card and nodded. "We'll be in touch?"

"Absolutely." His grin was huge. "I'll call you later."

"I look forward to it."

The minute I walked off, I heard Stella utter, "Who the hell was that?"

By the time I made it back to Lex's table, he was already gathering our stuff and leading me out the door.

Adrenaline surged through me as we walked to our cars.

Slow clapping had me turning around.

Lex leaned against his Benz. "You're hired."

"Hmm, rich evil genius tells innocent girl she's hired while standing in a dark parking lot? Should I be suspicious?"

"Hah!" Lex barked out a laugh, and the moonlight just made him look that much more sexy, dangerous. "I'm a put-it-all-out-there type of guy, no secrets."

"Bullshit!" I laughed. "Don't treat me like one of your whores, you have more secrets than the NSA!"

"Nice people, the NSA."

"My point exactly." I rummaged for my keys. "I gotta run, Lex. I'll see you later."

"Studying?" he guessed.

"Nope." New job, new scary job that was only hiring a young girl for nights.

"Date?"

"Nope." I forced my smile. "See ya, Lex."

His smile fell. "Where are you going?"

"None of your business." I slammed the door and drove off, hating that when I looked in the rearview mirror it was like leaving a magazine photo shoot. He really needed to stop being so good-looking.

Chapter Eleven

Lex

The week went by in a complete blur of boredom. There was nothing pressing going on with my classes, and since Gabs had aced my little test with flying colors, I was no longer needed as a trainer. But because Ian was still nervous about her handling male clients all by herself, I'd been promoted—or demoted, depending on how I looked at it—to her glorified babysitter. Though I'd like to think of myself as the Muscle.

Steve had signed up—and their second date was set for the following evening.

The drone of the TV was a welcome distraction from all things Gabi. My typical MO wasn't to sit around on the weekend, but going out just seemed exhausting, and, as if to prove a point, I yawned. Holy shit, what was wrong with me?

I clicked through the channels and was finally settling on *The Godfather* when Ian walked in the door with Blake. It was still hard to believe that this was the girl whose daily wardrobe used to consist of giant dude sweats and tube socks. Looking at her now you'd think she just stepped off the runway. She rarely wore makeup, but something about the midriff shirts and low-slung jeans she wore did something to a guy. Not me. Clearly, athletes weren't my thing. But Ian? Well, I think we discovered his kryptonite: tomboys who could challenge him to a pizza-eating contest and come out the victor while still being able to run a half marathon the next day. Funny that he'd broken one of his own rules by dating a client—then again, he was part owner and could do whatever the hell he wanted . . . within reason.

"Lex?" she called in typical loud Blake manner.

"Yup." I didn't look away from the TV.

"Are you sick?" She plopped down next to me on the couch.

"Blake, remember the rules: if your ass touches the couch, you aren't allowed to speak . . ."

She stood and then repeated the question. "Are you sick?"

I turned up the volume. "Can't a guy watch TV?"

I felt an itchy sensation spread from the middle of my chest out to my fingertips, like if I didn't go for a run or do something stupid I was going to lose my mind. But nothing sounded fun or entertaining; even hacking into Gabi's bank accounts seemed boring.

Besides, now she had money. I'd cut her first paycheck, a bonus, actually; it would be enough for her to get by for a few weeks.

"Dude." Ian sat on the other side of me. "It's Friday."

"Is it? Really?" I said in fake shock. "Cool, guys, we all have calendars and know what day it is."

Ian was quiet and then, "*Are* you sick?"

I looked up toward the ceiling. "Why the hell are you guys asking if I'm sick? Do I look sick?"

Suddenly self-conscious, I wondered if I really was coming down with something. That would explain the weird moods! Maybe I had a fever?

Ian's eyes narrowed again. "Lex, it's Friday."

"WHY THE HELL does it matter?"

"You're home," Blake said from my other side. "On a Friday night."

"Guys, if you can't respect couch rules, I'm going to have to kick you out of the living room without TV time."

Ian stood, then jerked the remote out of my hand. "So you're staying home? Tonight? On the weekend?"

I yawned. "I'm beat . . ." With a smirk, I added, "And when I say I'm beat, I mean—"

He held up his hand. "There he is. I was worried for a minute."

"Don't sweat it, Mom, I've banged the appropriate number of single females this week at least a dozen times. I'm not sick, nor am I finally on the straight and narrow. I'm also happy to announce I made at least three bad decisions this week and got drunk on a Thursday night."

Ian clapped.

Blake scowled and then let out a loud sigh as she stared at her phone.

"What?" Ian was by her side immediately. I made a whipping motion, but he flipped me off.

"Gabs," she whispered. They both looked over at me, then moved away from the living room, probably assuming that talking about her in my presence would put me in a bad mood. Normally they'd be right.

But things hadn't been normal for the past week, damn it.

My ears strained to hear their conversation but only picked up bits and pieces.

"She can't afford it."

What?

"No money . . ." And then I heard "Have you seen her cupboards?" More whispering. "Serena's talking about moving in with her boyfriend."

My body shook involuntarily. Serena—blonde, hot, with a nice rack—had been a horrible mistake. I'd taken one look at her and said, "She'll do."

Only she didn't.

I did.

She simply lay there and then burst into tears after everything was over, saying, and I quote, "That was the most magical moment of my life."

I couldn't get away fast enough.

And even when I said, "That's not magic, that's just good sex," she still didn't believe me and seemed hell-bent on believing that we had some sort of connection between our souls.

"I tried!" Ian said, raising his voice a bit. "But she won't accept it . . . and she won't tell me what's going on, but . . ." *Damn it, talk louder!*

More silence.

I stretched my body across the couch in order to get closer, but they'd moved to the farthest part of the living room, inconsiderate asshats!

After a few minutes, they came back into the room and said they were going to go out to dinner.

When I asked if Gabs was going with them, they both looked at me like I'd just spoken in Hebrew and asked if it was cool if I hosted Hanukkah.

"She's got work," Blake answered, while Ian made a face. Blake grabbed Ian's hand and led him out of the room.

I jumped up from the couch. "Work? I'm her work. What do you mean, work?"

"I'm shocked." Ian slammed his hand against his chest. "You mean you guys don't tell each other everything?" He and Blake joined in laughter. "Since when do you care what Gabs does? Last time you used her name in a sentence, it was paired with so many four-letter words that I'm shocked you even know how to have a civil conversation with her."

"Whatever." I know my response was immature, but it was all I had. "I'm going to go call a random."

"A random?" Blake asked.

"Don't . . ." Ian shook his head. "It'll just make you want to kill him, and I can't keep the peace between him and Gabs and him and you. I'm only one man."

"A random." I smirked seductively even though I knew it was lost on her. "When I go through the school website, pick a girl's number, call her, and then bang her in as many ways as possible, ruining her for all men."

"I'm sorry I asked," Blake mumbled.

I held up my hands. "Don't hate the player."

"Hate the game." Blake waved me off. "Yeah, I know."

"I was going to say hate the girl stupid enough to play with me . . ."

"Huh." Blake nodded. "Yeah, that too . . ."

"Have fun running away from commitment and your feelings!" Ian yelled back to me as they walked out of the house.

I waved with my middle finger. "Have fun picking out wedding colors and sleeping with the same woman for the rest of your life!"

The door slammed behind them.

The living room was blanketed with tension. Nervous energy trickled through me as my leg started its incessant bouncing, my fingertips drumming against the same bouncy leg. I crossed my arms, trying to get the nervousness under control. It didn't help.

I never used to be bothered by being alone; I wasn't really the typical party guy. I slept with girls, sure, but I didn't like crowds. I liked my computer, my sanctum, and I liked sex.

Anything beyond that didn't really matter to me.

The blare of the TV was grating on my nerves. I promised myself I'd stop obsessing over Gabi's personal life. It wasn't my issue, at all.

And yet I found myself turning on my heel and making my way into my bedroom, shutting the door quietly behind me, and pulling up a chair to my computer screens.

Hands shaking with excitement and maybe the adrenaline of how wrong it was to go snooping into the private life of my arch-nemesis, I hacked into her bank accounts again.

And nearly had a freaking heart attack.

Hearts Gentlemen's Club?

Two hundred dollars?

Wha-a-at?

"Oh, Sunshine, what have you gotten yourself into?"

Without a second thought I grabbed my phone, pressed the Home screen button, and said, "Siri, directions to Hearts Gentlemen's Club."

Hell, my night was just about to get all kinds of interesting. Thank God for really weak computer passwords.

CHAPTER TWELVE
GABI

My short black tube-top dress was itchy, not to mention extremely uncomfortable. Thank God I had black tights on; otherwise, every time I bent over I was going to be giving people a free show.

I blinked back tears. I hated it. Hated all of it. But my parents needed money, and this was the only job that would let me work around my school schedule and Wingmen Inc. Ian, being Ian, had offered to help me financially, but he'd already done way too much, and I wasn't his responsibility. Rich people didn't get it. Taking money from them had a way of making the less fortunate feel even worse.

Lex.

I was already in trouble. I had a very real fear that if I repeated his name three times in the mirror, or just in general, he was bound to show up and take possession of my soul.

"Hey, honey!" A drunk man waved a ten in the air. "Can we get some more drinks over here?"

"Sure." I forced a smile even when his eyes lingered longer on my chest than was appropriate. It was a gentlemen's club; what was I expecting?

The lights dimmed as one of the announcers went on stage and started getting the crowd pumped up for the next dancer.

At least I wasn't doing *that*.

Things could be worse, right?

I wondered if it was just a matter of time before I got that desperate. The manager of the club had already told me I could make a killing, but something about taking my clothes off for money sounded a hell of a lot like what Lex did on a daily basis, so . . . I refused.

Plus, my parents would be furious.

"Honey!" the drunk man called again. "The drinks!"

"Yeah!" I called back and made my way over to the bartender. "Can I get three rum and Cokes for table seven?"

"Sure." Jim was in his fifties, though he looked more like a thirty-year-old. He was really built and had a blinding white smile and no hair. "Here ya go, sugar." He slid the drinks onto my tray.

I heaved the tray up and walked over to the drunken table. "Three rum and Cokes. Will there be anything else?"

The man gave me a few dollars' tip and then crooked his finger for me to lean down.

Oh great.

"If you give me and my buddy a private dance, we'll double that." He pointed to the ten-dollar bill he'd given me.

Oh wow, twenty bucks to take off my clothes for Grandpa and friends? Where do I sign up?

"I'm not a stripper," I said through clenched teeth. "Just a waitress."

"Hah!" The men at the table erupted in laughter. "They all start as waitresses."

I swallowed the retort that I'm sure would have gotten me fired and smiled through clenched teeth. "Anything else?"

"You think about it," he slurred, and then he winked—or tried to, but it was really more of a blink.

"Yeah, I'll do just that," I lied and walked off toward the bar. It wasn't very busy for a Friday night, and I was thankful. I'd only been working a few days, and my feet already ached.

What I wouldn't give for a massage!

I reached into my apron and pulled out a candy bar. For the past three days I'd been getting baskets of food, mainly junk food and the odd protein bar or Red Bull here and there, but beggars couldn't be choosers.

Every time there was a note. And every time it said,

From your friendly neighborhood Spider-Man.
Just kidding. I'm way hotter.

Every. Single. Time.

I was too tired to research it, too tired to set a trap. I was just thankful I had enough Pirate's Booty to cause the rumbling in my stomach to cease, at least for a few hours.

"So," a familiar voice said above the music. "New job?"

Damn it! "I didn't even say your name three times!" I whined, turning around to face Lex. He was wearing a tight vintage black T-shirt with low-slung jeans on his hips and the ever-present sex-oozing smile.

"Three times?" He smiled wider. "You said my name three times out loud? Is it your new curse word? You know, like 'Oh, Lex! Holy Lex! Mighty Lex . . .'" His eyebrows drew together. "Somehow all of those sound like very familiar noises women make in my presence."

"Die, Lex," I said in an annoyed tone. "How about that one?"

"That's new." He snapped his fingers. "But it's growing on me. Maybe it's the way you say it, like you want me to die in your arms all *Romeo and Juliet* style . . ."

"Wow, ten at night and you're already wasted." I slapped him on the shoulder. "Take a cab." I tried to move past him, but he grabbed my wrist and pulled me back, pressing us together. Whether it was on purpose or not I wasn't sure, but he was warm.

And he felt . . . safe, familiar. My body was playing tricks on me; it was because I was vulnerable.

Like that night when . . .

I locked down my memories, especially that one, and threw away the key. "Lex, what do you want?"

"You," he said in a serious tone. "Now get up on stage and take off your clothes. I paid for a show."

I rolled my eyes. "Waitress, Lex. You'll have to call one of the many numbers on your phone to get a free lap dance."

"What if I pay?" His breath tickled my ear as my eyes burned with unshed tears. Normally, I wouldn't let what he did affect me. Normally, I brushed him off, but my armor had already been stripped. Call it exhaustion or maybe just the last remnants of pride I had toppling to the floor.

But I couldn't hold them in any longer.

One tear fell.

Then another.

I tried to wipe them, tried to jerk free from Lex's strong arms, but he turned me so abruptly that all I managed to do was soak the front of his shirt with my tears and smear it with mascara.

"Gabs?" His voice rasped as he hugged me tighter. "Come on, we're going."

"No." Panic surged through me as I tried to pull away. "You don't understand!" I'd given the last of my paychecks to my mom so she could pay the bills at the house, leaving me completely broke for this week's rent check. I was hoping to make enough money in tips for the rent.

Lex's eyes crinkled at the sides as he took one look at me and the rest of the seedy bar. I knew what he saw: girls dancing on poles, guys getting drunk and shouting at the girls while they threw dollar bills onto the stage, and a scared, stupid girl clinging to him like her lifeline.

Finally, he released me. "Gabs, I'm sorry, I was joking. We always—" He licked his lips and glanced down at the filthy floor, cursing. "Where's the money going?"

"Money?"

"New girl!" Dean, my boss, never called me by name, the idiot. "You working or flirting? If he wants time with you, he's gotta pay."

"Still a waitress?" Lex's eyebrows shot up.

I held up my fingers to indicate I needed a few more seconds, but Dean was apparently in a mood and stomped over to us.

"Problem?" he asked, crossing his arms over his skinny chest. The guy was small; Lex could probably break his face blindfolded.

"Yeah," Lex said, surprising me. "Your waitress just refused to dance with me because you guys are out of private rooms . . . so."

Dean's eyes narrowed. "You her boyfriend?"

"Do I look like a man who wants to commit to crazy?" Lex fired back. "But I do have this . . ." He reached into his back pocket and pulled out what looked like at least six hundred dollars in cash. "How long will that get me with your waitress?"

Dean's eyebrows kissed his hairline as he sputtered out, "At least three hours."

"I'll add in another six hundred if I can have table service and a private room, no interruptions."

"Done." Dean snapped his fingers above his head as one of his security guards came barreling over. "Please take them to the Diamond Room, no interruptions. Stand outside the door. One waitress goes in and out to provide drinks."

The security guard nodded.

And five minutes later I was stuck in a personal nightmare. A bottle of champagne rested on ice; two glasses were left on the table. Music pumped through the speaker system. A small stage was set up in the middle of the room, with two poles and some sort of swing that dropped down from the ceiling. I seriously didn't even want to know what it was for.

"That will be all," Lex said in a gruff tone. The waitress—I think her name was Holly—bobbed her head, then looked at me out of the corners of her eyes as if scared to leave me alone with the giant.

"It's fine." I waved her off and forced a smile.

The door closed.

"Stop pacing." Lex grabbed a bottle of champagne. "And that ass better give you part of that money . . ."

"Huh?" I turned. Lex had his feet up on the table and was texting. TEXTING!

He glanced up. "What? Something wrong?"

"Uh . . ." I lifted my arms into the air. "You sick bastard, you just paid for private dancing! From me!"

"No I didn't," he said calmly. "Nobody knows what goes on in here. Take a nap for all I care, drink some champagne—or you can shock the hell out of me and cry again, but fair warning, I only had one hug in me tonight and you stole it, so . . . I'll be reverting to the back pat."

"Who are you?"

"Lex Luthor, philanthropist by day and rescuer of hot waitresses by night." He smirked and held up the bottle. "Champagne?"

"Unbelievable." I choked out a laugh. "You just paid over one grand to sit in a crappy club and drink champagne with someone you hate."

"It's my good deed for the decade. Just don't tell Ian. He'll think I'm sick or something, and the last thing I need is Mother Hen helicoptering around my inner sanctum. He'll get pissed all over again if he finds out that I'm hacking."

My skin felt sticky and sweaty, and my feet ached. With slow movements, I made my way over to the couch and sat, not even wanting to know how many germs were on the leather.

"So," Lex said above the music. "Champagne? Or want me to order you something else?"

"Champagne's good." I swallowed and looked down at my hands. "I'm sorry I cried."

"As you should be. Big girls don't cry . . . they kick ass. Don't freak me out like that again, it's not good for my heart."

"Finally admitting you have one?"

Lex spread his arms wide. "Clearly, otherwise you'd still be waiting tables."

"Or dancing," I muttered.

"Hah." Lex laughed, actually laughed as if it was funny. "No offense, Gabs, but you're not like those girls on stage. You can't . . . You just can't."

"I can't?" Why the hell was I getting offended? "What do you mean I can't?"

Lex laughed harder. "Gabs, look, there's nothing wrong with being innocent. Lots of guys dig a girl who has fields that have never been touched, watered, planted, plowed—"

I held up my hand. "I get it."

"But those types of girls, the good girls, the ones who've never been . . ." He smirked. "Conquered? They don't typically know how to use their bodies in a way that mimics sex on stage. Get it?"

"No." I crossed my arms. "I don't get it! Dancing is dancing! A two-year-old can do it!"

"Bad example, bad mental picture all around, Gabs, again solidifying my point. Good girls don't dance, not like that." When I didn't say anything, he added, "Embrace your goodness; don't get pissed. It's a compliment."

"The hell it is!"

"Damn, I love it when you swear," Lex murmured, taking a long draw of champagne. "See, at least you do that right."

"I can't last in here for three hours," I muttered, jumping to my feet and starting my pacing all over again.

"Want to play games on my cell phone?"

"Like a child!" I blurted. "That's it! You're treating me like I'm . . . a toddler! Like I should be thankful you just saved me from hell. Be honest: If you had a sticker and a sucker, would you give them to me if I shut my mouth the entire time?"

Lex gave me a guilty look.

"I'm a woman!"

"Well, if you were a dude, we'd be having a different conversation and you probably would have punched the guys grabbing your ass earlier . . ."

Without thinking, I grabbed my glass of champagne, chugged it, poured another, chugged that one, then with shaky hands grabbed the little remote, turned up the music, and jumped on stage.

I expected Lex to say something inappropriate or at least roll his eyes. Instead, he looked . . . panicked.

"Gabs!" he yelled above the music. "Look, I'm sorry! Just get down!!"

"Oh, I'll get down!" I grabbed the pole with one hand and leaned back. "Just wait."

Chapter Thirteen

Lex

Warning bells went off in my head, but I still didn't move.

A freaking alarm sounded, and my hand twitched.

My body was paralyzed. Though my blood was still pumping, which I knew because I felt that blood hurry its way to all the wrong places as Gabs took a teetering step onto that stage.

My eyes . . . thank God my eyes were still working as they greedily searched for an exit, for an escape, because my body and my mind were not in sync, not at all. My body wanted to stay, while my mind told me it would be just one more thing, one more moment that would slide me farther down the hill. One day I was going to look back at all these moments and go, well, hell, it wasn't the first step that did it, or even the second, but the accumulation of all those moments and all those instances when I said yes—but should have said no and run like hell.

Ellie Goulding's voice filled the room as "Powerful" began playing. Shit. I gripped the leather sofa, then panicked. I didn't want her to think I was responding, but with the way my fingers were digging into the leather, I might as well have been Wolverine.

Gabs's heels were plain and black, but still spiky. The sound of them clicking against the floor next to the pole did something to my body, making my breathing pick up speed even though she hadn't started yet.

Bold, clear green eyes locked on mine, and then her hand touched the pole. I felt that touch as if she was grabbing me. My body gave a little jerk as her fingers slid down the metal. Jeans tightening, I had no escape, no choice but to watch and pray she wouldn't notice what that simple action did to my sanity.

"So?" I challenged her, praying it would make her lose her nerve. Hell, I'd even take the tears. "You gonna dance or just touch the pole?"

Her eyes narrowed.

Shit. I knew that look.

Too far, Lex.

She'd dance all night to convince me. I didn't need that; no man with my sexual appetite needed that sort of torture.

One sexy leg wrapped around the pole.

My mouth went completely dry as she slowly threw her head back, and then that little tease spun around the pole like she was born there.

What the hell?

Since when did virgins pole dance?

Knowing she was untouched, knowing that for the most part no man had ever seen her in the throes of pleasure, made the experience that much more raw. Everything about the way she slid around the pole—the way her body moved down it only to slowly move back up, making me notice every curve of her hips and ass—had me losing my damn mind.

I crossed my legs.

I coughed into my hand.

I thought of Ian's grandmother.

Nothing.

My body wanted.

Simple.

Hard.

Fast.

Slow.

In as many positions and ways as physically possible.

Patience wasn't one of my virtues.

My hands twitched at my sides as my cock swelled with painful need. I briefly closed my eyes, giving myself a break, but that was almost worse, because at least when my eyes were open she was fully dressed.

But when they were closed?

She was stripped of every piece of clothing—except her shoes. Bad idea!

I popped my eyes open again. Her hair had fallen in her face and one eye peeked out as her lips parted. Getting into it, she spun again and again.

Damn, I was beyond uncomfortable, getting rubbed raw by my own jeans while I tried to adjust myself without her seeing.

The song was coming to an end.

And so was I.

In more ways than one.

Ian would have laughed his ass off, and if it had been any other girl I would have told him.

But with Gabs?

He'd probably kill me.

And I'd deserve it.

Family.

Sister.

Best friend.

Holy shit, she just sucked her thumb.

My vision blurred as she stepped off the stage and took two steps in my direction. I leaned forward, body on fire.

The minute she was within reaching distance, I jerked her onto my lap. Gabs let out a little moan as her skirt hiked up past her hips. My hands followed the material as she rocked against me.

I wasn't thinking, I wasn't anything.

My response was primal, with this instinctual need to mark her, make her mine, and be the very first guy to do it.

The only guy to touch her.

Ever.

Heat surged between our bodies as I gripped her hips, moving her harder against me.

The song ended.

Another started.

I barely noticed. The entire bar could have burned down around us—probably was, because the explosiveness between our touches was enough to do that very thing.

"Gabs," I moaned out her name when she started riding me harder. "That's it," I encouraged, officially stepping outside of my own body as she panted against me.

My mouth found hers. I couldn't stop kissing her, tasting her.

And then a knock sounded on the door.

It wasn't loud enough to do anything except irritate me.

But Gabs froze.

My grip on her was still tight, as though my hands were begging for her to stay, just . . . stay.

Her eyes opened.

She sucked in her swollen bottom lip and let out a rough exhale. My entire body was buzzing.

Neither of us said anything.

I didn't know what the hell to say.

I just knew that I couldn't be an ass.

I wanted to be. It was my MO. Be an ass, push her away, stay in the safe zone with Ian.

The knock got louder.

With a curse, I slowly peeled her off my body, made sure her legs were covered, got up from the couch looking all kinds of turned-on, and opened the door.

"Sorry." The waitress looked apologetic. "The boss just wanted to know if you needed more champagne."

I had told the asshat not to interrupt us.

But in that moment, I was thankful, because I sure as hell had been about five minutes from screwing my best friend's "sister" in a strip club, on a red leather couch, in front of a stripper pole.

Holy hell, could I be any less human?

Any other girl . . . I wouldn't think twice.

But it was Gabs.

I hung my head and croaked out, "Yeah, um, that would be great." The waitress turned around, and I tapped the back of her shoulder and said, "A bottle of Jack would be nice as well, and maybe . . ." I was going to burn in hell. Alone. Fantastic. "Send in some more girls? I think Gabi needs to go home, and I've bought her for the rest of her shift so she's free to go."

The girl smirked. "I'm free."

Yay.

"Great." I forced a smile. "That's . . . great." It was so far from great, I wanted to puke.

When the waitress left, Gabs was already standing, arms crossed, face a mask of indifference as if I hadn't just insulted everything that happened between us.

"So . . ." Gabs nodded. "I can leave?"

"Yeah, you've done your . . . job." I don't know why I said it. Maybe because it felt like she was dismissing me when really it was the exact opposite, when I was saving us both from an epic mistake.

"Hah!" Gabs let out a little laugh and leveled me with a cold stare. "But you clearly . . . didn't do yours."

"Using me for sex?" I tilted my head in amusement. "You know all you have to do is ask, Gabs . . . but maybe wait until money doesn't exchange hands. Don't want to start that career too early . . ."

Her cheeks reddened. "I hate you."

"The feeling's mutual, believe me." I sneered.

She shoved past me just as three girls walked through the doorway. With a strangled curse, she pushed between them and left me alone with girls I didn't even care about.

I went back to the couch and sat.

Numb.

Girls started dancing around me.

Shots were poured.

And I couldn't give two shits about it. But I did what I always did, I tried to revert back into the guy I always was with girls. I flirted, I touched, I even kissed.

And felt like I was going to puke the whole time.

Because the only girl I wanted had just left.

Chapter Fourteen

Gabi

I was too angry to cry. What had I been thinking? I went over to my car and shoved my key in the ignition. It sputtered.

"Come on, baby." I clenched my teeth and tried again. "Come on."

Finally it roared to life.

I sent up a prayer of thanks and with shaking hands turned the steering wheel toward the general direction of the parking lot exit. Tears welled in my eyes, but I refused to cry over someone so stupid. Guys like Lex, Lex in general, didn't deserve my tears.

Why did I always do this to myself?

Why?

I'd been drunk on the power that the little cheap stage had given me. Lex hadn't looked at me like Ian's best friend or his most hated enemy. He'd watched me with a raw hunger that I'd never seen before. He'd tried to mask it, and then, after the mask had slipped, all I saw was . . . desire.

Finally. That was the only word I could think as his eyes hooded, his fists clenched, and his body so clearly responded.

I wasn't planning on walking toward him, but I'd gone halfway, and he'd pulled me the rest. His mouth was . . . Words couldn't describe the way Lex kissed, like he was pulling every inch of pleasure he could from me. Trying not to respond to him was impossible. Even his hands on my hips . . . I shuddered and shoved the memory into the box of *Never Again*. Damn, that box was getting full.

"Are you drunk?" I asked. Finals were over. Ian and Lex were hosting a party at their house. I was invited because I was invited everywhere Ian was. Ever since freshman year Lex had given me a wide berth, if wide meant he treated me like crap and I returned the favor.

"No." Lex's eyes looked clear. "Not yet."

"Got big plans for getting wasted and impregnating a nice young girl, only to have her drop out of school?"

Lex rolled his eyes. "Not tonight, Gabs."

"Whoa." I blocked his exit from the balcony. "Are you . . . okay?"

He licked his lips and stared at his shoes. Lex never stared at his shoes. He was an eye-contact sort of guy. It was rare to see him glance away from people. In fact, one of the few things I respected in him was the way he treated others—not me, but others. Everyone was important, everyone's opinion mattered. I clearly didn't count, but for whatever reason, I was okay with that.

"No." Lex huffed out a breath. "I, uh . . ." He scratched his head. "No."

"Anything I can do?" I touched his arm. I shouldn't have. That was my first mistake.

His eyes immediately locked on my arm.

My fingers tingled as if he had some sort of mental power, or laser beams coming out of his pupils, nailing my fingertips to his bulky forearm.

"What if I asked you for a hug?" he said slowly, then looked up. His eyes were clear, so hopeful. "Would you laugh at me?"

"Probably." I grinned. "But only after the hug took place. I'd still allow you your pride and all that."

Lex barked out a laugh, then held up a finger. "One hug . . . and then you can rub it in my face."

"Deal." I held out my hand.

He shook it, then without releasing it, tugged me against his body. Our chests collided, and my head nearly knocked his chin into submission.

And then his big burly arms wrapped around me.

With a sigh, I returned the movement.

We spent a few minutes hugging, and the hugging somehow turned into dancing, and one song turned into two songs, and then three, even though the music was barely audible from the house.

"Thanks," Lex whispered over my head. "For the hug and the dances."

I swallowed and looked up; our faces were inches apart. "It was nice."

"What?" He frowned. "No sarcasm? Did my hug drain all your superpowers?"

"Yes." I nodded seriously. "Apparently you're my kryptonite."

"Not Superman."

"No, I guess not." I lifted one shoulder and let it fall with a sigh. "What's Lex Luthor's kryptonite?"

"Superman."

I laughed.

"Or maybe Supergirl," he whispered. "Yeah, Supergirl . . ."

"And how does she get her superpowers?"

"Sunshine," he whispered. "Just like Superman, only . . . prettier." His head lowered while my chin lifted toward his.

"I like that."

"Me too."

"Are you going to tell me what's wrong?" I almost said it against his mouth. We were so close to kissing I couldn't stop shaking.

"I forget."

"You lie."

"No." He cupped my face. "For fifteen minutes . . . I forgot. Thank you."

He kissed me.

It was a quick peck on the lips.

And then another.

And another.

Until our mouths were fused together, arms wildly grabbing at one another. He didn't taste like beer at all, he tasted like . . . cinnamon, almost like he'd been drinking tea at his own party or something.

His tongue met mine in a whisper of a kiss. I let out a moan.

And then the doors to the outside burst open.

"What the hell!" Ian shouted.

Lex shoved me away so hard I collided with a chair, and my butt was nearly numb from getting hit so hard.

"Drunk," Lex blurted, and then the asshole winked at me with a dopey smile. "Thought she was Ashley."

My eyes narrowed. "Lex—"

"Ashley does have brown hair." Ian seemed to accept his excuse.

"You guys are both assholes and idiots!" I yelled.

"Aw, Gabs." Lex tried to reach for me. "Don't be mad, you're hot too."

Ian cleared his throat.

"In a flat-chested type of way."

Tears burned my eyes, and my mouth wouldn't work. Just like my brain couldn't come up with a nasty retort, something that would make him hurt just like he'd hurt me.

So I stomped off, to Lex's laughter, and swore I'd never let him in again.

I touched my face as tears streamed down in rapid succession. Ugh, I was a complete and utter failure. I needed to find a guy, one who actually knew how to treat a girl.

And stop whatever fantasy I had with Lex.

He wasn't for me. He would never be for me.

Over it.

Damn it.

My phone rang.

"Yeah?" I answered as I wiped my face with the back of my hand.

"Mija!" My dad's voice was just what I needed to hear. "How is your new job?"

Visions of me dancing around a pole, then riding Lex, hit me full force as a prickling shame crawled up my arms and settled in the center of my chest. "It's good, Dad." My voice cracked. "Really good!"

"Gabrielle?" He lowered his voice. "Are you alright? Have you been crying?"

"No, no!" I forced a laugh, and it sounded horrible, like a cross between a hiccup and insanity. "Just so tired, you know?"

"Okay, well, you take care of yourself, and your mother, and I thank you." He sighed. "Mija, you shouldn't be giving us more money." His voice was a combination of relief and stress. I chose to focus on the relief. I was young, I would bounce back from being tired. He wouldn't.

"Well, we need to keep the house, so . . ." I shrugged even though he couldn't see me. "Besides, I'm getting paid really well."

"Are you sure you're okay?"

"Yeah." My stomach chose that moment to grumble. It was so loud that I was afraid he'd hear it. "I'm fantastic. Gotta go, though!"

"Okay! Love you, and thank you, mija. Your mother and I are so proud!"

Uncontrollable sobs escaped me as the phone went dead.

What was I doing with my life?

I sniffed back more tears and wiped my eyes with the backs of my hands.

It was just a bad day. Everyone had them; this was mine.

At least I had chocolate at home and a bottle of wine, thanks to Spider-Man.

I pulled into the driveway and quickly let myself into the house.

Serena hopped off the barstool. "Oh good, you're home!"

Why was she so happy about that? She was rarely even there!

"Yup." I dropped my purse onto the counter and went in search of my Spider-Man basket.

"So . . ." Serena followed me through the kitchen. I located the basket and tore into it, only to find all the chocolate gone. "I'm moving out."

"Did you eat all my chocolate?"

"Oops." She lifted her shoulders into a guilty shrug. "Were you saving it?"

"YES!" I roared.

"Yikes. Maybe it's good we're breaking up."

"Wait, what?" What had I missed?

"Moving out. Me." She pointed to her chest. "So yeah, I'll give you rent for the month, but you're going to have to find another roommate."

Chapter Fifteen
Lex

"What crawled up your ass and died?" Ian asked as we parked in front of Gabi's house for dinner. It had been a week.

A week of pure hell.

A week where I had stalked her like the creepy insane person I'd officially become.

The only time she and I talked was when I sent her more info on Steve or when I needed to check in with her progress. Ian had never filled out progress reports, but since Gabs was new and we needed to know how the program was going with guys, she had to fill out a date sheet every time she went out with Steve.

So far they'd gone on two dates.

Both had been fine.

That's all I had.

Because Gabs refused to put anything other than "He was fine."

Question 1: How was dinner?

Fine.

Question 2: Did the client show any signs of nervousness? If yes, explain how you helped.

Client was fine.

I growled as I got out of the car and slammed my door.

"Seriously?" Ian glanced back at me. "What the hell is your problem? You can't treat this kind of car that way!"

I shrugged.

Ian's eyes narrowed. "You look like shit, too, just saying."

"Thanks, Mom, anything else?" I shoved my hands into my pockets.

Ian always saw through my bullshit, so I was suddenly thankful he was too in love to pay attention to me or my issues. He'd know immediately what it was, and then I'd be stuck apologizing to him while he tried to saw off my balls with a rusty fork.

The door to the girls' apartment opened in a flurry. Gabs was wearing the shortest damn Nike running shorts I'd ever seen. The hell? They sold those in stores? What did she do, shop in the kids' section and ask for an extra small? The outline of her ass was wreaking havoc on my already alarming attraction to her. I forced my eyes away for maybe three seconds before she turned and moved farther into the house, her tank top flashing smooth skin right next to her hip and a little shimmer of her belly-button ring. Mouth dry, I stared, looked away, stared again. What the hell was she doing answering the door with scraps for clothes? There were serious creepers in the world! Ones that would take advantage of all that . . . skin. I choked on my next breath as the dizzying scent of strawberries smacked me in the face.

I was already hot.

Things were about to get hotter.

She gave Ian a hug.

I got a fleeting look, and then she turned her back on me.

It was a great feeling—like being shot at. Not that I'd been shot at, but the pain was physical, real.

I'd never cared that she treated me like shit, because we had an understanding, a type of game, in which we both hated each other but at the end of the day, if she had a flat tire, I'd fix it.

If I needed a hug, she'd grudgingly give it, then step on my toe.

Except for that one time.

My stomach clenched at the memory.

"Seriously." Ian shook his head. "Are you on drugs?"

"Drugs?" I repeated. "Do I look like the type of dude who wants to drop thousands of dollars on something that only keeps me high for a few hours at a time?"

"So you've thought about it, then?"

"Yes, Ian, life is so horrible that I sat down at my desk with my calculator and figured out just how much money I would be losing if I took the plunge into addiction."

"You did?"

"Stop, just . . ." I moved past him and made my way into the kitchen. Gabs was leaning against the counter, and her petite little legs looked adorable in the shorts. I tried to look away.

But since she didn't know I was staring . . .

"Lex." Gabs didn't turn. "Keep staring, and I'm going to pull one of your balls until it pops."

"Oooo." I rubbed my hands together. "Promise?"

She didn't answer.

Ian brought in the two bags of groceries as per usual when we had family dinner. Blake couldn't make it because of practice, so it was just us and Serena.

Speaking of. "Where's Serena?"

Gabs turned and glared. "She moved."

"To?" I crossed my arms.

"And she ate my chocolate."

"So you kicked her out?" I laughed.

Gabs didn't.

Ian held up his hands. "Tread carefully, my friend. That look would get a lesser man killed."

"Good thing I'm not a lesser man, hmm, Gabs?"

I was pushing, pushing too hard, but I needed the verbal sparring, needed to know I still evoked some sort of emotion from her even if it was all negative.

She rolled her eyes and started unpacking the groceries. It was spaghetti night. Almost every family dinner was, because it was our favorite. "Her boyfriend's in a band," explained Gabs, setting the box of pasta on the countertop. "He's going to make it big someday—her words, not mine—and she wants to travel with him in his super-cool van to make sure no groupies try to steal his virtue."

"Hold up!" Ian busted out laughing. "Are you talking about the skinny emo dude who has green hair? That guy?"

"His voice is just—" Gabs placed a hand on her heart as her voice took on the high pitch of Serena's. "He gets me? You know? He gets life!"

"He has a song about hairspray," Ian pointed out.

"And its dangers to the ozone layer." Gabs grabbed the Italian bread and started slicing it. "Oh yes, I'm aware."

She was making me nervous with the knife, so I quickly grabbed it from her hand and pushed her out of the way.

"Wow, you're actually helping instead of drinking all the wine?" Gabi's eyebrows arched as a disbelieving smile crept across her features.

"I don't want blood on the bread." I drew the knife through the loaf. "I do this for all of us. My intentions are purely selfish, I'm starving, and you were cutting the bread like you thought it was . . . me."

"Bingo." Gabs winked.

At least she winked.

I shrugged and got back to cutting while Ian's eyes narrowed in on me and then on Gabs.

Shit.

"What's for dessert?" I piped up. It was always her job to get the dessert if we brought ingredients for dinner. I was still dropping off baskets, and I had specifically added in two boxes of brownie mix. "Brownies?"

Gab's mouth fell open, and then she closed it. "I, uh, actually forgot?"

"That's okay," said Ian, letting it go.

I'd just dropped off the basket that morning. How the hell had she eaten two boxes of brownies?

"Nothing? Really?" I stopped slicing bread and went over to her pantry, but her tiny body blocked me.

"What are you doing?" She crossed her arms.

"Um, what does it look like I'm doing?"

"Guys!" Ian held up his hands. "We don't need dessert, no need to start World War Three."

"You heard him," Gabs said.

"Move." I glared.

"No!"

With a grunt, I picked her up and tossed her over my shoulder, then opened the door as her little fists banged into my back.

Empty.

There was nothing in her pantry save for one box of mac and cheese.

Once the door was open she stopped fighting, slumping against me in surrender.

The kitchen fell silent.

What the hell? Pissed, I set her on her feet and carefully gazed at every empty shelf. The pathetic box of mac and cheese didn't even look new, like the boxes I'd given her.

"Uh, did Serena also take all your food?" Ian joked, though I could tell he was concerned from the way he hovered near Gabs. I was still too angry to say anything.

If she was starving, she should be eating what was in my baskets! Was she seriously that prideful? That she'd dump out free food just because she didn't want a handout?

With a scowl, I slammed the pantry door.

Gabs jumped a foot, then glared.

"You know what, I'm not hungry," I snapped, my eyes meeting hers, waiting for her admission, anything. But she was silent, crossing her arms again and staring back in challenge. "I'm gonna head out."

"I drove," Ian said.

"I'll walk." I needed to leave before I yelled at her or made her cry. Nothing made sense. I couldn't understand why she wouldn't just take the food.

Once I was outside in the middle of the sidewalk, I paused.

I'd grabbed a new basket each time.

Meaning if she was dumping the food, she was tossing the baskets in the trash, and it was Tuesday. Trash came Tuesday night.

Yesterday's and today's baskets would be in the trash.

I hurried to the back of her house, located her large green trash can, and found my inner raccoon.

Lifting the lid, I started digging through the black bags.

Nothing.

A throat cleared.

I must have been really into my trash digging, because I didn't hear a damn thing. How hadn't I heard the squeaky back door open?

"Um . . ." Ian scratched his head. "I'm sure you have a great explanation, right?"

Gabs was standing right behind him.

I snapped the lid to the trash closed as embarrassment washed over me, making my face heat with the awareness that I'd just been caught digging through my enemy's trash can like a homeless person.

"Yes." I nodded. "I do have a good reason."

Ian's eyebrows arched.

Gabs crossed her arms.

"But . . ." I took two steps back. "First, I have a question for the liar."

"Liar?" Ian repeated.

"Gabs." I barked out her name. "You get baskets every day. Baskets full of food. Where the hell are they?"

Her mouth dropped open and then closed. "I, uh, how do you even know about those?"

"Serena." She wasn't here to deny it, and I highly doubted Gabs would fact-check me.

"Didn't know you guys were still . . . cozy," she accused.

"Cozy enough." I fought to keep the smirk from my face. She wasn't jealous, was she? "Now, about those baskets."

Gabs shook her head, then glanced at Ian's back. Her eyes met mine again, pleading.

Something clenched in my chest.

"Actually . . ." I cleared my throat. "Serena did say something about a canned food drive . . . for the homeless."

Ian finally turned around and looked at Gabs. "That's cool, I didn't know you were doing charity work too. You should have told me. I would have helped."

She shifted on her feet before tucking her hair behind her ears and offering a nervous laugh. How he didn't see through the lie, I had no idea. "Yeah, well, I know you're busy . . ."

"Changed my mind." I made my way up the steps. "I'm starved."

"Great!" Ian rubbed his hands together and made his way into the kitchen, while I grabbed hold of Gabs's hand and tugged her backward, whispering in her ear, "I hope you have a really good reason for that lie I just told."

"I didn't ask you to," she hissed.

"Yeah." My lips grazed her ear, and her body relaxed against mine. "You kind of did."

Her head hung.

"Gabs!" Ian yelled loudly. "Lex!" He ran around the corner just as I released my hold on Gabi's arm. "Just got a text from Blake. She sprained her ankle and needs help grabbing all her stuff from practice. She's fine, but I'm going to go hang with her." He looked back and forth between the two of us. "Promise me that if I leave, both of you will still be alive tomorrow."

"Hah." I held up my hands in innocence. "Us? Fight? No . . ."

Ian rolled his eyes while Gabs let out a little grunt.

"At least finish cutting the bread so I know no weapons are present. I don't want to have to tell the police I left you both with sharp objects." Ian made his way back into the kitchen.

Gabs was hot on his tail and shoved him in the back playfully. "Just go! Your girlfriend needs you, and I swear I won't cut off Lex's balls."

Ian exhaled in relief.

"He'd be expecting it, and I like the sneak approach. I'd wait at least until he was sleeping."

"You wish." I pushed her out of the way and grabbed the bottle of wine we'd brought. It was time to drink. Especially if I had to be alone with her. But first I went over to the sink to wash my hands. "Believe me, the only way I'm inviting you into my bed is so I can suffocate you with my pillow."

"I'll just stay." Ian grabbed a chair.

"No!" Gabs and I said in unison as I threw my wet hands into the air, causing water droplets to land on his face.

Ian blinked, then shook his head in dismay.

I spoke up again. "Ian, go. Swear we'll be fine."

"If you're sure." He got up again, wiping his face with the back of his hand.

"Totally." Gabs nodded, too emphatically; we weren't very convincing. Then again, I wouldn't believe us either; legit hospital visits had happened because of us being in the same room together.

Ian's phone went off. "It's Blake." His shoulders slumped. "Just"—he held up his hands as a pleading expression overtook his face—"don't kill each other."

Within minutes he was gone.

When I turned, Gabs had a knife in her hand and a devious smirk on her face.

"Oh hell," I muttered. "We need more alcohol."

CHAPTER SIXTEEN

GABI

We were actually coexisting in the same space, breathing the same air, and not killing one another. We also weren't talking, so maybe that was the reason. It was horrifying to realize that the only time we didn't fight was when we were . . . kissing.

I let out a groan.

"Cramps?" Lex piped up. "Because if you want to forgo the whole family-dinner thing, I can leave so you and your tampons can have some personal time."

Lex's eyes were dark, soulless pits of hell. At least that was what I told myself whenever I found him attractive, which recently was every single time we were together.

Why was it so hard to focus on all the horrible things he'd done? It was like every time he was nice he erased all the bad with that one good deed. What an asshole thing to do!

Was it on purpose?

"Gabs?" Lex leaned forward. "You're pale, and you're staring at my eyes like you want to gouge them out with your fork."

I lifted the fork into the air. "The idea has merit."

"I'm too fast for your short legs. You'd end up forking my ass."

"True." I finished setting the table. "But it would still hurt, therefore, my life would be complete."

"Inflicting pain shouldn't be a life goal, Gabs."

"Neither should being an asshole, yet here we are." I smiled sweetly.

Lex breathed out a curse and poured his second glass of wine. I was still on my first. The last thing I needed was to be more loose-lipped in his presence; we really would get in a fight then—and probably burn the house down, leaving me homeless.

He tapped his fingertips against his glass, his full lips pressing together in a small smile. Everything about him sitting at the table with me felt right when it should have felt wrong.

I needed a fight.

Something to remind me that he was a horrible human being.

That the minute I let him in, he'd bite.

And not a good bite but the type that spread a life-altering infection, making it so you were never the same. I'd already nearly given my virginity to one asshole, there was no need to repeat history and actually follow through this time. I was afraid it might actually break me—that he would break me.

I shot to my feet, stalked to the stove, and turned down the sauce. The pasta was already on the table, ready for consumption.

"Need help?" Lex asked, his body heat singeing me from behind! A hand snaked around my body as his finger dipped into the hot sauce and then left.

I imagined his lips around his finger and nearly whimpered aloud.

"At least you can cook, Gabs."

"Meaning what, exactly?" I didn't turn around. I wasn't so sure I could trust myself not to launch my body in his general direction and beg him to kiss me.

My legs wobbled.

Gah! I hated him.

"Can't I give you a compliment?"

"No," I growled out, mindlessly stirring the sauce with the wooden spoon. "Because they're always backhanded. Like 'You don't look as fat in that dress as you did last time you wore it,' or 'Nice lipstick, I hope it was free'—"

Lex's hand cupped my face, and his cologne lingered everywhere like a cloud of sex that was impossible to step out of. I was afraid to breathe, afraid to move.

"How about this?" His body brushed against mine, our legs kissing, nearly intertwined as we stood in front of the stove. "I really enjoy your cooking. The end." He removed his hand.

"The end?" I whispered. "Is that going to be your new thing? I'll know it's real if you say 'the end'?"

"You'll know it's real because it's truth," he said, still not moving.

A door slammed, and Ian's voice rang out. "Forgot my coat and it's raining . . ."

I didn't listen to the rest of the sentence; I was too busy mourning the loss of Lex's body as he jerked away from me, leaving me cold, shivering, and completely turned-on.

Yes, folks, he turned me on by breathing.

Crap.

Someone needed to smack me in the face, knock some sense into me. I pleaded with fate to simply turn him back into his full-time assholeness so I could live a marginally normal life without losing my mind in his presence.

I turned around just as Ian ran into the kitchen, grabbed his coat, and then jogged back out.

The tension was thick.

Like the sauce I'd just let boil over. "Crap!" I turned back to the stove and quickly removed the pan.

"Correction." Lex sauntered over and took the pan from my hands. "You *were* a good cook."

"The end?" I scrunched up my nose as I looked down at the semi-burnt sauce.

"Yeah." He gave a firm nod and set the pan in the kitchen sink. "The end."

My stomach growled on command. He might dump the burnt sauce, but if he didn't, that sauce and I had a date later. I didn't care if it had charred pieces of coal in it, I was going to devour every last drop of it.

"I'll order pizza." Lex pulled out his cell. "It's not family dinner unless it's Italian."

I opened my mouth to protest, but he was already talking into his phone. "Yeah, can we get two extra-large Hawaiian pizzas, extra pine-apple on both of them and Asiago cheese on top?"

Curse him for knowing every weakness I have, starting with pine-apple and ending with cheese.

"Cash," he said into the phone, then fired off my address.

"Feeding an army?" I joked.

"Nah, just you, Sunshine." He smirked. "And I figure the fatter I keep you, the slower you are when I chase you."

"Smart." I nodded. "Prey on the weak, that's what I always say."

"Gabs," Lex said with a chuckle. "I thought you knew . . . I only spar with the strong."

With that, he walked into the living room and grabbed the remote, flipped on the TV, and set his giant feet onto the table.

"Sunshine!" Lex snapped his fingers behind him but didn't even turn around. "Wine me?" He held his hand out.

I rolled my eyes and grabbed his wineglass, contemplating only briefly, for maybe three seconds, dumping it on his stupid big head.

His stupid, close-shaved, sexy head.

Noooooo!

"Heard that foot stomp!" Lex called.

"Wine." I shoved it into his hand without spilling it and then sat with him on the couch and did a mental recount of all the horrendous things he'd ever done to me.

Chapter Seventeen

Lex

Typically I ate at least six pieces of pizza; some days I ate nine. But that night? I had two.

I was turning into a chick and growing ovaries. Hell, in a few weeks I'd probably start obsessing over Whine About It videos on Buzzfeed and crying over Nicholas Sparks novels.

Because as a dude, you aren't supposed to forgo any sort of food, especially that of the pizza variety.

Yet there I was.

Still hungry.

Lying about said hunger.

And praying the little liar would save the leftovers and make them her breakfast, lunch, and dinner.

"Thanks." Gabs patted her flat stomach. "I don't think I've ever eaten that fast before." Two pieces. She'd had two. What she needed was seven, eight—damn it, maybe the whole pizza.

I swallowed my question, knowing she wouldn't answer it anyway. Instead, I stood and pretended I was going in the general direction of her bathroom. When she was out of sight, I took a hard right by the hall closet.

I opened it.

Nothing.

Not even a flipping coat.

Did I have to start buying her winter apparel as well?

"Damn," I muttered, closing it softly before making my way upstairs, careful to avoid the third and sixth creaky stairs.

If I didn't hurry up she was going to think I was taking a shit in her bathroom, and that was the last thing I wanted her to assume—which was a first, considering I lived to piss her off.

I quickly made my way into Serena's room. It held only boxes, no baskets, and her closet was empty.

The upstairs hallway was the same.

And Blake's old room had nothing but dust in it.

When I finally made it to Gabi's room, I'd been gone around six minutes; things weren't looking so hot.

I pushed open her door and greedily searched around, my eyes zeroing in on seven baskets in the corner.

And the notes from the baskets in a small pile next to them.

She'd kept the notes?

"What the hell are you doing?" Gab yelled from behind me.

"Uh." I turned, offering an apologetic smirk. "Looking through your underwear drawer?"

"That's sick, even for you, Lex." She stomped over to me and tugged my arm toward the door. "Get out!"

"What does that mean, even for me?"

"You're a complete slut!" She rolled her eyes. "Seriously? I'm surprised you're not dead from an STD."

"Unfair." I held my ground, planting my feet against the wood floor. "I haven't even slept with anyone in over two weeks!"

She gasped. "Oh I'm sorry, was that supposed to be a personal record? Wrote that one down, did ya? Good job, Lex, you kept it in your pants for fourteen days. Your sacrifice has been noted. Hey, maybe the Catholic church will name a saint after you!"

My eyes narrowed as she uncomfortably bit her lip and looked at the baskets in the corner, then back at me.

"I already saw them, stop fidgeting."

She stared through me. "What do you know?"

"What don't I know?"

"Lex."

"Gabs."

Another foot stomp. "You drive me crazy!"

"And being with you is a picnic?" I sputtered. "You argue over everything! Why can't you just leave things alone?"

"Because!" she yelled, her pitch rising as she clenched her fists at her sides. "And why are you in my room?"

"Where's all the food?" I blurted. "I see the baskets, but your pantry's empty, and I know for a fact there were two boxes of brownie mix when it was . . . dropped off."

"You!" She jabbed my chest with her finger. "It's you? You're Spider-Man?"

"We've been over this before, Gabs. I'm the villain, try to keep up." I coughed into my hand and looked away, needing time to come up with a lie. "I, uh, was running this morning, because I run, and I saw the basket. That's all."

We were chest to chest, and she peered up at me from beneath her thick black lashes. "Now who's lying?"

"Calling my bluff?" A smile erupted before I could stop it. She was so tiny, and yet I experienced a bit of terror whenever she was angry, and whenever that anger was directed at me, which was daily.

"Lex." She backed up, and my body yearned to press against hers again. "Just . . . no fighting, no . . . whatever this is." She stared down at the floor. "Are you the one dropping off food?"

I licked my lips.

One of her eyebrows arched.

Damn it. "Yes."

Her face softened, and she managed to look both pissed off and slightly ashamed at the same time.

"Oh no you don't!" I held up my hands. "Do not give me that look! I'd rather you threaten to run me over with your car, Gabs. I am *not* that guy, so don't." I closed my eyes and turned around just as she wrapped her tiny little arms around my waist and squeezed.

"You found your heart!" Her teasing tone was back as she sidestepped the giant issue in front of us—where the hell the food was even going—and attacked me.

"Oh dear God, this is hell, isn't it?" I pried myself from her arms and turned around, gripping her wrists. "Gabs, don't read into this. This isn't a peace offering or any other friendship crap you've got going on in that tiny, small little head of yours." I dropped her wrists. "I just . . ." The last thing I wanted was to be her friend, for her to think it was okay for me to step into that territory while completely ignoring where I wanted to step, or lie, or just . . . screw. "Ian said something about you being short on funds, you took that extra job, and it just seemed like it might help. Besides, Ian's been busy with Blake and he doesn't notice shit anymore, which means all that shit piles onto my shit and stresses me out. Therefore, the baskets. Just filling in where he can't, that's all."

There, that sounded good.

Gabs's face fell. "Yeah, he's been really busy lately."

"Yes, let's talk about Ian. How do you feel about his newfound romance?"

"I'm glad you asked. Honestly, I don't think that—"

"Stop it!" I yelled. "That was a test! You failed! I don't have tits, this isn't a slumber party, and if you yell 'pillow fight,' you sure as hell better be naked!" I took a step backward, my legs colliding with her bed. "This changes nothing."

"It changes nothing," Gabs repeated.

The room fell silent.

If the baskets were our elephant . . .

The sexual tension between us was a freaking dinosaur.

Gabi's annoying ring tone went off. Thank God.

She reached for her phone and pulled it out. "Yeah? Okay, I can fill in. Sure . . . No, no, it's fine. I'll be there in fifteen."

"Who was that?"

"Oh, I'm sorry, were you under the impression we were friends?" Gabs tilted her head.

"I merely wanted to get the point across that I wasn't some chick you could gossip with, that's all."

"Exactly." She smirked. "Now out, I need to change."

"I'm really great at getting women out of their clothes. It would probably be faster if you let me help."

"Ahh, the asshole's back." She made a sad face. "I missed you."

I made a heart shape with my hands and held it out to her, then flipped her off and made my way out of her room. A pillow slammed into my head just as I was about to walk down the stairs.

"Seriously?" I roared.

"Stop being such a cheap ass and getting the small bags of Pirate's Booty. Girl's gotta eat, Lex. Just saying."

"Stop bitching," I grumbled with a grin that didn't disappear the entire night, not even when I woke up at two in the morning and made a quick shopping list.

Damn it.

She was in.

And there was no way I was going to be able to get her out.

Stupid heart.

Stupid, stupid, stupid, Lex.

My prayer that night was that Ian would at least let me explain before he shot me in the face.

Chapter Eighteen

Gabi

"Your attention to detail needs some serious work." Lex closed the binder that held all of my progress reports. "How about a trade?"

"I'm listening." I leaned forward, propping my elbows on his kitchen table.

Lex slid a grape over to me. "You give me better progress reports on clients, more than a one-word answer, meaning you separate business and personal, and I give you food."

I stared down at the grape. "Hmm, you gonna make me a rewards chart too? With stickers?"

His blank stare wasn't comforting. "That depends. Are you six?"

I popped the grape into my mouth. "I was kidding, Lex. And what kind of food are we talking about here?"

"Baskets of food." It had been two weeks of baskets. Two glorious weeks. I was so thankful I could cry, but for some reason it seemed to piss him off when I said thank you. So instead I pretended I deserved them, and he continued dropping them off.

The notes were getting more and more hilarious: "From the villain who lives under your bed."

Friday's was "From the badass antihero who kicked Superman's ass, which was sadly never recorded in comic book history."

"I'll let you pick what you want in your basket," Lex grumbled while I danced in my chair. "But!" He held up his hand. "Be realistic. Don't go asking for puppies and shit."

"I would never ask for shit." I held up my hand as if swearing to him.

"Gabs . . ."

"Or puppies." I slumped in my chair. "What about for Christmas, though?"

"I'm sorry, are you under the impression that I'm giving you baskets until Christmas? And why won't you tell me where all the food goes? You haven't gained thirty pounds in the last two weeks. Therefore, you're sharing it."

"A girl's got her secrets." I shrugged, suddenly uncomfortable with the entire situation. Guilt stabbed me in the chest. I was thankful, sure, but he was spending his own money because I was giving all of mine away.

It was for my family, but still.

"So." Lex pulled open his laptop. "Things with Steve seem to be going well. You've moved past making Stella jealous and straight on to her basically stalking him. Well done."

I grabbed another grape. "All in a day's work."

"When's your end goal with him? This weekend?"

Anxiety spread across my body. "Well, I took a double shift at the club this weekend, so . . . can I do it maybe Sunday?"

A muscle popped in Lex's jaw. "Gabs, I'm not trying to be an ass, but a key part of Wingmen Inc. is that we promise to get the job done fast, so I need you to be focused on that, not taking double shifts at the club. I know funds are tight, but once you're done with Steve we can talk about giving you more clients."

I hated that he was right. Shame made it hard to breathe. So did the fact that my dad still hadn't found a job, and my mom's job only brought in enough to cover the essentials. Last visit she'd cried when I'd dropped off my check.

Apparently, they hadn't been able to purchase groceries and, for the first time in her life, she had to go apply for state aid, only to find out that they still made too much.

And that was the sucky part about our system. They had no debt besides the mortgage and one car, but they lived on the other side of Lake Washington! It was even more expensive than Seattle. Their house payment was nearly three grand a month. Add in one car payment, food, and everything else, and things were tight, even without me living at home.

She said they'd missed the mark by a hundred dollars.

"Um, Gabs?" Lex tossed a pencil at me. "You paying attention?"

"Yeah, sorry, just tired." I yawned. I really was exhausted. Between working for Lex, trying to find a new roommate, being late on the last rent payment, and working doubles, I was done.

My classes were ridiculously hard, and I'd failed my last Human Anatomy test.

Things weren't exactly looking up. I'd even thought briefly about quitting school for a semester to work full time, but my parents would kill me.

"Just finish up with Steve this Sunday and let me know if you plan on taking any more double shifts with the club, okay?" Lex asked, his tone gentler this time.

I had to respect his business sense.

Just because I was Ian's friend and his . . . employee didn't mean that I got special treatment. He'd tell any of his employees the same thing. Be on time, get the job done on time, and don't waste his time.

"Got it." I nodded just as my phone rang again. I let out another groan. They were going to ask me to work.

"I gotta get this." I slid the phone out of my pocket. "Yeah?"

"You're late."

"What?" I frowned and looked at the house clock. "No, I'm not on shift today."

"Bell said you were taking her shift."

Damn Bell! That was the second time in a row.

"You need to be here in fifteen minutes or I'm going to have to let you go."

"What?" I yelled into the phone. "But I'm never late, I—"

"Get here, Gabrielle." The phone went dead.

Tears blurred my vision. "Gotta go, Lex." I grabbed my stuff and hurried out of the house.

My car was giving me trouble. I prayed it would start.

It did.

Luckily I'd been working so much I had my uniform in the backseat. I parked in front of the club ten minutes later, grabbed my uniform, and charged in through the double doors. My apologies fell on deaf ears—they always did, because even though I did everything right . . .

I was hated.

Because I was the only waitress in the club's history who had refused a promotion to the stage.

The girls called me goody-goody.

The men thought I was a prude.

And my boss thought I was ungrateful.

I really needed to find another job, but nothing paid me as well as this one did.

The next two hours were hell, and I still had two more to go.

"Your dress isn't as tight as it used to be." Lex's familiar voice was like a balm to my soul—words I thought I'd never think or say aloud.

"That's probably a good thing." I grabbed a napkin and placed it on his table. "What will it be?"

"A beer and water."

"Preference?"

"Anything that's going to get that asshole boss of yours to allow me to stay as a paying customer. Keep them coming."

His kindness floored me. Why was he even there?

"Are you, um, meeting someone?" I asked when I returned with his drink and water.

Lex burst out laughing. "I'm alone . . . Unless you're offering to join me?"

"Ha-ha." My laugh was awkward, uncomfortable. "I only have one break, and I was going to take it—"

"Now." He pulled out a chair and slid the water over to me.

Lex wasn't necessarily bossy; commanding was more like it. So when he said things, I either argued to keep myself from falling for him, or I listened because he was usually right.

And he was.

Right, that is.

My feet ached.

I winced as I sat my butt down and kicked off my heels.

Without any sort of warning, Lex grabbed both of my ankles, jerking my chair closer to his with a loud squeak, and then placed my feet in his lap.

"What are you—?"

Strong hands started massaging my right foot, hitting every single pressure point. With a shudder, I flexed my toes, then leaned back as a moan escaped my lips.

"Holy shit!" Lex burst out laughing. "Did I find your kryptonite, Supergirl?"

He hadn't called me that in years.

I opened one eye to stare him down, and I probably looked like an exhausted cyclops, scaring the super villain away. "Hmm?"

No words would come. It felt too good, and my feet hurt so bad.

His thumbs massaged up and down, pushing in around my heel. "I never knew you had an off button. I feel like I just discovered a new world or something."

"Yesss." I choked out the word as he pressed harder into my arch, making me nearly come off my chair.

The massaging stopped.

I opened my eyes.

And the hunger was back.

Lex's chest was heaving.

He slowly dropped one of my feet onto the floor and moved to the other, gripping my left foot hard and then pressing his thumbs into the middle while delicately caressing down the sides.

With a wicked grin, he twisted his thumb in the middle of my foot.

I arched off the chair, my foot landing on his crotch.

I tried to jerk away, embarrassed that I'd basically just kicked him in the junk, but he kept it there.

My eyes widened as I realized why.

Danger! Danger!

My mind screamed for me to pull back while my body remained perfectly still.

The logical part of my brain refused to listen to all the red flags popping up all over the place, instead focusing on his arousal.

And the fact that I'd been the one to cause it.

Again.

Was it me?

Or were all guys like that?

I didn't have enough experience to know.

All I knew was that I wanted Lex to look at me like that forever. His lips parted as he wet his lower lip and then huffed out a short breath.

I moved my foot.

His eyes closed.

I moved my foot again as his hands went limp.

"Gabi!" my boss yelled above the music. "Break time's over! You can flirt with your boyfriend on your own time!"

"He's not—"

"Now!" he yelled.

"Sorry." I fumbled for my shoes while Lex stared at me. I could have sworn his eyes were burning holes through my body.

"Thanks for the, um . . ." I couldn't look at him. "For that."

"Gabi." Lex said my name, my real name. "I'll be here."

That was it.

No snide remark.

No rude comment.

My shoulders relaxed, and with a nod in his direction, I grabbed my tray and walked off.

Chapter Nineteen
Lex

I went to work with Gabs for the next three consecutive days. And when I say I went to work with her . . .

I literally followed her like the pathetic loser I was, and even brought some of my work along. I probably looked like a freak, all set up with a laptop at a strip club.

The boss man came by twice to make sure I wasn't taking pictures. Like I'd record any of the dancing that went down on his stage? It was too depressing to even acknowledge.

Gabi's attitude changed drastically, almost as if when she saw me she was able to hand over whatever weight she was carrying and just . . . work, without being afraid.

I was planning on meeting Ian for a business dinner, so I couldn't stay for her entire shift.

And I hated admitting that I was a bit . . . reluctant to go. Ever since the foot-rubbing scenario, I hadn't been able to get her face out of my mind. Closing my eyes just made the erotic daydream all the more real.

She hadn't shied away. If anything, she needed little encouragement. Damn it, we couldn't keep playing the same game; it was destroying my sanity.

I waved Gabs over.

She bounced in my direction. "More beer?"

"Nah." I started packing up, knowing that it was probably for the best that I was giving us some space. "I've gotta meet up with Ian."

"Oh." Her face fell, but she quickly recovered. "Can you talk to him about me taking on more clients?" She made a face. "I sort of hate it here."

"It's already on our agenda." I grabbed one of my books and gave her a swift nod. "Try not to fall onto any poles in my absence."

A few girls started dancing on stage.

Gabs's shoulders slumped.

"Hey." I nudged her arm. "You know you can quit, right? It's not like Ian and I are going to fire you or anything. I mean, how much do you really make here?"

She gulped. "Seven hundred dollars a week."

"What?" I roared. "But your bank account—"

Her eyes narrowed. "I knew it! Stop hacking into my personal life, you ass!"

Offended, I blasted back, "Who else is going to look after you?"

"NORMAL people!" She threw her hands into the air, nearly hitting me in the face. "Ones who don't hack my bank account to check up on me!"

I took a protective step toward her. "I was worried!"

"Worried, my ass. You were just curious!" she spat. "Ugh, just go, I don't want to fight. I knew these three days of peace wouldn't last."

Okay, that pissed me off. "And it's my fault?" I smirked, anger dripping off every word. "Right? Like everything else between us? All my fault." *Damn it, Ian!*

"Yes!" She shoved my chest, and I tried reaching for her hands, but she was too quick pulling away. "Just stop . . ." Tears pooled in her eyes, giving them a bright sheen. "Stop being nice, stop hanging out here. I can't take it! It's like being told you're safe, only to have the net ripped out from underneath you. The net is always going to rip when it comes to you!"

"Is that really how you see us?"

"There is no us."

Four words. One sentence. Amazing how something so small could hold such power. I felt each and every one of those words slam through me, stealing the breath right out of me and inflaming my anger all the more.

"I'm so glad we've had this conversation," I said with a bitter edge to my voice. "You know, the last thing you need to worry about is someone like me falling for someone like you." I shrugged. "See? No harm done, safety net gone."

"Lex—"

"Whatever." Why the hell did it hurt to breathe? "I'm going to be late."

I stomped off to Gabs calling my name.

The logical side of my brain told me that she had a point, that I was just as hot as I was cold, but there was a reason! It's not like I wanted to be an ass! I had no choice, absolutely none! And now that I'd finally decided to jump in with both feet, I'd been met with nothing but air.

Safety net, my ass!

She had no idea that she was the one who actually removed it.

Not me.

I slammed my car door, started the engine, and attempted to keep myself from ripping the steering wheel off the dash. My phone started ringing. I hit my hands-free.

"What?"

"I, uh . . ." It was Gabs; I could hear the club music in the background.

"Spit it out, Gabs, I don't have all night."

"You know what? Never mind, I'll call Ian—"

"The hell you will!" I slammed my hand onto the steering wheel. "What do you need?"

"A ride," she croaked out. "One of the waitresses came in right after you left and said my back left tire was completely flat, and I don't have a spare, so I can't change it after work, and—"

"Take a breath," I commanded. "I'll take care of it. When do you get off, again?" I knew exactly when her shift was done. I just didn't want her to know I had every hour of her day memorized.

"Ten." She sighed. "Um, you can just drop off a bike or something."

"Really?" I fought and lost as a smile spread itself across my face. "And you're going to do exactly what with a bike, Gabs?"

"Ride it, you jackass!"

"Gabs, the last time you rode a bike, it had streamers and training wheels on it."

She let out a loud gasp. "I'm going to murder Ian."

"It's okay, Gabs, lots of twenty-one-year-olds don't know how to ride bikes. I mean, I can't think of any off the top of my head, and most of them probably can't walk in a straight line, either, so look, at least you've got that going for you!"

Another groan and then, "I gotta go before I really do get fired."

"Bitch better have my money," I sang, then turned up Rihanna in my car while Gabs mumbled a curse and hung up.

And just like that.

We were back to normal.

Ian's eyes narrowed in on me as the waitress cleared all of our food and brought out coffee. "You're hiding something."

I nearly spit my coffee onto the table. "What? Why would you think that?" Holy shit, was he a mind reader too?

Ian rubbed his chin with his hand, still refusing to look away. "Who is she?"

"Who?"

"The girl you're sleeping with."

I burst out laughing. "Don't you mean girls?"

"You haven't been with girls in weeks. I would know, because every damn time you come home smelling like skank, Blake has to Lysol the counters."

"One time." I rolled my eyes and looked away. "One time I had sex on the counters, and that was months ago. She was eager, what can I say?"

Leaning back, Ian reached for his coffee, then paused. "Not to change the subject, but . . ."

"What?"

He fidgeted with the ceramic handle of his mug. "Have you, um . . . looked into Gabi's . . . finances?"

"What do you think?"

"I think you can't help yourself, that's what I think."

"Then you'd be correct in your assumption." I wasn't sure how much to say. Gabs had been right: it was personal, none of our business. "Don't worry about Gabs. She's like a cat, always landing on her feet."

"Their rent is expensive, she's working her ass off, and Blake said Gabs mentioned failing her last anatomy test."

"She can't fail!" I blurted.

Ian laughed. "Since when do you care?"

"If she fails . . ." Shit. "If she fails then we'll be stuck with her forever, like one of those freaking mussels or clams that attaches itself to a wooden pole and never leaves!"

"Are you the wooden pole in this scenario or am I?"

"That's not the point." Panicking, I reached for my phone so I'd look irritated and distracted. "The point is that she has to graduate. Otherwise, we're going to be stuck with her forever!"

"As opposed to what? Her graduating and us finally being empty nesters?" Ian smirked. "Seriously, I've never seen you like this. Are you . . ." He leaned forward. "Are you sweating?"

"It's hotter than *hell* in here!" I choked out. "And I had jalapeños on my . . . shit."

"Jalapeños." Ian nodded. "On your shit? Hmm? I don't think I've ever heard you speak so eloquently."

"So . . ." I drummed my fingers against the table and checked my Rolex. It was already a quarter till ten. I needed to grab Gabs. "We need to find a way for her to work less, earn more, and stop failing her classes." And side note, I needed to discover why there was never any money in her bank account and why she was always starving as if I never fed her.

"Agreed." Ian frowned. "Actually, I had an idea. I wasn't sure you'd be okay with it, but since you guys seem to be, you know, both alive after working together for a few weeks—"

"Hold that thought." I checked my watch again. "Actually, I have to go . . . fix a tire."

Ian just stared at me like I'd told him I was going to flash my dick at the eighty-year-old sitting at the next table. "You?"

"What?" I stood. "I can change tires."

"Can you?"

"Stop doubting me."

"Okay computer science major, go crazy."

"I resent that."

"I resent the fact that you just made up some bullshit excuse about changing a tire in order to get out of answering questions about—"

His eyes did that thing where they got wide and clear. Shit, he was going to see right through me and Gabs if we were together.

"Look—" I tried for a half-truth. "Gabs knew you were busy, so she grudgingly called me and asked if I could change her tire after work. I told her yes, but only after she gave me a blow job."

Ian didn't seem fazed.

"She yelled at me."

He continued his staring.

"I yelled back." I released a long-suffering sigh. "She eventually wore me down."

Ian shrugged. "As she usually does."

"And I let her win round one, because I'm trying not to go to prison before I graduate from college, and if I keep fighting with her, well . . ."

"It's your future," Ian agreed.

"Right." I breathed out a sigh of relief. "So, can we take this up some other time?"

"Sure." He nodded. "But I think I already have my answer about my idea, if you're cool with me just making a decision for both of us."

He did that often, but he owned half of the company and I trusted his judgment, so why did I care? "Sure, whatever."

"Don't kill her." Ian called after me.

"Kill her?" My eyebrows rose. "What about me?"

"You always end up on top."

My jeans tightened to a painful degree. "Yeah, I wish."

Ian smiled.

The guy had no idea what he was saying.

But my body did.

What I wouldn't give to be on top—which really was saying something, since for once in my life, I'd be getting a workout in the bedroom. Not necessarily a bad thing, more like a sweaty adventure I couldn't wait to embark on.

Chapter Twenty
Gabi

Lex was late—only by a minute, but sitting out in the parking lot gave me the creeps. The club was still going wild with dancers throwing themselves around poles and patrons getting drunk, but outside it was dark, and the parking lot wasn't exactly well lit. Though the club stuck out like a sore thumb, all bright lights like an adult version of Candy Land or something.

Headlights blinked in my direction, and at first I thought it was Lex. The car was red like his, but as it neared I noticed that it was an older Mercedes. Lex's was basically brand-new and in impeccable condition.

The car parked a few feet away from me. I took a few steps back toward the club, making sure to appear like I wasn't afraid to be standing outside alone.

A tall man with a black beanie and graying goatee stepped out of the car. His black shoes were shiny, and his jeans looked tight and uncomfortable. A black T-shirt hung loosely on his body, and he smelled like he'd just taken a bath in aftershave. I almost had to hold my breath.

He took a step toward me. "How much?"

"Um." I pointed back at the club. "There isn't a cover."

He smirked, running his hand around his mouth. "Not for the club. For you."

Oh no. I swallowed the slowly rising panic as adrenaline surged through my system. "I'm a waitress. Not a hooker."

"Same thing." He nodded.

"No." I stepped back; only two feet and I'd be at the door. Never in my life did I ever think that I'd feel safer in a gentlemen's club than in a parking lot, but there it was. "Actually, it's not."

He moved too fast for me to react.

One minute I was standing.

The next, he was pushing me against the brick wall. "I asked how much, you bitch, and I always get what I want."

His breath smelled sour. I tried to turn my head away, but the grip he had on my chin was unbreakable.

"How much?" he repeated, his eyes crazed.

"You can't afford her," came a familiar voice.

I sagged in relief as the guy released my chin and turned to face Lex, who had at least sixty pounds on him.

The man scowled. "Back off. This is between me and the lady."

"You mean my girlfriend?" Lex crossed his arms, and I completely ignored the short thrill that ran through my body at hearing him say "girlfriend." It's like my body forgot to be afraid, because Lex was there. "I'm going to only say this once. Leave her alone, go in the club, grab a drink. There's plenty of girls in there."

The man looked at Lex as if sizing him up, then finally gave a firm nod and started making his way toward the door.

"Are you okay?" Lex moved toward me.

The man charged.

"Lex, watch out!" I yelled, but the man was already on Lex, ramming him into the wall.

Lex laughed. The bastard laughed as he shoved the man off him and punched him in the face, hard. Like so hard that *my* face hurt.

The man stumbled back.

Lex looked bored.

The man charged again. This time Lex landed an upper hook to the guy's chin, then followed up with a punch in the stomach. When the guy doubled over, Lex patted him on the back and whispered, "It's probably time to call it a night."

The man groaned and fell to the ground.

Just as the police showed up.

Seriously?

Lex and I shared a look of disbelief.

"Well, Sunshine." Lex grinned. "Looks like another trip to jail . . . What's this, twice now?"

"You aren't going to jail for self-defense." I rolled my eyes.

A police offer stepped out of his car. "Everything okay here?"

"It is now." Lex held out his hand, shaking the officer's, and pointed to me. "My girlfriend was just attacked by this dipshit."

"That true, ma'am?" the officer asked me.

I gave him a wobbly nod. "He asked how much I cost."

The look in Lex's eyes was pure hatred. "Clearly I didn't hit him hard enough, then."

"Do you work here?" The officer directed the question at me.

"I just got off."

"Alright, I'll need to file a report, but since it was self-defense and he was attacking you . . ." His voice trailed off. "I'd maybe invest in some Mace if you plan on keeping this job, or at least have your boyfriend pick you up at night."

I nodded.

After giving another account of what happened, we were finally in Lex's car. It was nearly midnight. I still hadn't eaten anything for dinner.

And I had a class and work the next morning.

Double shift.

Plus Steve.

Add that to being terrified from my attack, and I was just . . . done.

Lex turned up the heat even though it wasn't that cold out. I was grateful that he didn't say anything. I needed to think, decompress.

Nothing had happened.

But it could have.

"I'm sorry," I finally whispered when we were minutes from my house.

With a jerk, Lex pulled the car over to the side of the road, shifted into park, and faced me. "Are you serious right now?"

I nodded as my eyes filled with tears, and when I opened my mouth the only thing that came out was a pitiful croak.

"Shit." Lex closed his eyes, then unclicked my seat belt and somehow managed to lift me over the console and into his lap. My feet dangled on my seat while my body rested in his lap. He held me close and kissed my forehead.

And I completely lost it as tremors wracked my body.

"You're safe, Gabi," he whispered. "I swear."

"You know," I hiccupped, "you were totally more superhero tonight than villain."

Lex's chuckle shook my body, warming it, washing me with its rightness. "Yeah, well, don't tell anyone. I would hate to ruin a good thing, you know?"

I nodded.

"And I swear, if you ever apologize for getting attacked again, I'm going to spank your ass." His eyes were hooded as he stared down at me. "It wasn't your fault. I'm just glad I was there. You did nothing wrong."

"Well . . ." I broke eye contact. "I'm working at a club, so that's probably the first bad choice, then waiting outside—"

"No." Lex shook his head. "It doesn't matter. It wasn't your fault."

"Okay." I huffed.

"Okay?" He cupped my chin and then brushed a kiss across my cheek. His lips hovered near my ear, his breathing ragged. It matched mine.

"Okay," I said again.

His eyes met mine. "Okay."

And then our mouths touched.

Chapter Twenty-One
Lex

The contact was brief, almost like a whisper as my lips brushed hers, and then I retreated. I wasn't going to make out with her just after she got attacked. Vulnerability didn't look good on her. I hated it. She was strong. And when that armor cracked, it wounded me probably just as much as it hurt her.

"Have you eaten?" I blurted the first thing that came to my mind because if I didn't say something, I'd kiss her again and wouldn't stop there. I knew I had no self-control where she was concerned.

Because in that moment . . .

When she was getting attacked . . .

All I could think was . . . I've been waiting for this girl for four years, I sure as hell am not going to let anyone else touch what's mine.

Four years.

I was done waiting.

Gabi's big green eyes blinked back at me. Damn it, she was so beautiful it hurt to stare at her. "Actually, no."

"Great." I gently placed her back in the passenger seat. "Buckle up, Sunshine, I'm about to rock your world."

"Hmm . . . I wonder how many girls you've said that to?"

"That line? Too cheesy. I saved it for you."

"Touched." She smirked, then reached for my hand. "And Lex?"

"Yeah?" I was shaking, but I squeezed her hand back.

"Tonight." She licked her pink lips. "You were my hero."

I had never realized how badly I wanted her to see me in that light—until that moment.

"I should probably get a cape now." I nodded seriously. "You know, just in case."

"Red."

She didn't release my hand, so I put the car into drive with my left and took off. "You don't think black?"

"Black is too badass."

"Are you saying I'm not badass enough?"

"Eh." She made a dismissive motion with her free hand. "It's your major."

"Why is everyone hating on my major tonight?" I wondered aloud. "Did I or did I not just kick some dude's ass?"

"He probably had a weak heart and a fake hip," Gabs said seriously.

I nearly swerved off the road. "The hell he did! He was maybe fifty!"

She raised her hands in the air. "Whatever you say, Rocky."

"Did you know the *Rocky* script was written in three days?" I turned toward my house, completely passing Gabs's.

"Um?" She pointed.

"And"—I turned down my road—"also, the infamous running scene? Over eight hundred school kids used as extras." I stopped in front of my house and turned off the car.

"Fascinating," Gabs said in a dry tone. "Also, we're at your house?"

"Yup." I unbuckled my seat belt and then hers, and when she opened her mouth again, I silenced her with my lips.

"O-o-okay," she stuttered out when I released her.

"Okay," I whispered back, letting out a heavy sigh as she slowly opened her car door.

I followed her closely, my hands brushing her hips every few seconds, unable to keep myself away. Damn it, I was supposed to be staying away, not pulling her close.

Gabs suddenly stopped and I collided with her ass, nearly sending her sailing into the sidewalk.

"You need a warning button or something," I grumbled, placing my hands on her shoulders. "Suddenly scared of doorsteps, or what?"

"Yes." Her body tensed. "More like I'm scared of what it means."

"Nothing. It doesn't have to mean anything." I stepped around her and grabbed her hand, tugging her toward the door. "Or it could mean everything." Scary, how much I ached for it to mean everything.

Gabi's lips were swollen from my kisses even though I thought I'd been gentle; maybe it was a combination of her crying against me and my mouth pressed against hers. Regardless, she was gorgeous standing there blanketed in moonlight.

"Come on." I held out my hand. "It's just food."

"At your house." Gabs arched an eyebrow while the corner of her mouth twitched. "Don't you guys have a 'no girls allowed' rule at night?"

"Why yes, yes we do." I smiled wide. "But last I checked, you were a dude, so . . ."

"Ass." Gabs smacked me in the shoulder, shoved me to the side, and walked in, giving me a sideways glance before tossing her shoes off and dumping them near the neat little basket we kept by the door. I was surprised and a little stunned at my own raw reaction to seeing her feet, like she'd just flashed me boob instead of toe.

"See? Easy," I said behind her.

"Trickery," she grumbled, then made her way into the kitchen and sat at the barstool. "Okay, feed me."

I held up a finger and opened the fridge. "Okay, so I have . . . shit."

"Oh I'll take that, with a side of mayo, thanks." She laughed.

"Are you making fun of me?"

"I would never."

I rolled my eyes. "It's always going to be like this, isn't it?"

"What?"

"Arguing. You can't help yourself."

"I like to have the last word."

"Believe me." I shut the fridge door. "I know." I looked around the empty kitchen. "So, pizza?"

Gabs held up her hand for a high-five.

I slapped it, then sent a text to Domino's. Whoever was in charge of their social media deserved free pizza for life.

Within fifteen minutes we had three extra-large pizzas with enough pineapple to hold a luau.

Gabs was facedown on the couch, groaning, while I put the left-overs away and searched for wine.

She'd eaten two pieces.

I counted.

When I yelled at her to eat more, she threw a pineapple at my face and said that her stomach still felt weak.

I prayed it wasn't because of me.

But because of what happened in the parking lot.

Whatever. I needed to get over myself.

"I should get going," Gabs moaned from the couch, unmoving. "But for some reason my head is in love with this position."

I grunted. "You've probably just made that cushion's year."

She raised her hand above the couch and gave me the finger.

Laughing, I finally located two glasses and the wine I'd been hunting for and poured her a hefty glass.

She sat up when I turned down the lights and came around the couch. "What's this?"

"Peace treaty?" I handed her the glass, then clinked mine against it. "No insults until the morning, and then we're back to suiting up."

"Cover your man parts." Gabs took a long swig, and her throat moved as liquid poured down it. For some reason I found the entire movement erotic.

"Aw, but I thought you liked it when my man parts were all . . . exposed."

"Ew." Gabs took another drink and put the glass down. "Don't say 'exposed' ever again. Not alone, not in a sentence, not ever."

I rolled my eyes and reached for the remote, but Gabs suddenly shoved me out of the way, nearly spilling wine all over the floor in an attempt to beat me to the punch.

"Shit!" I yelled. "Are you four?"

"No!" Gabs yelled. "No ID channel!"

"Gabs"—I set my wine down and calmly tried to wrestle the remote from her hand—"it's educational."

"It's horrifying!"

"Only if you fall asleep with it on."

"Twice! Twice I thought I was getting murdered."

I tugged the remote harder. "Not my fault you have an overactive imagination."

She glared, then released the remote and stood. "I should be getting home anyway."

I smiled and leaned back against the couch. "Sure thing."

"Lex?"

"Sunshine?"

"Aren't you going to drive me home?"

"I've got a bike out back." I snapped my fingers. "Oh, wait . . ."

Her eyes narrowed. "Low blow."

"Mmmm." I put my hands behind my head and closed my eyes. "Say 'blow' again."

"Swear on Ian's life I will shove this remote control up your nose and cause more brain damage than you already have."

"That sounds really erotic. Fun fact: did you know the nose has more nerve endings than—"

With a shriek Gabs launched herself onto me, straddling my body with her short little legs and shoving a pillow across my face.

Laughter exploded from me. Did she really think she could suffocate me? She was a quarter of my body weight . . . Okay, not really, but pretty damn close.

"A little to the left," I instructed as she kept smothering. "Ah, right there, yes, yes, yes."

The pillow suddenly dropped, and Gabs huffed out a breath. "I give up. You're impossible to kill."

I shook my head. "If I had a penny . . ."

Gabs looked down at her hands, the hands she had placed against my chest. I was afraid to move.

I think she was too.

We'd crossed a line, but this time we both were very well aware that there was no net, no going back, nothing.

And the nothing was scary.

Even for sluts like myself.

Possibly scarier, because it was uncharted territory.

"Lex," she exhaled my name, sending shivers along my spine. "I—"

"Stay," I whispered.

"What?" She blinked as if she didn't quite hear me correctly. "Did you just ask me to—"

I pressed a finger to her mouth. "I believe I said 'stay,' the same command you give a dog—not that I'm making that comparison, just giving you the word in a sentence, sort of like, 'Spot, stay.' Doesn't mean the owner's going to take advantage of Spot or that Spot has to perform sexual duties in order to stay in the doghouse. Sometimes, Gabs, a word is just a word."

With a rough exhale, she crawled off me. "Only you could make something so asinine sound somewhat sweet. Okay, point me to the Fortress of Solitude, and I'll try not to sweat estrogen everywhere."

"Upstairs. And Gabs, I really mean it when I say . . . If you ever leave a tampon in my room, I will cut you."

"Aw . . ." Gabs placed her hands against her heart. "That's just so"—she wiped a fake tear—"thoughtful."

"I'm a thoughtful guy."

"Room?"

"Up."

"No . . ." Her word dripped with sarcasm.

"Gabs, my patience? Kinda thin right now, and even though you did just get attacked, I've tasted you—three times. I want to taste you again. Actually, I want to slam you against the nearest sturdy object and make you scream. So either get your cute ass upstairs or take me up on my offer and start stripping."

She ran.

Smart girl.

I, however, apologized to the lower half of my body . . . because it was going to be a long, cold, blue night.

Chapter Twenty-Two
Gabi

I almost went back downstairs to ask which room was Lex's, but then I remembered that Ian had a label maker and on one drunken night had labeled everything he could, including their rooms.

Sure enough, once I was at the top of the stairs I was able to locate Lex's room in no time. It also had a giant *L* on it while Ian's had a Superman symbol, proving yet again that boys never truly grew out of those Spider-Man sheets.

I pushed open his door and gasped.

What the hell kind of tech psycho was he?

Computer equipment filled the entire right half of the room. Three screens formed a little cave around one giant keyboard. Stickers covered most of the desk. His leather chair was more throne than anything, and I had to wonder, would this be where Lex sat when he finally overthrew the government?

A bathroom was attached to his room. I quickly went in and tossed some water on my face and stared at my reflection.

My normally honeyed skin appeared pale and lifeless, while my lips were swollen and pink. The memory of his kiss was enough to have me gripping the sink like a lifeline.

What the heck was I doing?

I was in his sanctum!

And I *knew* how nerdy that sounded, but I was in his most private secret place, and he had invited me there, and what did that mean?

I needed Ian.

I needed my best friend.

Hah, I'm sure that conversation would go just great: "Um, Ian, I'm totally in Lex's bedroom, he kissed me twice! *Eeek!* I know, right? So should I crawl into his bed naked? Short-sheet the bed and say 'gotcha'? You know, start off with a prank?" Ian would laugh, and then I'd hear a gunshot, and no more Lex.

"Get a grip." I pointed a finger at myself. "Stop being a girl."

"Damn it," Lex said from somewhere in the room. "Has the transformation already taken place? Am I too late?"

I slammed the bathroom door to his laughter.

While at the same time appreciating the fact that he was treating me like he always did.

Which meant . . .

My shoulders slumped. Nothing. It meant nothing. It meant he was extending an olive branch.

It meant he felt sorry for me.

And he was sharing his bed.

With his friend.

My replacement Ian. That's what Lex was turning into, and I hated him for it. I'd rather he treat me like crap again.

Than give me hope that sharing his room actually meant something.

"Ga-a-absssss." Lex strung out my name. "Hurry up. I'm exhausted, and I want to do a body-cavity check before you get in bed. I don't wanna get shanked."

I rolled my eyes and jerked open the door just in time for Lex to toss a large black T-shirt in my direction. "Cover yourself."

Normally I'd argue, but I was disgusting and I wanted to burn my uniform. The longer I stared at the short black dress with the club's insignia on it, the sicker I felt, until I thought I was going to puke.

With jerky movements I pulled the dress over my head and threw it on the floor, then, in a fit of anger, stomped on it. Unsatisfied, I started jumping up and down on top of it, until warm arms scooped me up into the air and carried me to the bed.

"I think it's dead, Gabs."

I didn't know I was crying until Lex wiped away the tears streaming down my face. He still had clothes on.

Meanwhile, I was in nothing but my bra and boy-short underwear.

But he wasn't looking at my boobs or anything else; he was staring at my face, which I imagined took extreme concentration on his part. I'd always known Lex to be a boob guy. Heck, he checked out a sixty-year-old grandma once.

To reference him yet again: tits were tits.

"You're not staring at my boobs."

"Nope." Lex's eyes didn't leave mine.

"Why?"

Eyes crinkling, he answered, "Gabs, if you want me to stare at your boobs, I will . . . But I'm not one of those guys. Never been."

"Huh?"

He leaned down until our mouths nearly collided, then pulled back. "Do I really seem capable of looking and not touching?"

"No," I breathed out in one whoosh. "You're handsy."

"Nothing wrong with a firm hand . . ." He slowly pulled away, then stood, padded over to the light switch, and flipped it off. He kept his gaze locked with mine as he made his way back over to the bed.

I leaned on my elbows and watched while he peeled off his cotton shirt and tugged down his jeans, leaving him clad in nothing but tight Nike boxer briefs.

My eyes widened.

He smirked, making his way back to the bed. Taking one look at me, he grabbed every last blanket he had and started piling them on top of me.

"Lex!" I yelled, already overheating as blanket number two was tossed in my direction. "What are you doing?"

His answer?

"Being a hero."

More blankets piled, until he was left with one sheet and I was cocooned. He proceeded to build a type of pillow fort between us, then yawned and mumbled out, "Good night."

"Lex," I hissed. "Are you drunk?"

"Nope." Another yawn. "Shh, Gabs, it's sleeping time."

"I. Can't. Breathe."

He pulled one blanket away. "There. Better?"

"How is suffocating me heroic?"

"I'm saving your innocence while protecting my own life. Ian walks in, sees you bundled up, doesn't kill me. You wake up, innocence intact, and don't shank me with one of your spiky heels."

"We aren't in prison. There is no shanking in bed."

"I could make shanking hot."

"You *would* say that."

"Gabs?"

"What?"

The tense silence crackled with awareness, like we both knew an inch of movement was the only encouragement one or both of us needed.

"Thanks for staying."

"Lex?"

"Yeah?"

"Thanks for not calling me a dude again."

He flopped over, his hand coming into contact with boob and about five layers of blankets. With an arrogant smile he whispered, "I always knew you were a C cup."

I shoved him off and pretended to be offended.

When really . . . I fell asleep with a smile on my face.

In my enemy's bed.

Chapter Twenty-Three

Gabi

Tap, tap, tap. I shook my head in an attempt to alleviate the irritating sound. *Tap, tap, tap.* With a grunt, I flopped onto my stomach and put a pillow over my face.

Silence.

And then: *tap, tap, tap.* A long pause, and then another *tap, tap.*

I jerked awake and glanced at the empty spot next to me, then frowned as I followed the empty spot up to the computer. Lex was sitting on his throne, probably hacking God-knows-who.

"You're an animal," I rasped.

"Gabs." He didn't look away from the screen. "I mean this in the nicest way possible, but you look like hell."

I growled.

"Kitty got bite?"

"Kitty will scratch your eyes out if you say 'kitty' one more time."

Tap, tap, tap. Lex's chair swiveled, revealing him in nothing but boxers, damn him for being so sexy. "Pussycat?"

I threw a pillow, narrowly missing one of his computer screens.

His eyes heated.

"Whoops?"

"Lex?" Ian called from the hallway.

My eyes widened in horror, while Lex jumped to his feet. "Just give me a minute."

"Dude, I've seen you naked. I just have a quick question—" The doorknob turned.

Lex threw the comforter over my head, jumped into bed with me, and shoved me underneath him.

I gasped for air that wasn't sweltering.

It didn't help that Lex's firm body was plastered against mine, even though his knees were up so Ian couldn't see the outline of his best friend.

Why was I hiding in Lex's bed?

Would Ian really assume the worst?

I thought back through Lex's track record.

Yeah, Lex would need to be fed through a straw for the rest of his life.

I decided against popping up like a jack-in-the-box and shouting "surprise!" I mean, there were moments when I hated Lex, but I didn't want his death on my conscience.

"What's up . . . man?" Lex asked, shifting his legs so his thighs nearly collided with my head. I pinched his ass. He jerked out a strangled cough.

"Uh . . ." I strained to hear what came next, but apparently Ian wasn't saying anything. I wished I could see what he was doing. "Are you sure you're feeling okay?"

"Great," Lex said, a little too cheerfully. The idiot sounded so guilty, I had a hard time not groaning out loud. "Did you say you had a quick question?"

"Yes." Ian sounded suspicious. "I just wanted to talk to you about Gabs for a minute."

"Or"—Lex started coughing wildly—"we could just—" Another two coughs. "Sorry, man, not feeling well." He pounded his chest. Meanwhile, I rolled my eyes and flicked his knee.

"Last night you said to make a decision, and I made one."

My ears perked up. Say what?

"I paid Gabs's last few days' prorated rent, and in exactly one hour I'll have a moving truck at her place."

"O-o-okay." Lex drew it out slowly. "Did you find her somewhere closer to campus?"

"Yeah." It was Ian's turn to sound guilty. "About a mile closer, and safer, and . . . cheaper."

"If it's cheaper, how the hell is it safer?"

"Bodyguards," Ian said simply.

"And it's cheaper?"

"Technically, it's free."

"Huh?"

"Anyway, just thought I'd let you know. Okay, see ya later!"

"Wait!" Lex yelled after him. "Come back here . . . What's the address of this glorious free place?"

Ian didn't answer.

I had a bad feeling.

I nudged Lex in what I thought was his leg but which ended up being something else completely, and he let out a low curse that Ian must have thought was directed at him, because he immediately started apologizing.

"Look, it's only for the next four months! We only have a bit of school left, and then we'll help her figure something out."

My brain wasn't working as fast as Lex's, because by the time my entire body went rigid with warning, Lex yelled.

"HERE?"

I pinched him hard in the thigh.

"You want her to live here?"

"It makes sense!" Ian shouted. "And it's already done!"

"What the *hell* makes you think we can keep the peace if we live within the same house?"

"You guys have been doing just fine," Ian said defensively. "Even you said you were worried about her."

"The way you worry about a dead raccoon when you drive by it!" Lex was sweating; his legs were actually sweating. "You don't save the raccoon, Ian! You let it go to raccoon heaven where there are shiny toys and . . . food!"

"You got me worried, man." Ian lowered his voice. "Look, if you are on something, there's help."

"Dear God," Lex grumbled. "It's not . . . Fine, if you want the French and the English hanging out in the same damn territory, that blood's on you. All on you."

Silence fell. What was Ian doing now? Had he left? A cough came from the doorway, so apparently not. "I hid the knives, so . . ."

"Oh great, Ian," snapped Lex. "Good. You removed the knives. Do you *hear* yourself?"

"She's staying. That's final. Even you admitted something was going on, but you apparently care more about your damn computer keyboard than Gabs."

"Unfair!" he roared. "You *know* I care about her!"

"Bullshit!"

I rubbed my hand up Lex's leg. He froze, and then I moved it higher, making little tiptoeing motions with my fingers. Curiosity killing the cat . . . Ugh, see? Bad omen. He'd called me a kitty, and there I was . . . exploring.

My fingers grazed him.

His entire body went slack.

"Dude, did you just have a stroke?" Ian's voice was laced with concern. "I've never seen a person's face do that before."

"What is this hell?" Lex voiced aloud, then started rocking against my fingers. I quickly figured out what felt good and gripped harder. "Shi-i-i-it, I'm going to burn."

"Oh, I hid the matches too," Ian said reassuringly.

"Just. Great," Lex said through clenched teeth. "That's just . . ."

"You look . . . strange."

"Go!" Lex shouted. "Just . . . I need time to . . ." He exhaled a curse. "Think."

The door slammed. I wasn't sure if I should stop. My answer came when Lex pressed his hand against mine and urged me on.

What was I doing?

And why did it feel good, even though he wasn't even touching me?

Lex's entire body tensed as his hips bucked off the bed. He quickly grabbed the sheet and wiped off his legs, then pulled up the blanket and stared at me, his face completely flushed. His shoulders rose visibly with each gasp for breath.

"I—" He closed his mouth and then frowned. "I—"

"So . . ." I quickly changed the subject. "Roomies, huh?"

He let out a groan and fell back against the pillows.

Chapter Twenty-Four

Lex

Twenty-four hours ago, I was a normal, sane—albeit teetering on the edge of crazy—guy. Now? Now, I was headfirst in crazyland as Gabs took the room directly across from mine.

And, within the first hour of being in our house, glued tampons to my door.

I responded with condoms.

And so started the first war.

If I had a friggin' cannon, I would fill it with sex toys, aim, and shoot, just to see how far I could push her.

We didn't talk about the bed.

We didn't talk about that night.

But it needed to be talked about.

Because every damn time we brushed past each other, which had been about a million times since she'd moved in that morning, it was sheer torture. I didn't just know what she tasted like.

She'd stroked me until I was spent.

Until I saw unicorns.

And freaking waved at a leprechaun while I skipped to the pot of gold at the end of the rainbow, only to be jerked back to reality.

A reality where Gabs and I still pretended we hated each other, yet . . . what? Kissed? Touched?

Yes. The answer to your question is yes. The morphing into an actual chick was taking place, and if I suddenly woke up dickless? Yeah, let's just say I wouldn't be that surprised. I'd yawn, look heavenward, and say, "Carry on."

The only bright side to her moving in had been that she was able to quit that horrific job, since she didn't need to pay rent.

Her car would be brought back at the end of the week. Ian and I made sure the mechanic did a full workup, though I'd never tell Gabs I had any part of it. I didn't want her to look at me like we were BFFs.

I'd rather have her hate.

Hate I could work with.

Friendship could go screw itself.

"Lex!" Gabs knocked on my bedroom door so hard I was surprised it was still intact.

Rolling my eyes at my computer screen, I got up as slowly as possible and made my way to the door, careful to open it only an inch just in case she had a weapon.

"Yes?" I peered through the crack in the door.

She shoved her way through.

"Of course, do come in." I spread my arms wide. "What can I get you? Tea? Arsenic? Sex? All three?"

Gabs opened up her leather jacket, revealing a low-cut white tank top. "Too slutty for Steve?"

I blinked . . . then blinked again, more slowly. I'd always known she had boobs. Why the hell was she just *now* showing me? "Gabs, are you asking as a friend? Because I think you wandered into the wrong room."

She pouted. "Please? Just say yes or no."

"I'll say this one more time . . ." I stalked toward her, backing her up against the nearest wall. "You ask Ian this shit. He's basically sexless now that he's with Blake. You ask me, and well . . . I may not play fair."

"Oh, Lex, when have you or I ever played fair? Do you even know what that word means?"

I took a deep, soothing breath, then lowered my head. She gasped as I licked between her cleavage and then set my hands on her hips and slid them up underneath her shirt, cupping her breasts, weighing them, teasing them, taking my sweet time.

Her mouth dropped open and then her head fell back.

"My opinion," I said, kissing the corner of her mouth, "is that you may kill young Steve . . . But this is your last date, right? The one where you fake a breakup in front of the object of his affection, only to make him appear like a superhero while she defends him?"

"Huh?" Gabs reached for me.

I pulled back. "Then sure, yup, that'll do." I slapped her ass and winked.

"I hate you." Her chest heaved.

"No, you don't." I smirked and let my eyes take a slow tour of her body, down then back up. My entire body tingled with awareness. Sweet torture. "But I'll be here. When you decide what you really feel . . ."

"I'm never coming to you." She crossed her arms.

"Halfway . . . I'm always willing to meet halfway." I reached for her, then jerked back without touching. "Have fun on your fake date, Gabs, and do make sure you fill out that progress report with more than one-word answers. Wouldn't want the boss getting all . . . hot and bothered."

She took a step toward me.

I took a threatening step toward her.

Ian swore from the hallway. "Is there blood?"

"Nah," I answered. "But I sense a war brewing."

"Shit," Ian mumbled.

"So, what will it be?" I whispered to Gabs. "Meet me halfway? Or are you too scared?"

"I'm not." She was, I could see it in her eyes. She was scared to let me in, scared I'd let her fall, scared of everything.

"Tonight," I huffed.

"T-tonight." She straightened her shoulders.

"Nobody likes a chicken, Gabs."

She licked her lips and leaned forward. Warm breath fanned across my neck as she whispered in my ear, "But everyone likes a bit of cock?" Sharp pain spiked from my earlobe as she nipped and then backed off.

What. The. Hell? She'd bitten hard enough to pierce my ear. I forced a smile to keep myself from rubbing it.

Gabs morphing into a vampire would have shocked me less.

I grabbed her arm with every intention in the world of locking her in my room and never letting her out of the damn house, but Ian was right there, waiting in the hallway, texting someone on his phone.

"Better not keep Steve waiting," I breathed out, then mouthed, "Later."

She gave me a weak, noncommittal nod and sauntered away. Meanwhile, Ian gave me a middle-finger salute and left with Gabs, while my body sagged with disappointment.

Chapter Twenty-Five
Gabi

"I haven't seen you in action yet. This should be fun," Ian commented as he drove me to the bar where Steve and I would have our final meeting. "Remember, the last date is what solidifies the girl's feelings for him. You have to break up with him while making him look like the better person, okay?"

I nodded. "Right."

"So, everything okay between you and Lex?"

My head jerked so far to the left, I was my own version of *The Exorcist*. "Sure. Why?"

"He taped a Costco-sized box full of open condoms onto your door, so excuse me for making sure you aren't pissed."

I waved him off. "No worries, I hid tampons in every nook and cranny in his room I could find. He'll be searching for them for years.

When he's eighty and still lives in that same room and runs the entire universe from his computer, he'll still be finding tampons."

Ian chuckled. "Lex hates girly shit. Hates it. Part of me wonders if that's why he's never really settled down. I swear anything that makes him think of cohabitation terrifies him."

"Oh?" I swallowed the lump in my throat. "You mean, you don't think he could ever . . . commit?"

"Lex has never even owned a pet. Not for lack of trying. He killed our last goldfish, simply forgot to feed it. Remember that plant we got freshman year? I put it in his room, thinking 'Hey, it's alive, if we can trust him with a plant, we get another fish.'"

"And?" I prompted.

"A week later the plant died, and when I asked him to throw it away, that took five weeks because he didn't have the time to mess with something so simple."

"But he's not really a plant guy," I said defensively.

"My point"—Ian turned into the parking lot of Maybe, the bar where we were meeting Steve—"is that Lex doesn't commit. Ever. His parents are legit mad scientists who grow opium for the government, and they're also divorced and still fight like hell. He's loaded. A certified genius who gets enough ass to keep him happy. Lex would probably convert to Catholicism and become a priest before he did something like settle down. The last thing he wants is to be unhappy like his parents."

"Ouch. Kinda harsh."

Ian frowned. "Are you defending the same guy you referred to as the Antichrist?"

"No!" I held up my hands. "Just asking questions. You know how I get when I'm nervous," I lied through my teeth. What was I doing? I knew Ian was right. But apparently I was a stupid girl because I was still toying with the idea of taking Lex up on his challenge. *Tonight.*

The whispered promise burned through my brain, only to turn into a flashing neon sign with arrows pointing to it.

I groaned.

"You'll be fine," Ian assured me, like all best friends should. "Blake's meeting us after her practice, so we'll just be at another table, alright? Get in, get it over with, get out."

"Right." I bolted out of the car, my mind a jumbled mess—and not because of nerdy Steve but because of stupid Lex.

Stupid. Stupid. Lex.

"Steve!" I smiled brightly when I saw him waiting at the bar. "You ready for a show?"

"Yeah." He was already sweating. "She's been texting almost every day. You think that's a good sign?"

"Yes, according to our research."

"Yeah." Steve called over the bartender. "Two vodka sodas."

"So!" I slammed my purse down onto the table. "You're gonna pull that shit again?"

"Uhhh." Steve looked around. "Gabi, are you okay?"

"What? You think I don't know?"

"Know what?" Guys were so stupid. I kicked him, urging him to play along.

Frowning, he rubbed his shin.

"I *know* she's been texting you. Who is she?" Stella was working at the bar that night. She quickly switched places with the other bartender and moved closer to us.

"She's . . . my friend," Steve said defensively. "So what? We talk."

"Well great, Steve." I said his name all whiny. "You talk? And what? We don't?"

"You don't understand me," Steve whispered. "I'm sorry, but you're just not . . ." He gulped. I knew it was hard for him to be cruel. "You're not like me . . . you're not like her."

"What is that supposed to mean? She's who you want? Is that what you're saying?"

The girl was seriously going to rub a hole through the counter, she was scrubbing so hard.

"Yeah, she is."

"I guess I'll go, then." I stood and turned. "You do realize you're saying no to the best sex of your life, right?"

"I highly doubt that." He laughed while his ears turned a pinkish color.

"Your loss." I shrugged.

The girl practically leapt to his defense. "No, I think it's his gain."

"Whatever." I sauntered toward Ian's table in the corner. Blake was still in her game sweats and eating a pile of nachos. It was beyond me how she could eat like a guy and not gain a pound.

Ian's slow clap was encouraging. "Another happy client?"

I turned back just in time to see Steve sucking face with the girl of his dreams. "Yeah." I laughed. "Honestly, it feels kind of good, helping them out."

Ian's smile turned serious. "I know Lex has been going over all the rules with you, but I want you to memorize the rules for dating and the top ten plays."

"Plays?" I repeated.

Blake snorted. "Like The Gentleman's Kiss."

"Huh?" I started frantically searching through the binder. "What's The Gentleman's Kiss?"

"In your case, The Lady's Kiss." Ian leaned back in his chair. "Blake, would you like to explain?"

"Get close, but not too close." Blake chomped on her chip and swallowed. Then she picked up another chip and waved it through the air as she continued. "And then brush your lips across hers, but not forcefully, and make her lean toward you. The hottest kisses aren't the passionate ones but the slow ones that allow a burn to take place, heating you from the inside out." *Crunch*. She smirked as she bit down on the chip.

"Who hurt you?" This I said to Ian as he rolled his eyes.

"It's easy." Ian pulled out a giant binder and pointed to a few graphs. They had graphs! Why was I never given this magical playbook before? "Just memorize all the main plays, and if you don't know what to do in a situation, reference the playbook. Always reference the playbook."

"Damn Lex." I slammed the top cover down. "What? Was he spouting all this bullshit training to see if he could break me?"

Ian was silent.

Blake looked away.

"Guys!"

Ian held up his hands. "He wanted to make sure that you could handle the job without our help, which you clearly did. So . . . welcome to the team." He held out his hand.

"Why does it feel like I'm shaking hands with the devil?"

"Don't be dramatic," Ian said as our fingers grasped. "We left *him* back at the house."

"Hah." My laugh was weak, my knees wobbly as I collapsed against the chair.

Blake scooted the guacamole in my direction. "Chip?"

"No," I grumbled, stomach suddenly upset. Stupid Lex, I was going to kill him. I'd kissed him to prove I could!

I kissed him.

To prove.

I could.

And then spent my valuable time following him around, hanging on every training word, terrified I'd get something wrong, only to find out I could have just memorized a stupid book rather than get thrown into the fiery furnace!

"No way!" I jumped to my feet. "That bastard! He kissed me! Pushed me!"

Ian cracked a smile. "It's standard procedure with our clients." He was clearly picking up on what I was pissed about. "We test their comfort in physical situations, ergo, the kiss. So Lex did the same with you as part of your training so you could experience it firsthand. Please, like Lex did that to make you mad. He probably took a bath in bleach afterward."

Blake and I glared in his direction.

"Not because he needs to!" Ian said quickly. "Because he hates you." He swallowed. "And now you both hate me?"

Blake rolled her eyes and chomped down on more chips, still not talking.

"No sex tonight, sweet cheeks?"

She tossed a chip at his face, and what followed was a very descriptive conversation about how Ian had instructed Lex to train me—including the playbook. He'd made him promise to do the physical tests like they do with all clients, but I was supposed to get the playbook to help so I'd have notes to fall back on, not be floundering in an effort to prove myself for Lex's entertainment! He'd basically made what should have been semi-easy extremely difficult! For his own amusement?

With each confession, I winced further until finally Blake reached across the table and grabbed my hand. "I take it that's not how things went down?"

I let out a low growl. "Let's just say I don't have the playbook memorized."

Ian's eyes narrowed. "But Lex said you'd been trained."

"Right." I nodded, then grabbed my purse and keys and ran out the door, thanking my lucky stars that it was a busy night and the street was crowded with taxis.

Lex had some explaining to do. Too bad I was going to kill him before he had the chance.

I smiled the entire way to the house.

CHAPTER TWENTY-SIX
LEX

The front door slammed.

Stomping commenced through the house until it suddenly stopped. The hair on the back of my neck rose slowly to attention as Gabi appeared in the corner of my eye.

The living room seemed a bit too small for both of us.

"Gabi." I nodded in her direction, then glanced back at the TV.

"Lex." She spat my name like it was the most evil thing to ever cross those lips of hers.

Oh hell, there would be blood.

She moved in front of the TV, hands on hips, eyes throwing ninja stars in my direction. "You bastard."

"Gabs . . ." I scratched my head. "Can we not do this now? *Dateline*'s on."

"Oh, you don't want to do this?" Her voice rose an octave. "Here? Now?"

I sighed. "Someone's granny panties got a bit twisted on the way up, hmm?"

"I don't wear—" She clenched her fists and marched over, stopping right in front of me. Curling her lip into a snarl, she shoved my chest so hard I collided with the back of the couch. "You made me think I had to prove myself with *only* the training you gave me! You LIED!"

"Well, you're in college, and life doesn't give you a manual for that—"

"I'm going to strangle you!"

A smile spread across my face. "Can I take a rain check? Erotic asphyxiation isn't really—"

"NO!" She yelled, slamming her palms against my chest. "You made me kiss you! You were basically waiting for me to fail with Steve! I was a ball of stress and nerves because of you! 'Playbook' ring a bell?"

I burst out laughing. "That's what you're pissed about? Gabs! I would train any employee that way; it was a test to see if you could take direction without the help of notes. You passed. Congrats. Now"—I gripped her by the hips and tossed her to the side—"time to watch serial killers."

She growled.

I shrugged and kept watching.

And then a couch cushion landed against my face, smothering me to death. I pushed back but she was on top of me, her fists pounding against the cushion.

"That's it!" I stood, grabbing the cushion, her little hands digging into it as she briefly dangled from it before crashing into the coffee table.

"My butt!" she yelled. "It's bruised!"

"It's not bruised!" I yelled right back. "Gabs, you fell half an inch."

She got up, rubbing her ass while glaring daggers at me. "Sleep with one eye open, Luthor."

"I'm disappointed." I tossed the cushion to the side and changed the subject. "Not taking me up on my offer? Too . . . afraid?"

"Afraid!" She cackled out "Ha!" and then limped toward me. Maybe she really had bruised something. "Maybe I'm just not interested."

"Aw, Gabs." I reached for her body and tugged it against mine. "Everyone's interested."

"I would rather punch your mouth than kiss it," she spat.

"I'll let you do both if you don't draw blood."

She drew back, jaw slackening, then sputtered, "You're sick."

"Make me well?" I was only half joking. I thought she'd laugh.

Instead, her face froze.

"Gabs?"

"You took care of me," she whispered, as if she was upset over the fact.

"Huh?"

"When I was sick."

"I distinctly remember that I had selfish reasons. I was truly terrified you were turning into a zombie, and I wanted to have dibs on getting a Presidential Medal of Freedom for stopping a worldwide pandemic."

"Right," she mumbled, then waved into the air. "I'll see you later, Lex."

I frowned. "Gabs, wait."

Her footsteps slowed, but she didn't turn around. "For what, Lex?" she asked in a small, tight voice. "What do you want from me?"

It was the perfect question.

I had the right answer.

I just didn't know how to get the words on my tongue from my mouth out into the universe. So I let her walk away.

Each step she took up the stairs felt like a choking sensation around my neck, as if she'd been my only source of air and I'd shut her off, shut her down.

"Shit." I tried to get back into my show, but it was just people moving around on the screen, and the girl I wanted—the only one I wanted—was upstairs, probably confused as hell because of my hot-and-cold tendencies.

"Damn it." I jumped to my feet and took the stairs two at a time as I went to her room. "Gabs?" I knocked twice. "Open up."

Nothing.

"Gabs!" I let out a groan. "Please, it's important."

"How important?" came her voice from directly behind me.

I turned on my heel, then fell back against her closed door, my ass kissing the doorknob as I took in her dripping wet form.

"My shower wasn't working, so I used yours and made sure to get all my girly parts all over the wall. So if you don't own bleach . . ."

"I like girly parts," I said as I slowly walked into her personal space, or my space, considering she was in my bedroom.

Wrong thing to say. Her shoulders sagged. "Lex, I think I speak for the entire female population when I say, yes, we know." She tried sidestepping me.

I blocked her way, pressing my hands against the door frame that led out into the hall.

"Why?" It was quiet, a desperate prayer as she glanced up at me from beneath those dark eyelashes. I'd always been an eye person, loved the way they revealed so much about a person, and I was an idiot for not noticing who she was four years ago.

And look how history continued to repeat itself.

"I'm an idiot." It felt good saying it out loud.

Gabs reached up and touched my forehead, then whispered, "Either the zombies got you or you're on drugs."

I grabbed her hand and pinned it at her side, then with my free hand flung her towel to the floor.

She didn't flinch.

Her breasts were perfect, her waist just made for a man's hands—my hands. But it wasn't her body that was doing the trick, it was her eyes, the trusting, knowing eyes that drew me in slowly and then all at once. I had no choice but to fall into the essence that was Gabi.

Trembling, I reached for her face and tugged it toward me, covering her mouth with mine—sealing our fate.

I silenced her gasp, lifting her into the air as our tongues battled one another for dominance. The girl just wouldn't quit—and I didn't want it any other way.

The energy between us exploded as she grasped my shoulders, digging her fingertips into my muscle like she was bracing herself for battle.

With a grunt, I collided with the side of the door, nearly taking it off its hinges.

Gabi was everywhere.

Naked in my arms, squirming, her scent in my mouth, surrounding me. I couldn't kiss her hard enough as I fought to regain control of the situation, to gain the upper hand I saw slipping away as her body rocked into mine.

Her hips drove against me.

"Damn," I breathed against her mouth, half expecting her to headbutt me and walk off. I had no idea the violence, the hatred, between us would end up sparking a flame that exploded wherever we touched.

She slid down me slowly, and my cock strained against my jeans as the pressure of her body teased me.

Once her bare feet touched the floor, she pushed me back, giving me the idea she needed space.

Hell, she wasn't the only one.

What the hell were we doing?

"I hate you," she finally said, breaking the silence.

I smirked. "The feeling is entirely mutual."

"Good talk?" Her smile transformed her entire face. Damn it, she was perfection.

"Yeah, Gabs." I reached for her again, grasping her wrist, waiting for her to come back into my atmosphere so I could breathe her in. "Good talk."

Nodding, she took one step, then two in my direction. She rested her hands against my chest, sending shock waves of heat through my system, then slid them up around my neck.

We were hugging.

Embracing.

All the tension left my body in that instant.

The rightness of the entire situation left me speechless about how a simple hug was exposing every vulnerability, breaking down every defense I'd ever laid in place when it came to Gabs. She might as well grab a knife, cut me open, and peer inside.

Because my weakness had always been her, it would always be her.

And now? It felt like she knew it.

I held her tighter against me, my hands slowly dancing up and down her back while I took a deep breath; the air was saturated with her.

"Your choice," I whispered hoarsely. "You still want this?"

Still want this. Please, God, make her still want this.

No answer.

Rejection washed over me as I frantically searched for every damn pebble from the wall she'd destroyed. I needed to rebuild, to fix the armor around myself.

I swallowed a giant lump in my throat as she stepped around me.

Leaving. Only this time, it was her leaving, not me, and I knew I deserved every moment of the rejection she was showing me as she moved past me, then tugged my body completely into the room and shut the door.

The sound of my door locking might as well have been a meteor hitting the earth.

I was afraid to turn around.

Small hands touched my sides from behind and then wrapped around my middle as Gabs planted her face against my back. "I still want this."

I hung my head. "Thank God."

Without giving her another chance to say no, I scooped her into my arms and carried her to the bed. "You know this changes nothing, right?"

Gabi didn't miss a beat. She smiled—still naked, mind you—and reached up to yank my head down to hers. "You're still a bastard."

"And you're still a pain in my ass."

"Okay."

I licked her lips.

She returned the favor.

"Okay."

Chapter Twenty-Seven
Gabi

The entire situation felt unreal, as if I was hovering over my own body, watching things happen, gasping, holding my breath, rubbing my eyes, and wondering if I was in a dream.

I'd always wanted him.

There was a tug-of-war between my head and my heart.

My head would remind me of all the situations when he'd been a completely horrible human being, while my heart kept the good memories sacred.

Like when we were younger and he beat up the kids who used to make fun of me because I wore hand-me-downs.

Or the time when he taught me how to dance so I wouldn't look stupid at my first junior high dance. Then he'd moved away from our school district, and we'd lost touch.

He and Ian had still hung out, but he had disappeared from *my* world.

Until my senior year of high school, when I came to that Christmas party on campus.

It was our game changer.

The trick play.

Be the Cinderella at the ball and the prince takes you home, right? Isn't that how life worked? Instead, the prince kissed me, then insulted me, rejected me, and so started the war.

I think I liked making love better.

"Lex," I panted as he invaded my mouth over and over again, as if he couldn't get enough of the way our lips slid across one another. The raw sensation of his rough hands rubbing down my ribs had me bucking off the bed every single time.

"I love that even now, when you say my name, I'm still a little terrified you're going to attack me." Lex chuckled darkly against my neck.

My laugh turned into a moan. "You . . . are . . ."

His lips found my ear, and then he was doing something with his tongue while his fingertips skimmed across my pelvis. "What was that?"

"No idea." I'd heard rumors that Lex was so good in bed he'd managed to give a girl three orgasms while studying for a poli-sci test at the same time. Something about the note cards being in the pillowcase.

The point?

The rumors.

Were true.

So . . . "Holy crap, Lex, that feels too much."

"Not a sentence, Sunshine." Lex hauled me up into a sitting position.

Confused, I looked around. He still had clothes on. I was naked, writhing beneath him like—

"None of those faces are allowed in the inner sanctum," he teased, his eyes dark. "Come here."

I didn't move.

"Fine." He peeled off his shirt, exposing me to so much masculine beauty that I had a hard time catching my breath. He stood, slowly unzipping his pants, before dropping them to the floor and kicking them away. "Vulnerability meets vulnerability, right?"

I nodded dumbly as he dipped his thumbs into his boxers and then removed them too.

My eyes stayed glued to the space in front of me, the space he occupied, as he very boldly and nakedly stood in front of me, muscles taut.

"You can say it: my stripper skills suck."

"Right," I croaked. "Because that's where my mind was going."

"Gabs . . ." He held out his hand, palm up. "We can take things slow."

"No." I shook my head vigorously. "No." Oh, no. I was going to do it. I was going to cry. No, no, no, no.

"Whoa, whoa, whoa." Lex pulled me into his lap. Now both of us were naked, and I was feeling way too many things—everywhere. Not to mention the panic that was rising in my chest that he'd walk away, that I wouldn't be good enough, that he'd laugh at my inexperience.

This would change everything.

Now if he made a sexual comment about me, it would wreck me, because he would know the truth.

"Promise me something," I whispered.

"Okay, Sunshine," he said gently, pulling me further onto his lap. "What kind of promise do you need? And is this one of those blood oath things? Will there always be blood?"

I smiled. "Be serious."

"Oh." He nodded and started moving beneath me, the slight pressure causing me to lose my train of thought. "What's this promise you need?"

"This stays here," I blurted. "Whatever this is, it stays here. It's a no-play zone, okay? When we walk out that door and still feel the need to yell and push and throw knives—"

"You have *knives*?" he repeated, incredulous.

I frowned. "Well, downstairs in the kitchen. We're getting off topic. This, between us, we can't use it against each other. No ammo. Keep the inner sanctum . . ."

"Sacred," he finished.

I relaxed against his chest without even realizing what was happening. I was in his arms, naked, sharing a moment of complete and total vulnerability as if it was normal, and Lex was responding like a human being.

"Agreed." He kissed my neck. "And I promise."

My groan of approval must have been encouraging enough for him to keep going as he moved his hand between our bodies. "Shh, don't panic."

"Panicking," I said dumbly.

"Relax." His mouth was hot against my ear. "This is natural. Normal . . . You'll like it."

"Are we sure? Maybe I won't, and then I'll disappoint you and get fired!"

Lex burst out laughing. "This isn't part of the test, Gabs. You won't fail."

I whimpered in embarrassment. "How would you know?"

"Because you're Gabi," he said simply. "You succeeded the minute you walked into my life and threw me on my ass. Failure isn't really an option where you're concerned. Besides"—he rocked against me—"does it feel like you're failing?"

"No." I pulled back to gaze into his eyes. "It feels like you . . . may have a thing for me."

"Big thing."

"Eh, small thing."

"Huge." He nodded.

"I don't know if I would exaggerate that much, but sure, to each his own," I teased.

"That's it." I was midair, and then he threw me back against the mattress and hovered over me. His head descended, and then all I knew were his kisses.

His touch.

His gentle whispers.

His breath as his air became mine.

Chapter Twenty-Eight
Lex

Pride cometh before the fall.

I'd always prided myself on being able to catalogue every type of woman into tiny little boxes with neat little labels.

Gabi had no box.

No label.

And whenever I tried to shove her where I thought she needed to be, she rebelled and came barreling back toward me.

I realized.

Sex would be the exact same way.

I couldn't be the usual Lex I'd always been in bed, because she was different—our situation was different.

And I needed to label it differently. As unromantic as that sounds, to me it was pure romance, because for a guy who thought in code—a guy who had a label, a place for everything in his life?

She.

Didn't.

Fit.

"Just tell me if it's too fast," I whispered against her swollen lips. "Tell me if it hurts, scream when it feels good. And I'm not against you just saying my name over"—I kissed the right corner of her mouth, where her lips spread into a wide smile—"and over"—I moved to the other side, not wanting it to get jealous—"and over again." I pressed my mouth to hers. The feel of her lips touching mine, the taste of her unique flavor, was so alarmingly arousing.

Then again.

I knew that.

I'd *always* known that.

"Okay." Gabs nodded, and a shiver tore through her. "For now, the kissing is good."

"Gabs . . ." I pulled back, regarding her with the most serious look I could muster. "The kissing needs to be great."

"Oh."

"Am *I* going to get fired?" I teased.

Gabi burst out laughing and then grabbed me by the back of my head, slamming our mouths together in such a hot kiss that I nearly blacked out.

Our lips teased and my tongue beckoned, sliding against hers, retreating, fighting for dominance, as I pressed my palm against her breast, my fingers splayed across her creamy flesh.

Moaning, she moved against me as I grazed my hand down her side, reaching between us, exploring, waiting for her body to respond to my exploration.

The minute my fingers brushed against her core, she stopped kissing me. I lifted my head, gazing into her eyes.

And continued slight pressure where I knew she needed it.

Her eyes locked on mine.

Watching my face as I pleasured her.

Making me desperate to join our bodies, to make this more than sex, more than a moment where shields were down and a white flag waved between us.

Her eyes snapped closed as she moved against me.

"That's it," I whispered along her neck, sweat beginning to make our bodies slide across each other. "Trust me."

I'd never asked for her trust.

Gabi opened her eyes and whispered, "I do." As she shattered right before my eyes, her body going taut before she slumped against my hand.

"That was . . ." I was jealous of every part of my body that got to experience her pleasure, jealous that I wasn't inside her when it happened. "Beautiful."

Eyes hazy, she brought my head down for a kiss. Her lips were tender. I pulled back and reached into the nightstand.

With wide eyes she watched me, and my freaking body responded like it was performing action stunts and deserved praise and adoration.

"You sure about this?" I murmured, tossing the wrapper onto the floor, praying she'd say no even as I longed for her to say yes.

Gabi reached for my hands. Our fingers linked together, and then I pinned them above her head, exposing her breasts to my mouth as I sank into her.

She arched off the bed.

"Relax." My lips made their way up her smooth neck, licked across her lips, then suckled the bottom one as I started rocking my hips in a slow rhythm.

Gabi's body went completely tense.

"Trust," I urged, slowing down.

She nodded her head, then met my kiss with raw hunger as she started moving beneath me on her own.

My body wanted to join the party, but I knew she needed to get used to me . . . And if I moved with her, it was going to be over with before it even really started.

"It feels . . . different," she said hoarsely, her hands clambering for my shoulders as she writhed beneath me. I watched, a smile spreading across my face as she used me without even really knowing it.

"You're beautiful," I said softly. "Just like this."

She opened her eyes. "Full . . . I'm full."

"Of me." I couldn't keep the pride out of my voice. "Now, are you ready?"

"Ready?" She frowned. "But . . . I thought that—"

"No mercy," I growled against her neck, sinking deeper into her, so deep that my vision blurred with the feeling of it. Why had it never felt like this before?

I moved slowly as Gabs clutched my biceps, her fingers imprinting my muscle, leaving marks.

I quickened my pace as she clenched me harder. Sweat dripped from my temple and landed on her chest.

I looked down at the small bead of sweat as it rolled between her breasts. The joining of our bodies was the most perfect thing I'd ever witnessed.

She tensed beneath me.

"Gabi . . ." I thrust faster, whispering her name over and over again as she jerked my head down to hers and our teeth clicked against one another as we fought for one another's kisses.

I swallowed her moan as her body tightened around me, and with one last thrust released four years' worth of waiting. I was torn between feeling complete because I was finally with her and pissed that I had waited so damn long. Every part of us being together felt right, even if I knew it was wrong to go behind Ian's back. This moment with her, this wasn't just sex. What exploded between us was . . . magic. Hell, one sexual experience with Gabs was turning me into a sap.

Our eyes locked on each other, and a lifetime of conversations took place in the look she gave me. It wasn't confusion, just pure want, desire.

When we slowly pulled apart, our noses still touched, and I still kissed her, didn't push her away, didn't even pull out.

Because she wasn't just any girl.

She wasn't a one-night stand.

She was the girl I'd wanted ever since she blinked her big green cat eyes up at me in defiance.

I love you, I wanted to say.

Instead I settled with "That was incredible."

Leave it to Gabi to pat me on the back and retort with "You did okay . . ."

Chapter Twenty-Nine

Gabi

What does a girl do after experiencing the most amazing bliss humanly possible at the hand of her sworn enemy? Throw a party? Jump off a cliff? Do it again?

Lex made the decision for me, when he got up from the bed and sauntered over to the bathroom. The sound of water being turned on was my only cue that things were done. Cold air bit at my body, reminding me that I was naked, that I'd just been naked for who knew how long with Lex's hands all over me. My body was still trembling with the realization that I wasn't the same.

Did I want to be?

Would I do it again?

Yes. Even if he was technically excusing me from his fortress. With a sigh, I grabbed the cold sheet and wrapped it around me as best I could.

Lex poked his head out of the bathroom doorway and held out his hand. "Come here."

"You gonna drown me, Lex?" I teased, teeth chattering with nervousness as adrenaline continued to settle across my body. I needed the joking to break the insane tension I felt after what had just happened. Holy crap, I'd just slept with Lex Luthor. Ian was going to kill us. I'd dated guys before, but I knew Lex was different; he was a certified whore, and I was in his bed. If Ian found out . . .

If he found out.

If.

"If" was my new favorite word. I was going to make a sign in big block letters and tape it to my door.

"Gabs, don't get me wrong, my dick really appreciates all the staring you're doing right now, but since it's not up for another performance for at least another hour, you need to stop before I get depressed."

"What?" Realizing my gaze had been glued below Lex's waist, I snapped my head up and caught a playful smile spreading across his chiseled face. "Holy crap. Sorry, I think I blacked out."

"Great." Lex nodded, making his way toward me. "That speaks really highly for my manhood, causing you to black out and all. Now get your sweet ass over here."

Slowly, I rose from the bed and walked toward him, so aware of my own nakedness that I almost dove back under the covers and hid. Maybe if I closed my eyes I'd disappear?

Chuckling, he grabbed my hand and tugged me the rest of the way into the bathroom. Now, normally, I'd be grossed out. Guys' bathrooms? Not always the cleanest. But both Ian and Lex were neat freaks, so Lex's bathroom was sparkling. He even had a separate soaker tub.

Being in Lex's bathroom was almost like being in a high-end hotel. Did that make me a hooker if I was naked in it twice in one day?

"Get in," he urged. His large hands dwarfed my shoulders as he gently pushed me toward the tub. "I promise you won't drown, but I'll grab a life jacket just in case."

"Ha-ha," I fake laughed. "Was that a short-person joke?"

"No-o-o." Lex chuckled. "I would never. The last time I made fun of your height, you threw a fork at my face."

"You're lucky I don't do worse." I dipped my toe into the tub; the water was deliciously hot. Suddenly chilled, I put my right foot in and then lifted my left.

"Okay." Lex hefted me up into his arms and plunked me into the tub, sending water sloshing up the sides.

"Hey!"

"Welcome." He smiled broadly, hands on hips, still gloriously naked and seeming not to care.

My eyes wanted to turn away, but he was so comfortable with his body and I still felt like a virgin. Nakedness was meant to be covered, right? But with Lex, it was like he wanted me on full display all the time. It was completely unnerving for someone who'd never even had sex before. And he was absolutely gorgeous and seemed to encourage me to drink my fill and come back for seconds—and he looked at me the same way. I licked my lips. He was just so . . . manly.

Everywhere.

"Gabs," Lex groaned, wiping a hand over his face. "What did I say about staring?"

"Er . . ." I jerked my head back and stared at the water pouring out of the faucet. "Don't do it?"

Lex poured in some bubble bath, which foamed into mountains of lavender-scented white puffs. As the bubbles crested the edge of the tub, he turned off the faucet. I thought he was getting ready to leave, but instead he closed the door to the bathroom and crawled in across from me.

"Lex." I licked my lips as chills erupted on my arms.

"Hmm?" He leaned back and exhaled. "What's up?"

"We're in the bathtub."

"We are."

"Together," I explained.

He looked around in fake disbelief. "No shit?"

"Lex!" I hissed, slapping my hand against the water, causing droplets to splatter across his chiseled chin. "This is *not* typical behavior!" For us . . . But I left that part out. It wasn't typical behavior for him either. We were laughing, joking, and completely naked in his bathtub. What alternate universe had I stumbled into? First, we didn't hang out and joke around, especially not naked. And I knew the type of guy Lex was. Bang and conquer, then leave with some lame excuse about his house burning down or his puppy getting run over by a scooter.

As the droplets made their way down his face, I wondered, how was he making bath water sexy?

"And you know . . . how, exactly?"

"He asks how!" I burst out laughing. "Ian's my best friend. I know all about your weird freak home disasters!"

"Huh?"

"Let's see . . ." I tapped my chin. "A few months back, your basement flooded."

"That it did." The jerk threw his head back and laughed.

"And before that it was, what? A windstorm caused a tree to barrel into the kitchen?"

"I was so upset." Lex looked down at the water and hunched his shoulders, giving the impression that he was trying to crawl into himself. "Do you know how much it costs to fix windows?"

"And I think one of my personal favorites: a bee infestation."

"Those happen all the time. Trust me, I looked it up on Google."

"Why doesn't it surprise me that you use Google to find stupid facts so that when presented with an opportunity to sleep over with a girl after sex, you have a legit excuse to leave—or at least one that appears legit?"

"Want me to make up one for you so you feel better?"

"What?" I blurted. "No. Wait . . ." Frowning, I narrowed my eyes. "Do you seriously just have random crap in your head that you can pull at any given time in order to get out of a sticky situation?"

Lex's face fell. "I was so worried . . ."

"Worried?"

"About Ian . . ."

"Huh? What are you talking about?"

"When he called and said that the fire had started in his room, I panicked. I mean, I'm the one who left the iron on; I'm the asshole who was trying to iron a shirt before my interview with Microsoft." He paused. "And it's my fault that part of our house, the house we've lived in since freshman year, is gone."

My mouth dropped open.

"We lost his goldfish, Kevin."

"You have a goldfish named Kevin?"

"He died," Lex explained. "Keep up, Gabs."

"Let me guess, smoke inhalation?"

Lex grinned. "How'd you know?"

"Fish don't breathe."

"Right, but most girls don't know that. Especially the ones who don't eat meat because they want to protect the rights of all animals equally." He paused. "One girl cried."

"Over *Kevin*?"

"He was Edgar back then."

"Your fish changes names," I said in complete disbelief.

"Well, I can't just use the same story with the same fish, Gabs." Lex grabbed some soap that was green and smelled like Christmas. "Sometimes it's Kevin that dies after the fire makes its way into the kitchen, other times it's Edgar in the living room."

"You're literally your own Clue game, aren't you?"

"The fish." Lex nodded. "In the laundry room . . . with the fire."

I burst out laughing. "I can't decide if you're a genius, a horrible human being, or a little bit of both."

"Turn around." He gripped my hips and slid me so that my back was against his chest. His lips grazed my ear. "A little bit of both, I suspect."

I didn't have to hide my grin since I was staring at the wall. "So I'm the lucky one, huh?"

"How do you figure?"

"No fake story?"

"I can't fake burn down the house you live in, Gabs, and I think we both know that if I had a fish, the poor bastard's survival rate would be, like, point one percent."

His hands moved smoothly across my back and then down my sides before he reached around my body and cupped me. "Are you sore?"

I froze. "I uh, no, maybe. I'm not sure. I can't really think right now."

"I'm sorry." His mouth hovered around my neck. "You may be a bit over the next few days . . ."

"I'll be sure to tell Ian it's because I went horseback riding," I joked.

Lex about died laughing, his mouth touching my neck, his lips sliding across my wet skin. "I guess you did ride, sort of, but next time I'll give you a better lesson."

My ears perked up. *Down, girl. Sleeping with the enemy, sleeping with the enemy!* "Next time?"

"I didn't burn the house down, Gabs."

"Ri-ight." I drew out the word. "Because I live here."

"That's not my only excuse. I have hundreds, thousands, but with you my only excuse is a mutual friend who may cut off my balls if he discovers I breathed in your direction."

I let out a breathy sigh. "Our secret, then?"

"For now," he agreed, turning me back around so we could face each other.

I don't know if I leaned in first, or if he did, but suddenly we were kissing again, his mouth covering mine as his hands slid across my wet body.

"Lex!" Ian shouted from just outside the bathroom door.

I shoved Lex away as water sloshed over the sides of the tub. "I thought the door was locked?"

"Bastard picked it. He's done that a few times, but only when he's feeling prickly." Lex hissed out a curse. "What, Ian?"

"Are you with someone?" Ian asked.

"Yes," Lex answered.

I smacked him in the shoulder.

He mouthed an "ouch." "But she's really . . . naked."

I slapped my hand against my forehead. *Idiot.*

"And sick."

"Sick?" I mouthed.

"What do you mean, sick? And what the hell, man? You know the rules about girls in the house at night!"

"Puking all over the place." Lex shrugged and then went, "It's okay, baby, let it out."

"Oh, good grief," I grumbled, and then made a whimpering noise, causing Lex to crack up and lose all composure.

"Like the flu?" Ian sounded horrified. Then again, Ian was one of those people who believed in quarantine if someone had as much as a head cold. He carried wet wipes with him everywhere.

"Yeah, maybe the swine flu. She doesn't look good, man, not good at all. I wouldn't come in—oh shit!"

"What?" Ian yelled. "What happened?"

"You didn't touch the doorknob, did you?"

Ian started cursing. "How else am I supposed to break in, you jackass? Why didn't you tell me?"

"Why would I need to? You're the one breaking and entering!"

"You weren't answering your phone, and it's important."

Lex shoved me, mouthing the word "cough."

I started coughing wildly and moaned.

"Dude, whatever it is, it's going to need to wait. In fact, if I were you, I'd go to the store and get some vitamin C mixes for your water."

"I can't get sick." Ian groaned. "I was just sick a few weeks ago. I nearly died from the plague, Lex. What the hell? You know the rules about girls in our house!"

"What did you want me to do? She was shivering!"

"Don't bring in strays!" Ian yelled. "Shit, I'm going to Walgreens. I'll be back and then we can talk, but I'm getting you a mask."

"Bye, Ian!"

"Son of a—" Ian could be heard cursing until a door slammed.

"Want to know another useless fact?" Lex asked.

"I'm listening." I ran my hands over his buzzed hair.

Lex leaned into me and pressed a kiss against my mouth. "The closest Walgreens is three point seven miles from our house. With traffic, it's a good fifteen minutes there and back, and then add in possibly ten minutes of Ian trying to locate what he needs. You know how he gets distracted."

"Are you telling me we have close to forty minutes until he's back?"

"Forty minutes, give or take a few seconds."

"If only we had something to do," I teased.

Lex smirked. "Here's a thought . . ."

My smile fell as his hands reached for my hips and lifted me onto his lap. "You know, just off the top of my head."

"You're right." I cupped his cheek. "You are a genius."

"That's *evil* genius to you, Sunshine."

Chapter Thirty
Lex

"You bastard!" Gabi seethed.

I yawned as I dangled her bra in front of me. "Gabs, you better hurry and get dressed; I mean, we only have around two minutes until Ian gets home."

Gabi's eyes flashed. "Lex. Hand over the bra. What the hell did you do? Rummage through my dresser while I was in the shower?" Gabs was in jeans and was in the process of putting on her T-shirt when I dangled one of her bras in the air.

Hell yes. I could die a sweet, lustful death in that underwear drawer. What should have taken one minute took about four as thongs begged to be picked up. Shrugging, I took two cautious steps toward her, holding the bra over my head. "What if I hide it here for safekeeping? Kind of like my insurance policy that you'll come crawling back across the hall and jump into bed with me?"

"You need my bra in order to get me back in bed?"

Her face met me mid chest. She was so short and flushed, it was . . . intoxicating, adorable, damn it. "Childish?"

"A bit." Her lips pressed together in a smile.

"One minute." I lowered the bra until it was at eye level. "Do you really have to restrain them?"

Gabi rolled her eyes. "Now you acknowledge their existence?"

"I've always known they existed; I suffered from forced forgetfulness."

"Forced forgetfulness?"

Yeah, as in I had to force myself to forget what they looked like, felt like. I adjusted myself and cleared my throat.

"Lex?" Gabi wrapped her arms around my waist. "Are you turning yourself on by holding my cheap little bra?"

"No," I lied, voice gruff. "I'm—just . . ."

"Lex!" Ian's voice sounded from downstairs.

Gabi smacked me in the chest just as I ran over to my bed and shoved her bra under my pillow.

"Seriously?" she hissed.

"What? It's not like I have any spare teeth I can put under there, and word on the street is, the F fairy only visits a select few."

"The F fairy?" Gabi repeated.

I shoved my hands into my pockets to keep myself from pulling her into my arms. "The Fu—"

"Lex!" Ian pushed the door open. His face was red, and he looked ready to set Lex on fire. "What the hell? Stop bringing home sluts!"

I nodded. "Won't happen again."

"Damn right it won't happen again. You can't just sleep with someone because they look lost! Or sad! Or hungry!"

"Right." I nodded slowly. "Or sick."

"Yes!" Ian agreed. "Or that." His gaze flickered from me to Gabi. "Wait. What's going on?"

The room most definitely smelled like sex.

Ian's eyes narrowed.

"I chased the skank out with my hair spray," Gabi lied flawlessly. "Sprayed it in her face and told her it was tear gas. She cried, fell down the stairs, and ran into the door making her escape, so the good news is, you're skank free. The bad news is—"

"She may sue," I finished.

"WHAT?" Ian bellowed.

"Relax." Gabi hid her smile behind her hand and barely managed to turn away from Ian in time to laugh.

"You think this is funny?" Ian's voice rose. "And why the hell are you in his room? If the skank is gone, your work here is done. Damn, Gabs, the last thing you need is to be exposed to—" His nose scrunched up, and then his eyes narrowed in on the bed. "You kept her bra?"

Shit! I thought I'd shoved it completely under the pillow. "She was probably too distracted by Gabi's screaming to grab all of her clothes."

"Thanks, Gabi." Ian sighed. "At least I can count on you to be the mature housemate."

Gabi's smile was sweet. "Oh, Ian, of course. The last thing I want is for Lex to die from some sort of incurable STD."

"Really?" Ian and I asked at the same time.

"And have the illness steal all my glory?" Gabi started walking toward the door. "Yeah, right. If anyone kills Lex, it's going to be me."

There we go. I rolled my eyes like I usually did, then flipped her off. Only this time, my heart was beating so fast I could have sworn Ian was suspicious.

"So, any broken bones?" Ian turned to face me just as Gabs made her way out, her middle finger proudly on display in the air before she slammed the door behind her.

"Not that I know of." I coughed into my hand. "And sorry, man, it won't happen again."

"What was her name?"

"When do I ever learn their names?" I countered quickly.

He still wasn't convinced. Shit, Gabi and I were going to have to rain hell on the house that night, get him focused on the one true thing he's always been able to count on.

Me and Gabs fighting.

After I finally convinced Ian to leave, I grabbed my cell and sent a text to Gabs.

Lex Luthor: He's suspicious . . . and Blake isn't here, so he's going to poke around. He does that when he's bored.

Gabs: If only we could just put a movie on for him or something.

I burst out laughing, then texted back right away.

Lex Luthor: We could try Game of Thrones, but last time he wanted everyone to watch it with him . . .

Gabs: Well, only one thing left to do.

Lex Luthor: ?

Gabs: You ready for WW3?

Lex Luthor: Bring it on, Gabs. Let's just see how convincing you can be after my mouth has been on you.

Gabs: Yawn . . . I've already forgotten what your mouth feels like. You sure you brought your A game tonight?

Lex Luthor: You're gonna pay for that.

`Gabs: Promise?`

I hesitated, my fingers hovering over my phone. What the hell was I doing? What were we doing? And why was I acting like a chick? Reading into everything? Damn it.

We were flirting.

Crossing into dangerous territory—no longer in one-night-stand land, but moving on to something more serious. Did I want that? My heart nearly burst at the thought, but yeah, I think I did. Because I wasn't feeling panicked. Maybe a bit confused and frustrated because Ian was my best friend, and you told your best friend when you were falling for someone. But I couldn't risk it. I couldn't risk losing the guy who had been like a brother to me growing up. And what if Gabi wasn't even thinking along those lines? See. Chick. I was a chick. I settled for something taunting and pressed "Send." Keep it simple, right? Keep it fun.

`Lex Luthor: Loser gets tied up.`

`Gabs: You're on.`

`Lex Luthor: Hope you don't mind rope burn.`

`Gabs: Says the loser . . .`

I nervously chucked my phone onto the bed and crossed my arms. Ian walked by my room again, this time pausing in the doorway. "I want to talk to you about business stuff, and then after, you wanna watch a movie?"

"Sure." I didn't turn around, mainly because my conversation with Gabs had caused a serious problem that I didn't need Ian commenting on.

"Cool, I'll see if Gabs wants to watch too."

"Great." I waved him off. "See you downstairs in a few."

Chapter Thirty-One
Gabi

I ignored the warning bells going off in my head, right along with the elation I felt the minute I made my way into the kitchen and saw Lex grabbing a beer.

My body was still humming with pleasure.

"Gabs," Lex said gruffly. He slapped me on the butt, then squeezed it right before Ian walked into the room.

Lex jerked away from me and winked over his beer bottle as Ian started talking.

"Action or horror?"

Well, here went nothing. "Since Lex has already had enough whores"—I lingered on the word—"why don't we watch action?"

"Jealous?" Lex fired back, though his eyes were twinkling, bright, like he was enjoying the fight.

"Oh, so jealous." I nodded dumbly. "If only I didn't know how to count to four! Then maybe, just maybe, the godly Lex Luthor would sleep with me!"

"The last girl could count to five." Lex grinned wickedly while my belly heated. "I let her count orgasms."

"How charitable of you." I clenched my teeth. The bastard! Had it been five? He held up five fingers on his free hand, then dropped all but one and mouthed "six" when Ian turned around to grab a beer from the fridge.

"That's what I do up there, Gabs. Charity work, helping save girls from poor bastards who can't find their G-spots, one sexual experience at a time."

My eyes widened while my body jerked to attention. "Gross, Lex."

"Gross, Lex?" he challenged. "That all you got, Sunshine? How about please, Lex? More, Lex? Yes, Lex." He started grinding against the counter, damn him. "Right. There. Lex."

"Careful, Lex, you're going to get the granite pregnant," I joked, even though my voice came out hoarse. I knew I sounded turned-on, and I was going to *kill* him.

"One time a girl said I got her pregnant by looking at her." Lex winked. "Another threw me her bra because she was convinced I was famous . . . I signed it."

"You're a regular Boy Scout," I said with heavy sarcasm.

"I learned all kinds of things in the Scouts," Lex said seriously. "Want me to show you?" He tilted his head, then held out his fingers and counted. "I'm pretty sure it would only take me three minutes, since you're so . . . new."

"New?"

"Virgin-like." I noticed he didn't say "virgin," and my face heated even more.

"Aw . . ." Two could play that game. I slapped him on the shoulder. "Not anymore."

Ian's eyes went wide and then crazy as water spewed out of his mouth. "What the hell do you mean, 'not anymore'?"

"Oh, I took off my chastity belt. It was getting really uncomfortable," I joked.

"The hell?" Ian leaned against the counter. "Who is he? The bastard! Who touched you?"

Lex's panicked expression helped my mood immensely.

"It was a small"—I smirked so Lex would know I was kidding—"little—tiny, really—moment. I hardly remember it, Ian."

"Good." Ian nodded. "That's . . . good. But no more." He paced in front of both of us. "You can't. That is, you can't sleep around and work for me."

My eyes widened as I burst out laughing. "Are you being serious right now? Lex sleeps around every day!"

"Lex is Lex! It's like controlling a horny tomcat! Eventually it's going to break out of the litter box and get some."

"That was the worst example I've ever heard." Lex shook his head. "Can we get back to the problem at hand?"

"Which is?" Ian's crazed eyes met Lex's.

"Well, I should think that would be obvious." Lex shrugged in my direction. I really wished I could read minds. "We need to lock Gabs in her room, away from the dangers of the opposite sex."

"Yes." Ian snapped his fingers and began nodding. "We'll leave bread and water by the door."

"I'll take the night shifts." Lex's lips twitched, while I covered my mouth with my hand and turned around so Ian wouldn't see me laugh.

"The problem is the day," Ian said in a serious tone.

"Guys!" I turned back to face them. "Can we please stop talking about my sex life and watch the movie?"

"As long as Gabi sits on the floor—you know, where all canines belong—I'm down for that." Lex shoved my shoulder, so I reached around and pinched his ass.

He let out a little yelp while Ian stared at the ceramic tile.

"Dude!" Lex popped him in the head. "It's okay that she's finally hit puberty. I mean, at least now we won't have to pay someone to date her, you know? That list was getting mighty short."

"Oh good grief." I shoved past both of them and found a spot on the couch, then winked at Lex. "Look! Your spot."

I could have sworn his eye twitched. "But that's where I always sit."

"Hey, Lex, who did you have in your room before Ian got home?"

Lex growled and then jumped into the spot right next to me, his hand reaching beneath my blanket and gripping my thigh as he hissed out, "Don't play with fire, Sunshine . . ."

"I'm made of fire." I licked my lips as his eyes narrowed. "Don't get burned." I was referencing the Sunshine nickname, but I think Lex's focus was on something else completely as he leaned in.

"Can you guys stop bickering? For ten minutes?" Ian made his way into the living room with two more bottles of water and then turned on the TV.

"I'll get the lights." Lex stood and walked over to the light switches, then flicked them off.

Something about being in the darkness made the air crackle with electricity—with awareness, especially when Lex sat down next to me, his palm pressed against my thigh underneath the blanket.

I squirmed beneath his large hand, trying to get comfortable, hating that my body was responding to a hand.

That was it.

Lex's hand was magical.

Ian had decided on *Scream*. Something we'd all seen and could quote and make fun of.

But I wasn't paying attention to anything except the fact that if Lex's hand moved up a few inches, it would be exactly where I wanted him.

My heartbeat pounded in my ears as I slipped my hand underneath the blanket and pressed it against the front of his jeans, then gingerly dipped my fingertips into his waistband.

Every muscle in his body went taut.

"Right, Lex?" Ian elbowed him.

I quickly pulled my hand away, embarrassed. What was I doing? I tried to move away from Lex, but his grip on my thigh made it impossible.

"Right," Lex agreed, then turned to me and mouthed, "Go with it."

"Huh?"

"What the HELL!" Lex jumped up. "Are you kidding me, Gabs?"

"What's your problem, you jackass?" I yelled back.

"You!" he roared. "You're my problem, and I'm tired of dealing with your shit all the time!"

"So close." Ian groaned, leaning his head back against the couch.

"I was trying to be nice, letting you have my spot and the blanket, and you pinch me the entire time? Name-calling? Really, Gabs?"

"Oh please! Like you weren't doing worse!"

"That's it!" Lex gripped my hand. "You wanna fight? We'll fight, away from Ian, whose only crime is wanting to watch a movie with his best friend."

"Friends!"

"Friend," Lex said, louder. "You're just the third wheel we put up with because Ian feels guilty."

My eyes widened. "You bastard!"

"Guys!" Ian shouted.

"Stay out of it!" we both fired back.

Lex grabbed my hand, dragged me toward the nearest downstairs bedroom, and slammed the door behind him. Then he lifted me into the air and pushed me against the door.

"You dirty . . ." He kissed my mouth hungrily. "Wicked . . ." Another kiss. "Girl."

I yearned for him, my body stretching out to meet him, my hands tangled in his shirt as I tried to yank it off his body.

A knock sounded on the door. "You guys alive?" Ian asked.

"Barely," I whimpered as Lex braced me against the door, his knee sliding between my thighs. "Just . . . barely."

"No blood." Ian sounded bored. "Want me to pause the movie?"

"No." Lex's eyes pierced mine. "This is gonna take a while."

"Take your time." Ian's footsteps grew fainter as he went back into the living room.

"Oh, I intend to." Lex's grin was evil as he pulled me down on his leg. The sensation of straddling a part of him was too much for my body to handle. I was ready to explode from his touch, his strokes.

"Bed," I commanded.

"No time." He jerked down my leggings while I reached for the button on his jeans.

"What happened to taking your time?"

"Can't," he panted, pressing another hungry kiss against my neck, his lips moving against my skin as his hands gripped my bare ass. "Need you."

"Then take me," I begged, finally getting his jeans past his hips. He let out a groan as he freed himself and locked eyes with me. "Tell me you're on the pill."

"Since I was fourteen."

"I'm clean. I know you think it's a line, but I get tested, and I need you, all of you, every part of you. I need"—his hands dug into my flesh as he brought my body near his heat—"you. I've always needed just you."

"Always?" I asked, confused.

His clear eyes looked panicked as he whispered, "Since Christmas . . ." He sighed. "Four years ago."

It was exactly what I needed to hear, what I'd craved, and I let go, completely let go and gave my heart to him. But the joke was on me, because Lex had always had it. I was just too stupid to realize it.

And now, he had all the power.

And I knew, if he left . . .

It wouldn't just break me.

But ruin me forever.

"Gabi." He thrust into me, filling me so deeply that I let out a gasp, gripping his shoulders for balance. But there was no balance with him, no calm, only crazy, wild, frenzied movements that caused foreign moans to escape between my lips as I clenched my thighs together in order to contain him, contain what was happening between us.

"Lex—" I exhaled as my body shuddered against his, unable to keep up with his pace, not sure I even wanted to as he took complete control with his movements. I was dizzy with feeling, with yearning. "I need you closer."

"Sweetheart, we can't get any closer."

"Try!" I whimpered.

He chuckled and then, with a grunt, tugged my leggings the rest of the way off my feet and helped me wrap my legs tighter around him. "Hold on tight."

"Drop me"—I sighed in rapture—"and I kill you."

"You're killing me right now." Our mouths met again, one way, then another, each new angle causing me to lose my mind as he continued his rhythm. With a curse, he pressed me against the wall and pinned my hands above my head. With one final thrust, I shattered against him, my body exhausted as I tried to catch my breath.

"You guys done fighting yet?" Ian knocked again.

"Yeah." My voice was husky. "We just signed a peace treaty."

"Thank God," he muttered. "I'll go make popcorn."

"Peace treaty, hmm?" Lex's mouth covered mine again, and again, before he finally pulled out of me and helped me grab my clothes.

"Yeah . . ." I whispered sheepishly.

"I have an idea." Lex handed me my leggings. "Make war every day . . ."

"So we can make love every night?"

"And sign a peace treaty in the morning?" Something about Lex's smile was different. Like he was allowing me to see past the guarded Lex I'd always witnessed, like he'd let me in.

It was the perfect time to ask him what he meant about Christmas four years ago, but I wasn't sure my heart could handle it if he laughed it off or said he brought it up in the heat of the moment.

Four years ago, I had fallen in love with Lex and given him my heart.

And I was beginning to think it was his turn to do the same.

Chapter Thirty-Two
Lex

"New clients." I approached the bench near the student union building where Ian and I always did our morning business, only this Monday morning, Ian was not alone.

Gabi was holding her coffee in the air, her usual smile replaced with a distracted frown as she texted someone on her phone. Did I also need to hack her phone records and find out what idiot was making her sad?

I raised my eyebrows at her, but the minute we locked eyes her smile was back, and the text was forgotten as she dropped her phone in her purse.

"Ian." I tapped my phone against his. "Just sent you the info regarding Caylin."

Ian glanced down at his phone, a smile spreading across his features. "Looks pretty easy: been in love with her best friend's brother since she was six and followed him to school. Pretty, smart, and an athlete. I do well with those."

"We know." I shook my head. "She's also on the volleyball team, so I figured we can have Blake help out a bit."

"Yup." Ian shoved his phone into his pocket. "And the male client for the week?"

I pulled up his application on my phone and tapped the corner against Gabi's phone. We had a file-sharing app that made business so easy it was ridiculous.

Her eyes widened.

In shock?

Horror?

A little bit of both?

"Something wrong, Gabs?" I smirked, trying to remember that I wasn't her boyfriend, I wasn't her anything, and that if Ian found out about us he'd drown me in the fountain. "Losing your nerve?"

"No, it's just . . ." Gabi held out her phone to Ian. "Did you know about this?"

"No chance in hell." Ian stood and faced me. "How did he make it through the screening process?"

"Easy, the program picked him and his stats looked good. How else do you think applicants make it through? I don't see a problem."

Ian rolled his eyes. "The problem is that he knows Gab—"

"No problem!" Gabi interrupted and stood. "I'll make contact and designate the meeting place. Don't worry, guys, I've got this."

She walked off without another word. I wanted nothing more than to push Ian into the dirt and chase after her, but it would look suspicious, and Gabs and I had already made our own rules for our relationship last night before we left the room to watch the rest of the movie with Ian.

"Everything is fair play, but no bringing up our private moments in public." Gabi nodded as if I needed reminding again. "Okay, your turn."

"I can't believe we're making rules like we're five."

"Most five-year-olds' rules revolve around no hitting and snack time," Gabs pointed out.

"I could use a snack."

"You've had three today." She placed her hand against my chest. "Now, what's your rule?"

I swallowed down the shock at what I was about to say, then scratched my head in wonderment as I sat on the bed and stared at her. "Exclusivity."

You'd think I just told Gabi I preferred men.

"Exclusivity?" she repeated. "Between us?"

I bristled. "Why is that so weird?"

"You're Lex."

"I know my name. Helps that you shouted it a few minutes ago while I pleasured you, but thanks for the reminder." I shifted, suddenly uncomfortable, and looked away. Was I that bad? Really?

"Fine," she agreed quickly. "What happens between us is private, and we're exclusive."

I nodded.

"Should we put a time limit on . . . this?"

"No," I said quickly. "But when it needs to end, it ends. No asking why, no fighting about it, no arguing. We just let the other person go, and everything goes back to normal."

"When do you think that will be?" Gabs sat next to me, and the bed dipped under the pressure of both of us sitting on the edge of the mattress.

Never. Because I'd never get enough of her. I couldn't imagine that day ever happening, but I couldn't tell her that, and I sure as hell couldn't make things official between us without first talking to Ian. Since I valued my life . . .

"Seems easy enough," she finally said. "We fight in public and—"

I burst out laughing.

"What?" She shoved me in the arm.

"This!" I pointed at her hand. "You just shoved me, Gabs. When do we not fight? Even in bed? I kiss you senseless and you even try to outdo me with that! We will always fight."

She slumped against me. "That's true."

"Hey, don't look so defeated." I tilted her chin toward me. "I'd rather fight than be bored out of my mind going to the same restaurant for date night and knowing what to expect every day. Hell, tomorrow you could wake up and decide to run me over with your car or set my goldfish on fire. The world is full of possibilities."

"You don't have a goldfish," she grumbled.

"If I did, either it would die from starvation or you'd kill it—or better yet, steal it and hold it hostage and demand I be nice to you before giving it back. But knowing you, you'd get attached and keep it anyway."

Gabi burst out laughing. "You know me too well."

"You have no idea," I whispered under my breath.

"What?"

"Nothing." I stood and offered my hand. "Let's go before Ian calls the police on us—"

"Again," Gabs finished.

"How do they know each other?" I massaged the back of my neck in annoyance.

"Easy." Ian shoved his Ray-Bans on his face and shrugged. "They dated for two years."

I prided myself on being a relatively calm individual, able to process the facts before acting, but two hours later, while I was in Advanced Physics, I was still attempting to process what the hell I was going to do about Gabi taking on an ex-boyfriend as a client. I nearly lost my mind as all the possibilities lined up to one giant catastrophe.

What if she still liked him?

What type of douche let her go in the first place?

Did he somehow know she worked for us?

Was this a ploy to get her back?

"Hey, Lex." Ruby, a girl I'd banged once upon a time, rubbed her lips together, then thrust out her chest. Her white T-shirt strained against her full Cs. "Wanna study?"

Code for *Wanna see me naked?*

I opened my mouth and then frowned as the whole idea of going back to her dorm room played out in my mind. She'd moan, I'd take off her clothes, she'd say something cheesy while her long nails dragged along my back. We'd kiss, I'd add in a little foreplay for her benefit, and then what? Sex? Boring-as-hell sex where she'd try to keep me in bed and then make a futile attempt to get my number—then pout.

"No," I said gruffly. "Sorry."

The shocked look on her face would have been alarming enough, but her two friends looked as though I'd just backhanded the entire female race.

I had said sorry, right? Besides, I was exclusive with Gabi. Holy shit, I had a girlfriend. Is this what that was like? Saying no to girls I didn't want to sleep with in the first place? It wasn't so bad, and not how I imagined it. Then again, in my daydreams it had always been Cameron Diaz propositioning me and me cursing the girlfriend who was waiting at home in mom jeans and frizzy hair.

"But . . ." Ruby reached for my arm. I stepped away.

Hell, I never skipped class, being a nerd and all, but I was going to be skipping now, especially since I couldn't seem to focus on anything except Gabi.

Shit.

I scrambled out of the room and texted Gabi.

```
Lex Luthor: Skip with me.

Gabs: Some of us need to pass classes without
sleeping with the professor.
```

Lex Luthor: One time.

Gabs: I hope she gave you an A.

Lex Luthor: A-, apparently she didn't . . . okay never mind, not having this convo. Come over after class.

Gabs: And what? Bake cookies?

Lex Luthor: Yes. That's exactly what we're going to do, and when we're finished baking cookies, we'll make pot brownies and see how many we can feed Ian before he catches on.

Gabs: REALLY?

A marijuana leaf wearing a goofy smile blinked at me on the screen.

Lex Luthor: It worries me that they actually have a pot emoji, but what's more concerning is that you found it within two seconds.

Gabs: Oops, gotta go, class starting.

Lex Luthor: Live a little! Break the rules.

Gabs: I did. Last night and again this morning.

I smirked and typed back my response.

Lex Luthor: Tell me you didn't love the extra-long shower time.

Gabs: I wasn't the one moaning . . .

Lex Luthor: If you don't stop texting me people are going to think I'm looking at dirty pictures on my phone.

Gabs: Why?

Lex Luthor: I'd take a picture, but then it would be like sending you porn during class, and since you don't like to break rules . . . see you soon, Gabs!

Gabs: No fun.

What wouldn't be fun was me sending her a picture of my suppressed arousal and having Ian find it on her phone.

Two hours. I had two hours to burn before she was going to be at my house, and my focus was scattered at best.

I pulled up the asshole's information on my phone, and then all was right in my world as an evil plan hatched tiny little dinosaur eggs that would one day eat the rat bastard and spit out his bones.

I was going to hack his ass.

I cracked my neck and smirked the entire way home.

Chapter Thirty-Three

Gabi

It was the longest class of my life, made worse by the fact that I kept glancing at the clock every few seconds only to discover the hand had moved a quarter of an inch.

When class finally did end, I bolted out of my seat so fast my legs nearly tangled beneath me.

By the time I reached the door, a heavy dose of logic had seeped into my otherwise frantic and overly emotional brain.

Lex. It was Lex. I nearly skinned both knees and caused a domino effect of students also rushing out the door.

Lex could wait. I could be a mature adult and walk to my car, then drive the few miles to his house without breaking every traffic law in the state.

I could.

But did I want to?

My text alert went off.

```
Asshole Lex: Yawn . . . are you walking
backward toward the house? Really, Gabs?
```

I really needed to change his name on my phone . . . Or—I smiled wide—keep it, since it still made me laugh.

```
Gabi: You do realize who you're talking to,
right? Legs are a bit short.
```

```
Asshole Lex: Didn't feel short wrapped around
me last night . . .
```

I shuddered and slid my phone into my pocket. No way was I going to keep texting him and run into a tree, causing permanent damage to my nose and all four front teeth.

My car wasn't parked far away from the building. I half ran, half skipped to it and prayed it would start.

It did. Thank God.

And so began the three-mile drive to the house. Three miles that should have taken me maybe seven minutes, tops, with traffic.

It took eight.

I pulled up to the house, opened my car door, realized the engine was still running, turned the key and pulled it, then grabbed my bags and got out. After I locked the door, I turned and ran down the sidewalk.

When I made it halfway, the front door opened. Lex stood there, shirtless, with sweats hanging low on his hips.

His smile was so blinding, so perfect, I had to keep myself from doing a little twirl in the air before launching myself into his arms.

"Miss me?" He caught me midair and pulled me hard against his warm chest.

"Yes." I sighed against his neck. "A perfectly unhealthy amount, you ass."

His dark chuckle caused shivers all the way down to my toes. "Good. Also, we're out of flour, so . . ."

"Huh?" I pulled back, my feet dangling in the air still. "What do you mean we're out of flour?"

"Oh, when I say we're out of flour, what I meant is, I tossed away all the baking ingredients so that we'd have no choice but to go to my room and . . . study."

I nodded. "You didn't have to go to such extremes."

"I didn't want to take any chances that you'd actually rather make cookies."

"Does it look like I'd rather make cookies?"

"Gabs . . ." He placed me on the ground and kissed the top of my head. "You're practically starving to death every time you eat, so yeah, I thought it was a fifty-fifty chance."

Guilt gnawed in the middle of my chest like a stupid parasite. I should tell him about my parents; heck, I should tell Ian too, but . . . Well, it wasn't just pride. It was the fact that they were both loaded, and they'd feel guilty and maybe even a bit hurt that I hadn't shared with them earlier.

"I'm probably starving because sleeping with you is like joining a sports team. I hardly ever get Gatorade, and you rarely give me time-outs."

"I was under the impression that time-outs were frowned upon."

"Whatever would give you that idea?"

"You pinched my ass when I told you I needed air and then said, 'You'll be fine. Man up and kiss me.'"

I shrugged. "Are you . . . complaining?"

"Is the team captain complaining? Hell no!" Lex scooped me into his arms and carried me up the stairs.

"Wait!" I laughed as he juggled me around his buff arms. "Does that make me cocaptain?"

"Sorry." Lex winced. "The team already voted. You're the towel girl."

"It's a two-person team," I pointed out.

He ignored me. "Your sole purpose is to serve at the captain's pleasure."

"Oh really?"

"Yup, it's in the rule book."

"What rule book is this?"

"Lex's Rules for Bedtime Sports, Section One, Part A."

I nodded slowly as he set me on my feet in his room. "Did you clean?" It smelled like bleach and Lysol, which was weird, since his room was spotless on a regular basis. I hadn't even seen so much as a sock on the floor. Odd behavior, even for Lex, to clean what didn't need cleaning.

"I clean when I'm upset."

"And throwing out the flour got you all tied up in knots?" I frowned, glancing around the spotless room, and my eyes homed in on his computers.

Lex's eyes widened. "No!"

"Lex!" I hissed out his name like a curse and stomped over to the main screen. "Have you been hacking him?"

Mark Dawson was printed across the top of the screen. Beneath that, his Social Security number, credit score, and last three addresses were listed. Slowly, I turned to Lex, expecting him to look guilty. Nothing but pride washed across his features.

"Oh good grief, Lex." I rolled my eyes. "You're a sick man."

"You know, hacking is an addiction . . ." He nodded slowly, and his eyes crinkled as his full lips pressed together in a toe-curling smile. "Just like you."

"Good one." I pinched his arm. "You can't just go around snooping into people's private lives!"

"He had a penile enlargement," Lex said in a low voice.

"No way!" I gasped.

Lex shook his head. "Yeah, I'm lying, but these are the types of things we need to know, Gabs! He's your ex. I'm not sending you out into the field with God-knows-who! I mean, he could be a sociopath!"

"Out into the field," I repeated. "I'm sorry, do we work for the CIA now?"

"I'm ignoring your sarcasm, which, by the way, is harder than it appears. Just let me do my research so I know you'll be safe."

"Safe, safe, safe." I tapped my chin. "Wonder what Ian would think about my safety now, hmm?" I sauntered over to Lex and grabbed one of his hands. "Am I safe now? In your room?"

"Are you asking if being with me is dangerous?"

"Seems like a risk to me."

He swallowed, his eyes darting between me and the floor. "A risk worth taking?"

"I think I already took it . . . a few times," I joked.

"Let me go check my bedpost. I've been carving out notches."

"Ass!" I slapped him on the arm and motioned back to the computer. "Can you please just . . . trust me to do my job? Remember, you and I are exclusive, and my official job for Wingmen Inc. is to help him get his dream girl, who just so happens to be some chick in his business class. Give me a week and then he'll be gone."

"I love a girl who's confident in her abilities to seduce."

"That's me: seductress." My phone started buzzing. I frowned and shoved it back in my pocket, planning on ignoring it.

Instead, Lex reached into my pocket and pulled it out. "Answer it. I'll still be here when you're done."

"It's my dad. I can call him back."

"Exactly." Lex pressed the phone into my hand. "It's your dad. Talk to him. I know how close you are."

With that, he kissed my temple, walked back over to his computer, and exited out of all the screens.

Leaving me speechless.

Because the Lex I'd always known would choose sex over anything.

And unless I read it wrong, I thought that's why he'd texted me. I thought I was a glorified booty call.

Instead, he was pulling up the Wingmen Inc. software while I held my phone in my hand.

"Gabs . . ." Lex sang, without looking at me. "Call your dad."

So I did.

And when my dad answered and wanted to know how I was doing in school, I ignored the pang of guilt. And when he once again thanked me for the money but voiced his concern about my working too hard, I brushed it off like I'd been brushing everything off lately.

Lex was polite enough to put on his headphones while he worked, and it kind of made me fall a bit harder—that he'd provide me privacy and that, without realizing it, he knew exactly what I needed.

I needed to tell them, not just because they were my friends, but because I was beginning to realize I wanted to—I wanted to open up to Lex, and if Lex found out and Ian didn't . . .

He'd kill us both.

My nerves were completely shot—I'd never been in this type of situation before, lying not only to my best friends but my entire family. But as far as lies went, there were worse things to lie about, right? At least that's what I kept telling myself.

CHAPTER THIRTY-FOUR
LEX

"So." Gabs walked back into my room and placed her phone on the nightstand. It was weird, constantly having her in the only sacred place I had. What was weirder? Had she announced that she was going to redecorate it with hearts, flowers, and Ryan Gosling unicorn heads, I probably would have allowed it.

What. The. Hell?

"So?" I put my computer to sleep and swiveled in my chair, lacing my fingers behind my head.

Gabi's gaze fell to my naked chest.

"Gabs, up here."

"Shh, the towel girl's looking for sweat."

I burst out laughing. "Find any?"

"Not yet. Give me ten minutes, maybe fifteen."

"If you start breathing heavy I'm cutting you off."

She gave me a dismissive wave through the air and slowly approached. With a look of pure concentration on her face, she crawled into my lap and straddled me. Her legs went under each of the chair's arms, which was so freaking adorable I fought to keep myself from just hugging her.

Right, hugging her.

Like a sad bastard who didn't know how to kiss and was afraid to make the first move.

"My parents' anniversary is this weekend, and they specifically asked if you and Ian could come hang out for Sunday dinner."

"Hmm, that depends . . . Is your mom making her famous tamales with homemade salsa?"

"I'm pretty sure I can convince her to."

"Sure, I can go as your . . . friend."

She let out a heavy sigh—of what? Relief?—as her forehead touched my chin. I kissed her head, waiting for her to say something.

"This is . . ."

"I know." I tightened my grip on her arms. "I know."

Maybe we knew each other too well and that was the problem. We'd launched our little enemy ship into an entirely foreign land, and neither of us knew what to do.

"I don't want you kissing him," I admitted softly.

Gabs pulled back, her eyes narrowing. "I won't, or at least if it can be avoided, I'll avoid it."

"No tongue."

"Getting kinda bossy for a *friend*." She emphasized the damn word.

I gripped her ass and jerked her against me. "We were never friends."

Gabs let out a little whimper. "And now?"

"We're so much more." My mouth found hers in a heated kiss as she snaked her arms around my neck.

I kissed her until my lips hurt, until my ass felt like it was going to sleep, until the need to have her was so intense it was all that consumed my thoughts.

"Lex . . ." Gabi pulled back, her green eyes locked onto mine. "Four years ago—"

"Four years ago"—I looked away, breaking all eye contact—"I was an ass."

"Yes."

"Hell, four weeks ago even . . ."

"Yup," she agreed.

"I . . ." Cursing, I gave her hair a little tug with my right hand, then let her dark locks slip through my fingers. "Have I ever told you how beautiful you really are?"

Gabi's eyes filled with tears.

And I realized in that moment just how much of a dick I really had been to her, that behind all the teasing, she never truly realized how wonderful she was.

"I wanted you then." I cupped her face. "I want you more now, only because now I know you. And every day since knowing you, I've fallen a little bit harder, a little bit deeper, a little bit more . . ." I didn't say "in love." But I wanted to.

Gabi blinked back tears. "I don't understand. Then why didn't you say something?"

"One word," I confessed. "Ian."

"Right, he'd be pissed, but . . ." Her eyes narrowed. "Has he said anything else about us?"

"Other than telling me I'd never be good enough for his best friend? Someone he considers a sister? He told me that if I touched you he'd cut my hand off, or what's worse . . . if I pursued you, our friendship would be over."

"WHAT?" Gabi roared. "Are you serious?"

"Yeah," I croaked. "Look, I'm not proud of the way I treated you, but I keep my promises, and the idea that he would just cut me out of his life, well, I felt like I had to choose you or him."

"But it doesn't have to be that way!"

"Doesn't it?" I fired back. "Do you *know* Ian?"

"He'll get over it!"

"Gabs, you are the only family he has other than his sister, and you and he are closer than they've ever been. You were there when his parents died, you were there for all the birthdays they missed, and when I moved away, you were still there for him. You are everything to him, and as stupid as it sounds, he's like a brother to me. Hurting him . . ." I sighed.

"What do we do?"

"Sex." I nodded confidently. "It solves everything, like coconut oil."

"Huh?"

"Coconut oil. Premed, hmm? And you don't know the many uses of coconut oil?"

"Guys!" Ian's voice traveled from downstairs.

Gabi panicked while I tried to lift her out of the chair only to realize her legs were stuck under its arms.

"Help!" she squeaked.

"Stop squirming!" I hissed as I shoved one leg out of a hole and nearly fell on top of her. "Bend your knee!"

"If I bend it any further it's going to snap!" she yelled.

"Gabi! If there was ever a time to impress me with your flexibility, this is it!" I tried to ease to the right at the same time she went left.

"Ouch!" Gabi smacked me in the leg. "That hurts!"

"Oh I'm sorry, did you want our best friend to find us pretzeled up in my room?"

Gabi's eyes widened as we heard Ian climb the stairs. "Maybe if you push my foot left, I'll pull right—"

"Shit!" I was about to give up when her leg came free, causing her to tumble to the floor with me on top of her as the chair slammed backward against the bed.

"Whoa!" Ian stepped into my room. "Have we moved past the verbal insults? Are you guys getting physical now?"

"Yes!" Gabi shouted as she started pounding my chest with her tiny fists. "Now get off, you ass!"

"YOU LOVE IT!" I yelled back, unable to think of what else to say while my body responded so exquisitely to her wiggling. I tried to send her a silent plea to stop moving, but her hips rocked.

Damn it!

"Dude, get off her, she's a quarter of your size. We're lucky we don't have a Gabi-sized pancake on the floor."

"Hah," I laughed in fake amusement and moved away from Gabi, trying to stay hunched on the floor so Ian couldn't see just how much I enjoyed our little wrestle time.

"Geez." Ian held out his hand to her. "Are you okay, Gabs?"

She took it and stood. "Sure!"

"You look . . ." Ian's eyes narrowed. "You're seeing the guy again, aren't you? The one who stole your treasure!"

"She's not a pirate," I commented as Gabi smacked Ian in the chest.

"My treasure?"

"Your booty." I laughed.

"Not helpful, Lex!" Gabi glared and then turned to Ian. "And why do you even care? I'm a woman. I have needs!"

"Oh, hell no!" Ian raised his voice. "You can meet your . . . needs in other ways!"

"How's that?" I loved Angry Ian. He usually made no sense at all, and it was hilarious as hell to watch.

"There are . . ." He gulped and looked to me. "I'm not going to sit here and talk to you about sex toys."

"Oh, so you want me to use sex toys? Is that what this conversation is about?" Gabs crossed her arms.

"NO!" Ian roared. "Just—" His helpless gaze found mine. "No guys, no toys, no sex. Aren't you Catholic? There really aren't enough nuns in the world, Gabs."

"I'll become a nun the day Lex becomes a priest."

I stood and held out my hand to Ian. "Bless him, Father . . ."

"You're not funny," Ian said through clenched teeth.

"You're such a . . . dad!" Gabi blurted.

Ian sucked in a breath. "That's it! Go to your room!"

"But—"

"Go!"

Gabi stomped away from us and slammed the door to her room.

"Chin up, it's like practice for the future." I chuckled. "Want me to go talk to her?"

Ian's shoulders slumped. "You'd do that? I mean, you were already fighting before I came in."

"Eh, she's exhausted most of her energy trying to get me off of her and verbally sparring with you." I shrugged. "I'll wear a cup just in case."

"Thanks, I just . . ." Ian wiped his face with his hands. "I can't lose her."

"I know." *Me either, Ian. Me either.* "I'll, uh, just go over there."

Ian watched while I knocked on the door twice. Gabi opened it wide and let me step in. I turned around and nodded at Ian while he slowly made his way down the stairs.

The minute the door slammed behind me, I looked up at Gabi. "He's just scared."

"I know the feeling."

"Yeah, I think we all do," I whispered as we reached for each other and picked up right where we left off.

Chapter Thirty-Five

Gabi

I braced myself for what I knew was most likely going to go down as one of my least favorite experiences ever. Lex had tried to prep me the night before, but no amount of prepping could make a girl totally comfortable with helping her ass of an ex get a girl he thought the deserved. I honestly felt sorry for the girl he liked. Then again, maybe she was just as bad as he was? Lex said the program had judged them a good match, so who was I to argue with science?

My nails dug into the palms of my hands. I didn't just despise Mark, I loathed him. Every girl has one. The Game Changer. The one guy in your life who, when you look back on things, makes you want a total do-over. Mark was mine, because in my immaturity I'd allowed him to chip away at my confidence until I was consumed with making him happy.

My life had been Mark.

In a completely unhealthy way.

I was so worried about upsetting him I even stopped answering Ian's phone calls, which lasted all of a day before Ian came over to my house and unleashed hell. Mark earned a black eye—and later that day told me I probably wasn't even worth it.

Right. I wasn't worth getting hit over.

Desperate to keep him, I offered the one thing I'd always held close to me: my virginity, my innocence.

I could still remember his cruel smile.

And the fact that later that night—the night I had promised to go back to his parents' house while they were out—I mistakenly picked up his phone, thinking it was mine, and saw a naked pic of one of the cheerleaders on the squad.

The text that accompanied it read: "Last night was great. Repeat?"

Ugh.

So the fact that I was sitting with Mark—a guy who still, somehow, had a way of twisting me up inside just by me looking at him—yeah, let's just say Lex owed me big. Then again, who needed Mark when I had Lex? That thought alone gave me enough confidence to straighten my shoulders a bit and march into the restaurant.

Mark was sitting in the back corner of the dimly lit coffee shop, hunched over a book, his eyes squinting as if he was trying to figure out a complicated puzzle. Years ago that look used to do me in. I'd thought it was adorable, the way he scrunched up his nose while he was concentrating.

Then he'd gone and called me Sara. Another girl's name. The girl he was cheating on me with, and well, everything about him had just made me feel like strangling someone—him, mainly. I guess it was a stroke of luck that I'd found that picture and text a few minutes before to prove that he was cheating. At least I wasn't stupid enough to believe it was a Freudian slip.

I ordered a scone, then made my way over to his table. "This seat taken?"

"Yes." He didn't look up. "I was actually expecting someone."

"Hmm." I sat down anyway. Last night, after Lex had grudgingly left my room, I'd pored over Mark's folder. A lot of the stuff I knew, except what he'd been doing for the past four years. The gaps weren't hard to fill, and after two hours I knew exactly how I would help him get the girl.

Then again, the guys' handy playbook was really helpful in regards to the steps someone like him needed to go through in order to gain a girl's trust and affection.

"Hey, I said—" Mark's eyes met mine. "Gabi?"

"Mark." Was it wrong that saying his name out loud made me wince a little? What had I ever seen in him? His sandy blond hair was way too long, his blue eyes a little too light. Even his face was too round.

He was Lex's opposite.

Huh, imagine that.

"Gabi." The gap between his two front teeth appeared more pronounced. "I can't believe you're here. I mean, we should catch up sometime." He swallowed and nervously glanced around the coffee shop. "But really, I am meeting someone and—"

I slid the Wingmen card across the glass table, then took a large bite of my scone. "You were saying?"

"You?" he blurted. "You work with Wingmen? I highly doubt you're the brains." Sigh. And we were off to such a promising start.

"The brawn, actually," I corrected, half tempted to flex. "And my best friend owns the company. Now, why don't we talk about the object of your affection?"

Mark's ears burned bright red as he quickly averted his eyes and drummed his fingers against the table. "I, uh, wow." He coughed into his hand. "This is awkward."

You're telling me. But I offered a professional smile. "Only awkward if you make it awkward, and I'm here to help."

I didn't trust him. But that didn't mean I could walk away either. If he'd applied to Wingmen, Inc., and if the stats matched him, then I needed to follow through.

Besides, I needed the paycheck.

Especially after my dad's text that morning. I shook it off and tried a different approach. "Charlie's pretty."

Mark snorted. "She's gorgeous."

"Smart too."

He started playing with the straw in front of him, twisting the crap out of it before finally dropping it onto the table. "Look, Gabi, how exactly are you supposed to help me, when—" He pointed at me. I looked down. Did I have something on my shirt?

"When . . . ?" I prompted.

"Well, I'm not trying to be rude, but how's a seven supposed to get me a ten?"

I almost gasped out loud. The rat bastard! Was he insulting me? To my face? I gripped the bottom of my chair to keep myself from grabbing his straw and stabbing his throat with it a few hundred times.

Four years ago that comment would have wrecked me.

Maybe even a few weeks ago.

But . . . funny thing. Even though being with Lex was leaving me torn up inside—mainly because of the lying—I knew from the way Lex looked at me I wasn't a freaking seven.

I was an eleven.

Hah! Seven-eleven.

"Why are you laughing?" Mark asked. "I wasn't kidding."

I pitied the woman who ended up with him. Then again, he'd always been very literal, dry, smart—almost too smart—and, if I was completely honest, one of the most narcissistic individuals I'd ever met.

"Look." I eyed the door just as Charlie made her way in, her eyes zeroing in on our table and then flickering away. Ten? If she was a ten, I'd hate to see what constituted a one.

Love is blind, folks. Love is blind.

And suddenly, I wasn't insulted, not one bit.

Charlie was adorable, beautiful even. Something clicked into place, because it didn't matter if I thought she was a one, zero, six, five . . . Who cared? What mattered was that to Mark she was a ten, the best of the best, and he wanted her.

"You like her, right?" I asked as I stood to my feet.

"'Like' is such a weak word for what I feel in here." He slapped his chest, his eyes widening as if trying to show me how big his love was. "I would die for her. She's just . . . She doesn't even know."

"Oh, I bet she knows." I held out my hand. "Now, do exactly as I say."

The playbook specifically said that jealousy mixed with confusion was the easiest way to get the opposite sex to notice you, because it forces them to look at you through a different lens. If I found him amazing, even if the thought had never occurred to her to do so, she'd do a double take, confused about what she was seeing. And she'd peel back layers of his personality, curious as to what else she'd been missing out on.

Layers!

Ah-hah! Lex had said something about layers, and Ian had immediately referred to *Shrek*, but I had tuned them out shortly after that.

"I'm going to lean in, alright? Don't stiffen up."

I did just that, leaning over his shoulder while my eyes locked on Charlie. She didn't look away, but her face fell just enough for me to know that my actions were working.

"Hmm . . ." I wrapped my arms around him, hating that I was basically acting like my ex-boyfriend's wingman. He returned the hug, then stood to embrace me.

Charlie slowly made her way over to us. "Hey, Mark."

"Oh hey, Charlie." Mark turned bright red. "I didn't see you."

Her lips pressed together in a firm line. "Who's your friend?"

"I'm an ex." I held out my hand. My response was perfect; she'd wonder about our history. "We dated for two years."

Mark swallowed hard as he glanced between the two of us.

"I'm surprised he never mentioned me." I laughed. "You know, since there was talk of marriage."

"M-marriage?" she repeated, crossing her arms over her chest. "Wow, you guys must have been serious."

Channeling *Legally Blonde* more than the Wingmen Inc. playbook, I shrugged and let out a long sigh. "Yeah, best two years of my life. I mean . . . maybe this is inappropriate, but I compare every guy's kisses to Mark's, every man's touch." Another sigh. "Well . . ." I tried to appear dejected. "Are you, um . . . his girlfriend?"

"No." Mark's lips turned up into a smile. "She's not."

"But"—Charlie's forced smile wavered a little—"we're really close."

"Hmm, what did you say your name was, again?"

"Charlie," she mumbled.

"Sorry, Charlie." I smirked. "So, Mark, we should catch up, tomorrow night maybe? There's this sushi place near campus that's amazing!" Mark hated sushi, so in a way that was my payback. "Maybe we can ride bikes after?" Mark also hated exercise and anything that messed up his emo hair. "Since you're allergic to chocolate, we can't do that kind of dessert, but I have something else in mind." I bit my lip.

Charlie looked ready to punch me in the face, while Mark rocked back on his heels in silence as if contemplating my idea.

"Here." I shoved the Wingmen card into his hand. "If you wanna take me up on my offer, just send me a text or e-mail. Cool?"

"Yes," he blurted. "I mean, I want to. I just have to make sure I'm not doing anything tomorrow night."

"Great." I really had to force myself to look happy at the prospect of sacrificing one of my free nights so that Mark could get the girl of his dreams, the girl he'd already told me was way prettier than I was. *Thanks for that, Mark.* "I'll see you guys later."

I excused myself before he could have any second thoughts and smiled brightly down at my phone when it buzzed two minutes later with Mark's number and the enthusiastic text:

`You're hired.`

"Looking at porn? Dirty girl." Lex fell into step beside me.

I recoiled sideways and stopped short when I found myself heading, nose-first, for a fat tree. "Lex!" I gasped, as my heart struggled to pound free of my chest. "You can't just . . . lurk!"

"Gabs, I'm over six-three. I can't help but lurk."

I was still having a hard time catching my breath when he reached for my hand. "So, how did the meeting with Dickface go?"

"Lex, tell me you weren't spying through the window."

"Fine." He was so beautiful. I loved the way his smile spread to his eyes, and I hated that we had wasted so much time fighting that I was only now noticing the way his face lit up. "I wasn't spying through the window."

I breathed out a sigh of relief.

"I was spying through the back kitchen."

"Lex!" I released his hand. "Come on! I'm a big girl. Gotta cut those apron strings."

He stopped walking and braced me by the shoulders. "If I cut the apron strings, can I substitute them with rope? I could do a lot with rope."

"You aren't tying me up either."

His face fell.

"Be serious." I slugged him in the chest. "And I'm happy to announce that I didn't kill my second male client, though he did call me a seven."

Lex crossed his arms. "A seven? So you were reciting numbers in order to turn him on? Weird kid, but okay, whatever works."

"No." I looped my hand through his arm as we kept walking. "He said, and I quote, 'How is a seven supposed to help me get a ten?'"

Lex jerked to a stop and I stumbled forward, nearly tumbling head over heels onto the itchy grass.

"Come again?" he whispered hoarsely.

"Lex," I groaned. "It's fine. He's always been an ass like that. I was offended for maybe a minute."

"I'm offended for you," Lex snarled, throwing his hands into the air as if he was ready to charge one of the nearby trees and break it down with sheer body weight and will. "What the hell kind of person says that? Does he even realize how gorgeous you are? What a little prick!" The more he talked, the angrier he appeared, and then he turned on his heel and started marching back toward the coffee shop.

"Lex!" I yelled. "Client! He's a client!"

"Son of a bitch is gonna need someone to chew his food for him in five minutes." Lex's fists clenched at his sides as he took purposeful strides back toward the building.

"No!" I jumped onto his back. "Lex, be reasonable!"

"This is me being reasonable," he said in a deathly calm voice. "I'll ask him if it's true, he'll say yes. I'll give him maybe sixty seconds to defend himself, and then I'm going to kick his ass clear into next year and wave as his head detaches from his body."

I was still banging on his muscular back when the door to the coffee shop opened and Ian stepped out.

With a sigh, he looked at me, then Lex. "We're in public, guys, show a little decorum."

"He, uh"—I slid slowly down Lex's back—"was being mean."

I rolled my eyes and covered my face. Really? That's all I had? He was being mean and pushed me off the swing? Good, Gabs, real good.

"Dipshit in there"—Lex jabbed his finger at the door to the coffeehouse—"called her a freaking seven."

Ian's eyebrows drew together as though he was trying to process what Lex had said. "And you're pissed because the only one who can insult Gabi is you?"

"He's a total asshole!" Lex yelled as the door opened and a customer scurried by.

Ian burst out laughing. "Yeah, okay. Look in the window, Lex. What do you see?"

"Huh?"

"It's your reflection . . . and yet another asshole. Sorry to break it to you, but you're kind of a dick."

"But—"

"Gabs." Ian held up his hand for a high-five. "I was in the area when we got an e-mail from Mark—seems he's super impressed with how things went down, so good job. Now . . ." He slipped on his sunglasses. "You guys want pizza?"

"Sure!" I forced a giant smile because I didn't know what else to do, but Lex didn't move. It was like someone had put glue on the bottom of his shoes and told him to stay while it set. "Lex?"

"Ian"—Lex's nostrils flared—"we'll meet you there. I need to talk to Gabs real quick."

Ian looked between us. "You do realize she was just beating you, right? With her bare hands?"

"I can handle Short Stack." Lex clenched his fists.

"Alright," Ian said, grabbing his keys. "I'll grab pizza and meet you guys at the house, cool?"

"Yup," we said in unison.

As soon as Ian drove off, Lex reached for my hand and jerked me toward his car. Once we were inside, he didn't say anything, but I could tell he was still pissed by the way his jaw kept clicking. Any minute, I truly expected him to start spitting out teeth.

We drove for two miles in silence.

He stopped down the road from the house at one of the neighborhood parks.

And turned off the car.

"Lex." I reached for him.

"Don't," he hissed. "Just—give me a minute."

My anxiety tripled because I had no idea why he was still so pissed, but I was a bit terrified that it was my fault.

Chapter Thirty-Six
Lex

I will not punch my best friend, I will not punch my best friend. I'd been serious as hell, repeating that same mantra over and over again in my head as my fists clenched at my sides while Ian continued insulting not only me, but the entire freaking situation!

If a dude calls your best friend a seven, you sure as hell do something about it, right?

He'd brushed it off.

The way Ian brushes off everything that has to do with Gabi and me. I was sick of it, sick of having to pretend in front of him.

"You"—I found my voice, unbuckled my seat belt, and turned to face Gabi—"are absolutely gorgeous."

A red blush stained her cheeks. "Lex, it's fine. I mean—"

I held up my hand. "Let me finish."

She swallowed, her eyes darting to the center console while she wrung her hands together.

"You have the most amazing smile I've ever seen. It's like staring at the sun . . ." I sighed. "I get lost in your eyes every time they lock onto me, and I'm ashamed to admit that some of the reason I've pushed you away lies in the fact that those very trusting eyes saw too much. Damn, they still see too much, but I'm done." Another sigh slipped out. "Gabs, I'm so done with this, whatever it is."

Gabi looked horrified, as if I'd just run over her pet. Her eyes got so huge it was hard to concentrate. Damn, she was gorgeous.

Her breaths came fast and harsh as she searched my eyes. With a mumble she said, "Okay then."

I cursed and ran my hands over my buzzed head. "I like you. A lot. And if Ian can't handle that, then screw him! I'm . . . just . . ." I shrugged. "I'm making a total ass out of myself right now . . . But I refuse to let another minute go by with you believing you're a seven, or even a ten, when you're a twelve, hell, a fifteen. When every time you look at me, it's like seeing the sunrise over the mountains, its rays lighting up everything around it so even if someone wants to stay in the darkness, they won't, not for long, not when you're around."

I'd stopped looking at her—probably wouldn't have had the balls to say any of it if I did look—so I stared at my steering wheel. Something wet dropped onto my hand. I glanced up and found she was crying.

"That's why you call me Sunshine?"

I smirked. "Even when I insult you it's a compliment, Gabs."

She punched me in the shoulder.

"I deserved that."

"You really mean . . . all those things?"

"Yeah." My voice cracked. "I really do."

"You know I hate you, right?" She reached for me, grasping the front of my T-shirt and tugging my body as close as possible.

"Oh, I know." I nodded smugly. "I hate you too."

"Good."

"Great."

Her lips twitched. "Okay."

"Okay." My mouth met hers in a searing kiss.

Gabi's hands pressed against my chest, then spread around my shoulders and hooked behind my neck. "You taste good."

"Like sunshine?" I joked.

"Yeah." She laughed against my mouth. "Like sunshine."

I couldn't pull her into my lap, even though that was all I wanted, and the idea of hopping into the backseat had merit, except it was Gabi, and she was more than a quick screw in the back of a car.

Our tongues tangled together as our mouths synced with kiss after dizzying kiss.

"Ian's going to think you killed me," Gabi breathed, mouth swollen. She broke away and then rested her chin on my shoulder, running her hands up and down my neck.

Shivering, I returned her hug and closed my eyes, breathing in the scent of vanilla and wildflowers. "Yeah, probably."

"Pizza?"

"Can't I just eat you?"

"Why do you have to ruin every moment?" She laughed against me.

"According to Ian I'm an asshole, so . . . from here on out, let's just assume the worst, shall we?"

"You're not . . ." Gabi chuckled, then made a face. "Only sometimes . . . like a few hours out of the day."

"Good to know you have such a high opinion of me."

She winked. "Always." After buckling her seat belt, she spread her arms wide and smiled. "Okay, let's get home before he calls the cops."

I snorted and started the car. "Wouldn't be the first time."

"Won't be the last."

"Nope."

She reached for my hand. "Lex?"

"Yeah?" The last thing I wanted was to share her with Ian. "What's up?"

"We'll tell him together . . . But let's wait until after my family dinner this weekend, alright? He's going to take it hard, and I don't know, I just think we should wait. I'll tell Blake first. That way, when he does find out, she can talk him through it."

"Whatever you want, Gabs, you know I'd agree to anything."

"Anything?"

"Gabs," I warned.

"My car's been acting up. You should probably go see what's wrong with it . . . shirtless . . ." She nodded. "Maybe rub a bit of oil on your face . . . No." She clapped her hands, scaring the shit out of me. "Oil on your abs . . . Oooo, can I put it on?"

"How did we go from telling Ian about us to me suddenly playing auto-shop porno in the front yard?"

"You did say 'anything.' It's your own fault."

I kissed her hand, then regretfully let it go as we pulled up to the house.

As expected, Ian was standing out on the front step, his eyes worried.

"He'll make a great mom someday," Gabi joked as she slowly unbuckled her seat belt and got out of the car.

Shit.

I wouldn't go so far as to say that Ian knew, but the minute he pulled Gabi in for a hug, he locked eyes with me.

It was a warning.

I'd seen that look on his face before.

And I sure as hell didn't want to see it again, but this time? I wasn't backing down; I couldn't.

I just hoped our friendship could survive what was about to go down.

Not for my sake.

For hers.

Sleep wasn't happening, not with Gabi right across the hall from me. Hell, it was like living at my parents' house all over again, only this time Ian was the parent, and I knew he wouldn't just be disappointed if he found me in bed with her.

No, he'd save the disappointment until after he pushed me out the window and chased me down the street with his car.

I let out a sigh and stared up at the ceiling.

Gabi had her date with Mark tomorrow evening, and that pissed me off. The entire situation made me want to physically maim him.

I'd even gone so far as to do a background check on the guy, and not the legal kind either.

He was fine. She was safe with him, but the bastard did have some weird fetishes.

And in my book a weird fetish for old libraries basically meant he was one bad choice away from snapping and needing to be institutionalized.

I really hoped Gabi did a good job so she could be done with him and move the hell on.

Was this how every client was going to be?

My fingers itched to do damage to the prick's credit score, just like they itched to check Gabi's bank accounts and discover where all her money was going.

And food.

She'd eaten her pizza like a ravenous cougar, devouring three pieces before coming up for air and locking eyes with me.

When I asked her when she last ate, she shrugged me off and started asking Ian about Blake's next game.

A light tapping at my door startled me, before it opened. Gabi shut it quietly, locked it, then tiptoed over to my bed. "Room for one more?"

I pulled back the duvet. "Thank God you can read minds."

"You're not the only superhero in this house."

"Super villain," I corrected.

"Nah." Gabs sighed against my chest, her soft breath warming my skin. "This afternoon . . . when you said I was a twelve . . ." She yawned. "And told me why you called me Sunshine . . ." Her nails danced along my chest. "Hero."

"I did save a frog once."

"We should probably notify the chamber of commerce, just in case they want to throw a parade or something."

"It was a long time ago."

"Heroes never die."

"Truth or Dare?"

"Games in bed? And no rope? Losing your touch, Mr. Luthor . . . and I choose truth."

"How many times have you thought about me in the shower?"

She pinched my nipple. I let out a little yelp. "Twice today while rubbing myself down with my loofah."

"Say rubbing yourself down, again."

"Nope."

"Damn it! Another opportunity lost!"

"Truth or Dare?"

"Dare."

"He wants a dare, hmm?" Gabi leaned up on her elbows. "I dare you to . . . knock on Ian's door naked and ask him if he has towels."

"That's a daily occurrence. I'm always out of towels, always naked. Next?"

Gabi's eyes narrowed. "Let me wrap you in a blanket for five minutes, arms pinned."

I shivered. "Hell no."

"Aw, you said dare. This is it, no take backs!"

"Oh look, you won the game, we should probably sleep or have sex. I'm down for either."

"Loser."

"The last person who called me a loser was Ian. We were in fifth grade. I rest my case."

Gabi made the *L* sign with her fingers against her forehead and burst out laughing.

"Are you serious right now?"

"Lex . . ." She moved to straddle me, and my entire body jumped to attention. "Please?"

"Stop that," I hissed as she rocked against me. "Play fair!"

Gabi leaned over, her hair kissing my chest as her hips ground into me. "Is it still no?"

"Hmm . . ." I laced my fingers behind my head. "Take off your shorts and move a little to the left, then the right, up and down a bit, and we'll see."

"You really need to burn all those manuals."

"Hey! Some people need direction!"

"Do I?"

"Hell no!" I gripped her ass with my hands. "Honestly, even if you accidently fell onto my dick, it would still be the best sex of my life."

"I'm trying to find romance in that."

"You won't." I nodded. "So I'd stop trying."

She moved her hips again while I hissed out a curse.

"Still no?"

"Fine," I grumbled. "I'll let you pin me underneath the blanket for *three* minutes, and then my dare is over, deal?"

She nodded.

"And then I get sex as a reward, lots of sex, and you can't complain when I ask you to channel your inner gymnast."

"Seriously, you're so romantic I can hardly keep my clothes on," she said in a dry voice.

I slapped her on the ass and closed my eyes. "Okay, I'm ready, but for the record you're doing this against my will. I have a totally legitimate fear of being trapped beneath things. It's called claustrophobia, not to be confused with medorthophobia, which I clearly don't have." I wouldn't have had claustrophobia either, except that Ian had contributed to my irrational fear by trapping me in sleeping bags during our childhood camping trips.

"The fear of erect penises?" She wrapped the blanket around the front of my body, then sat on me while my arms stayed pinned to my sides. "How would I confuse the two?"

I squinted at her face. "How do you even know that?"

Gabi squirmed, and then her cheeks stained red. "We were talking about phobias in my psych class, and well, let's just say that a certain ex-boyfriend said he had a friend who suffered from it."

"Bullshit!" I burst out laughing. "Please tell me Mark's afraid of his own junk. It would make my life."

"We never had sex, so I wouldn't know." Gabi leaned across me, using her body weight to pin me down. "Maybe he's just afraid of the sudden . . ." Her cheeks reddened more.

"Oh no you don't." I squirmed beneath her. "The sudden what?"

"Er, the sudden . . . ness." She nodded. "You know, like, oh look, everything's totally fine in the world, and then *boom*. Erection."

I fought like hell to keep my laugh in. "Yeah, that's not how that works."

"It isn't?"

"Maybe if you're on a shitload of Viagra. It's more of a slow . . . rise, you know, like when you do the Pledge of Allegiance and the flag—"

Gabi covered my mouth with her hand. "If you keep talking, I'm never going to be able to say the Pledge of Allegiance without thinking about man parts." She pulled her hand away.

"My theory is this." I tried to focus on her instead of the terror of being trapped. "Good ol' Mark was giving a presentation in front of the class when his very hot, very single teacher looked at him . . . and that's all it took—or to put it in your words, *boom*, erection. Traumatized for life as kids pointed and laughed."

"Huh." Gabi nodded. "Good theory."

"I am a genius, so . . ."

"A genius who used to cry when Ian trapped you in sleeping bags."

"Bastard used to zip them all the way up, Gabs!"

"Okay." She pulled away from me. "All done, see? Aren't you glad you didn't punk out?"

"Yes. Thank you." I rolled my eyes as my hands were freed. "Pay up, woman."

She scurried off the bed, laughing. I chased after her and pulled her against my body. "We can do this the easy way or the hard way."

"I like hard."

"Well, lucky for you"—I kissed the side of her neck—"I'm already there."

She turned in my arms and whispered, "Truth."

It was on the tip of my tongue to ask her about the food, the money, everything, but . . . Part of me felt guilty, and I didn't want to kill the moment, so I gripped her by the ass and lifted her in the air. "How good does it feel when I do this?"

I jerked her shorts off of her body and kissed her.

"So"—she slammed her mouth against mine for a brief kiss—"good."

"Truth or Dare?" She pulled back, a coy smile on her lips.

"Truth."

"How many girls have been in your bedroom?"

"One," I whispered. "The only one."

"Good answer."

"Heroic?"

"Don't push it." She giggled as we fell against the bed, tangled in one another.

Chapter Thirty-Seven

Gabi

Asshole Lex: Truth or Dare?

Gabi: Truth.

Asshole Lex: Are you wearing any underwear?

Gabi: Aw, are these your "ass" office hours? I'll be sure to text you once they're over.

Asshole Lex: Seven to ten every night, expect no gentleman . . . only full asshole man, hell bent on offending your delicate feminine sensibilities as much as he can.

Gabi: Noted. Now stop texting me during my date.

Asshole Lex: Truth or Dare.

Gabi: Seriously?

Asshole Lex: Just one more . . .

Gabi: Dare.

Asshole Lex: Good to know we communicate telepathically now. I was chanting dare in my head . . . Slip the word erection into your dinner talk and see what Mark does. Also, record it. Give the audience what it wants, that's what I always say.

Gabi: No!

Asshole Lex: I trapped myself in a blanket for you last night. Say erection and you'll be the hero.

Gabi: I hate you.

Asshole Lex: I await the video. Don't let the good people of earth down, Gabi. Think of the children.

Gabi: Too far.

```
Asshole Lex: Sorry, I was on a roll and just
went with it.
```

I burst out laughing.

Mark frowned. "Everything okay with your mom?" I may have lied and told him my mom was sick and texting me.

I cleared my throat and shoved my phone back into my purse. "Just great. How's the sushi?"

He stared down at his plate, where the salmon rolls festered. "It's . . . cold."

"Sushi is cold," I pointed out as I stabbed a tuna roll and watched Mark's nose scrunch up. "So, I'm assuming Charlie didn't want you going out with me tonight?"

He put down his fork and leaned back in his chair, and his black T-shirt hung on his toned body. I could appreciate that he had an okay form, but he was nothing compared to Lex, not even close.

"She was pissed."

"Good." I nodded. "So, now that you're an official client, let's just go over the next few days. I'll make sure she sees us together a few strategic times, and she's most likely going to start texting you more, showing up randomly, calling. Be busy during those times. Don't necessarily brush her off, just say you have a lot going on, alright? When she pressures you to hang out, tell her you can do it next week, you're busy now, but next week you're free. You have no social life this week, got it?"

Mark sighed. "Look, I know you guys have a crazy success rate, it's just . . . I don't see how this is going to work. She has to be legitimately jealous of you."

My stomach clenched as I tried to keep my face a mask of professionalism. "It worked the other day."

"True," he finally admitted.

"I'm the best." Okay so that was a lie, but still, I needed him to trust me. "You have nothing to lose. I promise that by the end of the week you'll have her ready to lose her mind over you."

His posture stiffened, and as he glanced up a small smile teased his lips. "You think so?"

"I know so," I said confidently. "Now, as for the um . . . physical part of Wingmen Inc., a situation may pop up." I was going to kill Lex, because that entire sentence just reminded me of our conversation: erection, *boom*! Noooo! I coughed into my hand. "A situation may arise." Nope, that made it worse. "A situation may magically appear." There, better. "Where I need to touch you." And back to bad. "Or kiss you." The thought made me want to puke. "You can't shy away if that happens, alright?"

He shrugged.

"Mark?"

"Fine."

"Great." I exhaled a sigh of relief. He really was an ass. Worse than Lex had ever been. You couldn't even compare the two! "So, any weird . . . issues I need to know about? In reference to a sexual relationship?"

He froze in his seat.

And then Mark started shaking as he grabbed his fork and attacked his sushi like he hadn't eaten in months.

"Anything at all?" I prodded.

"Nope," he said, mouth full of fish.

"Oh good! You have no idea how many weird things we come across. You know, people who don't know how to kiss, aversions to feet . . ." I cleared my throat. "The fear of arousal or . . . erections."

Mark choked on a piece of fish and reached for his water as soy sauce exploded all over his plate.

"But good to know that you don't deal with any of those things, hmm, Mark?"

His eyes narrowed. "I didn't write anything on my sheet."

"Wingmen Inc. . . ." I offered a fake smile. "Even if you don't write it down, our job is to know."

He looked away.

"Is your *little*"—my lip twitched as I emphasized 'little'—"problem going to be a . . . problem?"

"No," he said a little too quickly. "It's not. I swear it's not even what you think."

"I don't think about your penis, so you're right, it's not."

"Can we just drop it?" he pleaded, a desperate edge in his voice that I'd never heard before. Then again, I'd never known the word "erection" to be a buzzword, but you learn something new every day!

"Fine." I wiped my hands on my napkin. "So, tomorrow I'll stop by your first class so she sees us, and we'll go from there depending on her reaction, okay?"

He hesitated, cheeks full of sushi. "Fine." His mouth was full, and I had a sudden vision of him kissing Charlie and nearly puked. Revulsion crept over his face as he fought back a gag, then swallowed. "But if this doesn't work, I get my money back, right? That's how it works?"

I sighed loudly and stood. "Look, Mark, you either need our help or you don't. You signed a contract that locks you in for at least seven days. At the end of the seven days, if you aren't happy, you'll get your deposit back, but that's it."

He snorted.

What did I ever see in him?

"So?" I crossed my arms.

"Fine." He wiped his mouth with his napkin and stood. "I'll meet you tomorrow morning."

The minute he stood, my eyes widened, unable to look away from the front of his pants.

"Er, you have a"—I gulped—"situation."

"It's called priapism," he grumbled, slinking back down into his seat. "It's not you." His words were like venom.

"So . . ." I held back my smirk, just barely. "Is this another reason you need our . . . help?" Oh my gosh, it was still there! Lurking! Under the table! I couldn't look away. Face, he had a face. I jerked my head up so I was making eye contact.

"It's a simple blood-flow problem."

"I'll say," I whispered.

"Happens when I'm upset or nervous," he grumbled. "Or turned-on. I just . . . It takes effort to control, alright? Especially around Charlie."

"Hey!" I held up my hands. "Maybe she'll like it? You know, screw the guessing game and all that."

Mark gave me a defeated stare.

"Or," I said, trying again, "we'll just make sure that your first date together is at a restraint—er, restaurant—with really long tablecloths? Dark setting? I'm thinking no light whatsoever?"

He exhaled loudly. "Gabi? No offense, but the last thing I want to be talking to you about is my inability to control . . . things." He cursed. "Especially with someone like you."

"Someone like me?"

"Yes." He gritted his teeth. "Just. Like. You." A heated look crossed his face. "A cock tease. What is it? Do you only open your legs for athletes? God knows you never did it for me."

Without thinking, I grabbed my water glass off the table and threw the contents in his face.

"What the hell!" he bellowed, jumping to his feet.

"You know what?" I grabbed his water and repeated the motion. "As of two seconds ago, your contract is officially dissolved. We don't need you as a client, not now, not ever!"

"Like hell!" he roared. "I paid good money! I'll sue!"

"Just try it!" I yelled right back and stomped out of the restaurant, tears streaming down my face.

I was too angry.

Too hurt.

Too anything to even react beyond the tears.

It wasn't that I liked him. It was that his comments had hit home. They were the exact comments I'd gotten all through high school from jealous girls who had always assumed Ian and I were more than just friends. When I wouldn't sleep with Mark, he pulled away and later cheated on me, then blamed me for the cheating, claiming that I was probably already sleeping with Ian anyway.

What was even worse: the one weak moment I had, where I just wanted to get sex over with, it was Lex. *Lex* who'd appeared in my time of need.

Only to make what had been a surface cut a full-blown wound as he, too, passed me by and found another willing girl.

Every insecurity I'd had came back to the surface full force as I made my way to my car and turned the key. Logically, I knew I was a different person now. I knew it, but words still had the power to hurt, and his words just reminded me how stupid I'd been and how easily I'd fallen for a guy's words instead of his actions. Which was crazy, since I'd fallen for Lex's actions more than his words. His words had always been cruel, but his actions?

When I was sick, he took care of me.

When I needed him, he was there.

He'd always been there—maybe not emotionally, but physically, he'd been there every single time I needed him—and I was lying to him.

I turned the key again.

Nothing happened.

"Come on!" I tried again. Nothing. Not now! "Come on, baby, you can do it."

But it couldn't.

My car was dead.

No lights.

Nothing.

How was my car worse off after coming back from the shop?

I was just about to call Lex when someone banged on my door.

With a curse, I looked out the window and saw Lex, hands in pockets, staring at me.

And the minor tears trickling down my cheeks suddenly turned into a deluge as full-fledged sobs began.

CHAPTER THIRTY-EIGHT
LEX

It's not stalking if you just happen to be strolling by the same restaurant, walking your imaginary dog, or, you know, trying out a new bar in the exact neighborhood the maybe girlfriend is in.

Right?

"Idiot." I'd never been *that* guy. Hell, I'd always openly mocked *that* guy. Clearly, Gabi was tying me in knots. I wasn't even spying to see if she was doing a good job.

Somehow trying to get her *not* to work for Wingmen Inc. had turned into me wanting her to be such a blinding success that even Ian would be impressed with her skills.

I'd given her all the coaching I could.

And now she was sitting with Dickface while he leaned in way too close and pressed his fingers against the table, nearly grazing hers.

If I had a knife, I would throw it.

At his shit-eating face.

Instead, I was stuck watching *them* together.

The only bonus was making her laugh with my texts and then being able to see that he did, in fact, have a slightly small problem with getting his body to pay attention to his mental signals.

"Down, boy." I chuckled, then about died when he stood and saluted the entire freaking restaurant. That shit should have been on TV.

Gabi looked like she was trying not to laugh, and then it looked like they started fighting after he sat down. Whatever he said, it pissed her off enough for her to throw water in his face.

Twice.

She stormed out of the restaurant without looking to her left or right and made a straight shot to her car.

Which didn't start.

If I could buy her a car and not have her get pissed off at me, I would, but where would I even find a basket big enough to stuff a car in? And what would I do, put it right next to the Pirate's Booty like, oh, just saw this at Costco, thought you might need it?

Not only would Ian have me by the balls, I figured she had too much pride to take a gift that big.

And guys didn't just buy their girlfriends cars.

Right?

Holy shit. She was my girlfriend. Girl. Friend. When did that happen? And why wasn't I freaking out? Instead, my reaction was the exact opposite. I was elated, ready to sprout little Red Bull wings and take flight. Well, shit.

The car refused to start. With a smirk, I jogged over to her and knocked on her window, only then noticing that she had tears streaming down her cheeks.

"Gabs?"

The window was rolled down. I unlocked the passenger-side door and let myself in, only to have her start sobbing as she launched herself from her seat into my arms.

"Aw, Sunshine," I clung to her as tight as I could while the scent of her strawberry body wash floated into the air. "He must have one scary dick."

This only made her cry harder.

"Too soon?" I mumbled against her hair while the heat of her body started making me sweat. "Sunshine, look at me."

Finally, she pulled away, her eyes swollen. "I just . . . He's a complete jackass."

"I know those types well," I said softly while wiping the still-flowing tears from her soft cheeks. "I'm pretty sure I used to be their president."

"Used to be?" she teased, hiccupping out another sob.

"Yeah, well, the rule of jackasses goes like this." I tucked her against my chest, pulling her feet across the console so that she was fully in my lap. "You have to be an ass at least three times a day. I won't bore you with more numbers, but there's graphs and a very technologically advanced computer system that ranks us against one another. Looks like Mark just weaseled his way to the top, hmm?"

"Yes," she hissed. "He just . . . caught me at a low point without my armor on, you know? Like if you're prepared for the jab, you block it, but he caught my chin and then got in a few good left hooks."

"Did you—?" I pulled back and stared at her. "Did you just use a boxing reference to explain life?"

Gabi frowned. "Weird, but yeah, I think I did."

"Kinda hot." I brushed the hair out of her face. "And just what type of jabs and hooks are we talking about? The typical insult to a girl's self-esteem, or low blows?"

"Low blows," she huffed. "Ones I wasn't ready for, ones about me not putting out in high school and how I probably spread my legs for everyone now, but you know, especially athletes. He was always jealous of my relationship with Ian, but he was just so mean about it." She sagged against me, her hands curling around my neck as they started making lazy circles against my chest. "I threw water in his face and then basically told him we didn't need his business." She sighed louder. "He threatened to sue."

I choked out a laugh. "I'd like to see him try. We had a very expensive lawyer draw up our paperwork. He's an idiot if he thinks he can sue us."

"That's what I said, but what if he exposes your and Ian's identities? Or worse, exposes me? What we do? The whole reason Wingmen Inc. works is because it's a secret."

"While you do have a point," I said slowly, careful to choose my words so they wouldn't scare her, "what's the worst that could happen? We still have the app, and we'd just stop offering Wingmen services."

"But!" Gabi pulled away. "You and Ian *love* being wingmen!"

"Ian's busy making babies with Blake," I pointed out while she made a face. "And if you haven't noticed, I don't necessarily appreciate kissing other girls anymore."

"No?" Her lips quirked into a tiny smile. "Why's that?"

I offered a casual shrug. "I'm gay."

"Lex!"

Chuckling, I hugged her tighter. "There's this really hot girl who dressed up like a sexy elf one day . . . She kind of had me at hello."

"Did I say hello?"

"You really think I remember that shit? I saw boobs, which is not exactly the most romantic story if you look at it my way, Gabs. I wanted to have sex with you, not share secrets and paint each other's toenails."

"Aw, too bad. I would *love* to paint your toenails. It's my sexual fantasy."

"Oooo . . ." I licked the side of her face, causing her to burst out laughing and squirm in my lap. "Tell me more."

"Lex!" She shoved my chest. "You suck."

"Don't you forget it." I kissed the top of her head. "Also, your car's a piece of shit. You're driving mine from now on, and I'm taking my bike."

"You ride a bike?"

"When I say bike, I mean my Ducati."

"Oh." She blushed. "I didn't know you had one."

"It sits in the garage a lot because let's just say I've seen way too many motorcycle accidents. Besides, what villain drives a motorcycle?"

She squinted. "The Riddler?"

"Nope."

"I'm thinking."

"Let me know when you have the answer." I sighed. "Until then, grab your shit. I'll take you home and draw you a bath."

"Really?" She perked up.

"Sorry, I can't lie to you with that face." I opened the door and helped her out. "I have no intention of letting you in a bath until I've been inside you and erased every last Mark memory you've ever had."

Her cheeks reddened.

I glanced up just as Mark made his way out of the restaurant.

"But first." I moved away from Gabi and stomped toward Mark. I had at least four inches on the guy and could probably kick his ass drunk. "Hey, Mark."

He glanced up, his eyes narrowed. "Do I know you?"

I smirked. "Well, you're about to."

"What the—"

I punched his face so hard that my knuckles hurt. He went down in one giant heap, while blood trickled down his nose.

With a sigh I leaned over him. "You disrespect my girl ever again and I'm going to make sure you have to pee through a bag for the rest of your life. Mm'kay, pumpkin?"

Mark's eyes watered, but he said nothing.

"Come on, Gabi, he's not worth your time. Oh and Mark? Erection!" I screamed it as loud as I could and reached for Gabi. "Now, hopefully every time he has an erection, his face will remember the sting from being punched. One can only hope this experience is traumatic enough to condition his psyche."

I pulled Gabi into my arms and kissed her head. She smiled up at me and whispered, "Hero."

"Twice in one week. Does that mean I get extra hours of sex? Should we start a chart? Just in case? You know, so we don't lose track."

She punched me in the stomach.

Funny how some things changed, yet others stayed exactly the same.

Thank God for that.

Chapter Thirty-Nine
Gabi

Lex claimed his hand didn't hurt, but bruises don't lie. When Ian asked, Lex told him in graphic detail about Mark and also informed Ian that he was going to rewrite the entire program that involved male clients. He didn't want to take a chance that some guy like Mark could use Wingmen services and try to get a girl he didn't deserve.

He worked on it all week. I barely saw him.

Unless I was bringing him food, which he ate without even looking at.

Finally it was the weekend, and he was taking time off from writing code so that we could all go to my family's dinner in Bellevue.

Ian drove, which left me in the front seat and Lex in the back. It would have been fine except that I kept catching him staring at me through the rearview mirror.

Luckily, Ian was in a bad mood because Blake had an away game, so it seemed the only things he was able to focus on were listening to the game on the radio and how many days until she was home so they could be together.

He'd gone from being a player for life to some guy I didn't even recognize. That morning he'd asked me about wedding rings, causing Lex to choke on his cornflakes and almost need the Heimlich.

"So," Ian said as he took the turn down my parents' street. "How's the new program coming along, Lex?"

"Good."

I turned around so I could face Lex. He looked exhausted. I hated how much I missed being in his bed, but he needed to concentrate, and my absence was good—good because Ian kept checking on him throughout the night.

"I've hit a few snags, but it will be fine." Lex's voice was deep and gravelly like it always was when he got tired, but man, even exhausted he was still beautiful. "Give me two more days, tops."

"Good." Ian let out a breath. "Gabs?"

"Hmm?" I jerked my body back toward the front seat but stayed half turned so I could see Lex in the corner of my vision.

"You'll be happy to know that Mark hasn't tried anything."

I snorted out a laugh. "Probably helps that Lex almost killed him."

Ian grabbed my hand. "Had I been there, I would have done worse."

Did Lex just growl from the backseat? I stole a glance in his direction. His fists were clenched at his sides, a slow tick starting in his jaw.

"Um, well." I pulled my hand away from Ian. "Lex handled it. You know how super villains are . . ." It was my try at killing some of the tension in the car. It didn't work. If anything, it made things worse as Ian clenched the steering wheel harder and Lex suddenly found great interest in the passing trees. Had something happened between them? Suddenly nervous that Lex had gone back on his promise and mentioned something to Ian, my stomach heaved. "So," I tried again. "My parents will be so happy to have everyone."

"Can't wait for real food. There better be tamales or I'm walking," Lex said in a strained voice.

"Her mother only makes tamales for the holidays," Ian corrected. "Trust me, I tried to get her to make them for me last time, and she said they were only for special occasions."

"Their anniversary is special," I pointed out, sensing that it was more of a pissing match than anything. Was Ian jealous of my relationship with Lex? Was he finally seeing that we weren't fighting? Oh no!

"Tamales or I can't go inside. Sorry, Gabs!"

I rolled my eyes. "Lex, stop being a child. I already told her to make them."

"What?" Ian pulled up in front of their house. "For Lex? You called in a food-related favor . . . for Lex?"

"It's because Lex is awesome," Lex said, his huge trademark smirk firmly in place. "Come on, Ian, I tell you every day how awesome I am, now someone finally recognizes it and you're angry?"

Ian slammed his door and glared at him. "You're pissing me off more than usual."

"You always say that when I'm on my best behavior. It's confusing."

"That's actually true," I agreed.

"Stop!" Ian held out his hands between us. "What the hell is this? You said you had a freaking peace treaty, but to be honest it's scaring the shit out of me! Stop . . . smiling at each other!"

"We aren't!" I said defensively.

"She's still, er . . . stupid," Lex said lamely while I tried not to groan out loud and give him a what-the-hell look.

"And Lex is an ass, he's always an ass."

"I really am." Lex nodded. "She told me so this morning."

When he caught me in the hallway and gripped my ass, but not the point!

"Hell," Lex said as he fell into step behind us, always the third wheel. How had I never noticed that before? "She's screamed my name more in the past three weeks than . . . well, ever."

I told my cheeks not to heat.

Thankfully, my mom was already at the door, throwing it open and jumping out to pull Ian in for a hug. "Oh, *mijo*! You've grown!"

Ian hugged her back. She'd always been like a mom to him, the only mom he really knew. "Ha-ha, you said that last time!"

She pulled back and pinched his cheek. "It was true then too, my handsome boy. Where's Blake?"

Ian hung his head. "Stupid volleyball game."

"Oh." My mom's long black hair was pulled back in a braid. She tossed it over her shoulder and held open the door. "You need food. Food will make you feel better."

Ian trotted off in the direction of the kitchen, leaving Lex and me on the porch.

My mom held up her hand, stopping both of us. "What's going on here?"

Eyes wide, Lex stared at my mom, then at me. "Uhhhh . . ."

"Gabrielle Francesca Sava!"

I hid behind Lex.

"Coward!" he hissed, trying to get me off him.

"You." She thrust a finger at Lex. "You have been . . ." She leaned in and sniffed the air above us.

"Mom!" I wailed.

"You . . ." My mom's eyes narrowed. "You have been with my daughter."

Lex gulped. I felt it. Was he trembling? "Yes, ma'am, but nobody knows . . . and we haven't told Ian yet. I will tell him. But your daughter asked for time. I care about her. A lot. And I care about him too. I want to do this right, so please don't say anything until we're ready."

She leaned back and smiled. "I'm happy you are doing the right thing by both Gabi and Ian. My lips are sealed. Now run along into the kitchen, young man, and find your tamales."

Lex bolted away from me before I could stop him, leaving my mom and me staring at each other on the porch.

"Gabrielle." She sighed, then opened her arms. "You don't just 'care about' him, do you?"

I hadn't realized how much I was holding in until I was able to sag against her. Tears flowed freely. "I really, really like him. I've liked him since—"

"Oh, mija. I still remember when you stormed into the house four years ago yelling about him. I know." She patted my head a few more times, then stopped. "Ian. He will not like this."

I stiffened up again. "I know, Mom."

"Okay, you'll need to be careful." She pulled away from me. "Is Lex worth losing your best friend?"

I didn't answer.

How could I?

It wasn't a fair situation. Part of me was so angry that Ian had that much power over my relationships, yet another part knew it made total sense. He was, in all essence, my brother. Nobody would be good enough, and he had firsthand knowledge of how much of a whore Lex had always been.

"Mija." My mom laughed. "Don't hurt yourself, all will be resolved. Go eat."

The answer to everything. A full stomach.

I rubbed mine as I made my way into the kitchen.

"Mom?" Food was everywhere. How were they able to afford it? All the money I earned was going toward groceries, but this was too much. I didn't make enough to line the tables with hot, steaming Mexican food.

"Oh, Gabi . . ." My mom shrugged. "It was the most wonderful thing. Ian offered to do the grocery shopping yesterday. I told him I was going to go by myself, but he wanted this to be his gift to us for our anniversary!"

My eyes filled with tears.

Damn, Ian! He had to go and do something nice and make me remember yet again why I loved him so much—why he was like a brother to me.

Why I couldn't lose him. No matter what.

Chapter Forty

Lex

"I've never met a tamale I wouldn't devour." I grabbed a fourth helping, then balanced a Corona in my other hand as I joined Gabi's dad, Earl, in the living room.

"You sleeping with my daughter?" he asked without looking up.

Luckily, I had no food or drink in my mouth, though choking to death sounded a hell of a lot better than having that conversation. "Sir, I don't know what Gabi has told you, but—"

"My wife. She has been suspecting for a while, and she says today she sees proof in how you stare at Gabi."

I set down my beer and stared down at the floor, then back up at him. He had a dark salt-and-pepper mustache that curled around his lips. His white hair was cut close to his head and his stature was bulky, well fed. "Sir, I like your daughter, but—"

"Marie told me." He motioned for me to lean closer. "I figure I don't have to kill you; Ian will do the job for me. That way I don't have to get my hands dirty."

"Throwing your own son under the bus?"

"He'll do better in prison."

"He's prettier, he'd get wrecked. Whereas you're old, senile." I smirked while her dad waved me off with a chuckle. At least I'd broken the awkwardness. "I give him two days, tops."

"Boy wouldn't last twenty-four hours."

"Maybe we should just toss Ian in, take bets on his life?"

"Toss me in where?" Ian walked in, his eyes darting between us.

"Prison," we said in unison.

"Who'd I kill?"

"Nobody." Earl stared me down. "Yet."

"You know"—I stood and patted my stomach—"I'm just gonna go find the restroom."

I darted out of the living room and nearly collided with Gabs in my desperate escape.

"Whoa!" She tilted her head up at me. "Why are your eyes so big?"

"Honest moment, Gabs, was your dad ever involved with the Mexican mafia?"

"My dad voted for gun control." Her cute little forehead furrowed.

"Yeah, he may be whistling another tune now." I sidestepped her. "I had to make a quick escape. All the talk of prison and bets got me nervous."

"Prison?" She laughed. "He threatened prison?"

"No." I turned and smiled. "It was more along the lines of killing. Death. I'm sure dismemberment."

She covered her mouth with her hands and choked out a strangled laugh.

"Oh, you think this is funny?"

She nodded her head while I charged her and carried her down the hall. "Where's your room?"

"First one on the right!" she squealed. I deposited her on her feet in her childhood bedroom.

"Gabs . . ." I tsked. "Easy access? First floor? I could have just waltzed in here without a ladder? Man, I wish I would have stayed in Bellevue and gone to high school with you. Things would have been so much easier."

"Scaled a lot of houses, did you?" She leaned against the doorframe, her smile wide, eyes happy. God, I just loved seeing her like that.

"You have no idea." I fell back onto her bed and let out a loud exhale. "I have the slivers to prove it. Scaling walls isn't for the weak, Gabs."

"Good to know." Waves of her laughter hit me square in the chest as she moved casually to the bed. Once she sat down, I moved to the side and hovered over her, needing to touch her lips so desperately that I'd completely forgotten the door was open.

"Gabi." Her mother cleared her throat from the door. "A minute?"

I jerked away from Gabi as if we'd just gotten caught having sex, while her mother's lips twitched in amusement. At least I had one fan.

I refused to count their dog, since it sniffed my ass and walked away as if I was a lesser human.

"Be right back." Gabi tugged her T-shirt down over her thin frame and on wobbly legs made her way to the door. Too cute. It did something to me, something . . . powerful, to know I affected her that way.

I stood in the room for a few minutes, then realized I really did need to use the restroom. With a sigh, I walked out and blindly made my way down the hall, hoping I'd discover a bathroom.

Two more doors on the right, and I found what I was looking for.

Five minutes later I was just getting ready to go back to her room when I heard hushed whispers.

"Mom, I love you guys! Let me help!"

"It is too much, mija," Gabi's mother said softly. "You can't keep giving us all of your money. You are not eating. You're skin and bones! You even bring us food! Do we look like we need food?"

"Yes!" Gabi raised her voice. "You do! You have to take care of Dad, and I know you're both tired, and it's only until he finds something!"

"Gabi, he will find something, but in the meantime, you need to take care of yourself. It's not that we don't appreciate it. We do. We appreciate that you would sacrifice so much for us, but I'm worried about you." Her mother sighed heavily. "Your father did find a small job working on the construction of the new Victoria's Secret at the mall. The pay isn't great, but he'll be fine."

"Construction?" Gabi repeated. "Mom, he's so much better than that!"

"I know. But we do what we must. Now, take back your envelope full of money and fill your pantry with food and buy yourself a new dress."

"But—"

"Mija." Her voice was more stern this time. "Do as I say or I'm going to tell Ian."

All talking stopped, and then, "I love you, Mom."

"You too, mija."

I quickly backed up a few steps and then ran down the hall so I wouldn't get caught.

My head throbbed with sudden realization. The food I'd been giving her, she was giving to her parents.

The money she'd been earning at the club.

The money she was making from Wingmen.

All going to her parents.

"Hey." Ian slapped me on the back. "You look like you're about to be sick."

"Do I?" My voice sounded hollow. Why the hell was I so pissed? I should feel sorry for her, right? I should feel bad, pull her in for a hug, tell her I'd help in any way I could.

But it wasn't that.

It felt intense.

I felt like I'd been betrayed.

Like she'd . . . lied to me.

I had her body.

Did I have anything else?

Because I realized, in that moment, I wasn't happy with just parts of her. I wanted every last piece.

And she'd purposefully withheld parts of herself. Was that life's final cruel trick? I finally settle down with someone—find the person I care about the most in the world—only to discover that she's been sharing the surface level of her heart and refusing to let me hold the rest.

It sucked.

It hurt.

More than it should.

But I wasn't that guy, the one that got pissed and bailed. I deserved answers and I'd demand them—before I had a freaking nervous breakdown.

Chapter Forty-One

Gabi

I wiped the tears from my cheeks and then splashed more water on my face. It would have to do.

I still looked semi-puffy, but knowing the guys, they'd probably be too focused on eating to notice.

Lex wasn't in my room when I returned. Then again, he probably didn't want to get caught hanging out on my bed where Ian or my dad could find him. It would look too suspicious.

My stomach clenched.

I was keeping secrets from Ian, secrets from Lex, and both sucked. I felt like I was ready to burst from it all.

"Hey." Ian pulled me in for a hug once I was back in the living room. "You okay?"

Now he notices? Whoa. Where had that come from? I was ready to lash out at my best friend. For what reason? I took a step back from him.

He'd been so preoccupied lately.

And I'd purposefully pulled away because of Lex.

"Gabs?" Lex rounded the corner. "Can I talk to you for a minute?"

"Have you removed all pointy objects from the kitchen?" Ian teased.

Lex's jaw ticked. "Laundry room. Safer there."

He didn't look amused.

I tried to read his expression, but he turned around and started walking away before I could do more than stare after him.

"Better go see what he needs. Just try not to kill him." Ian pushed me after Lex.

The laundry room was small. There was only space enough for a washer and dryer and a small sink. It smelled like Tide.

"You lied." Lex's eyes met mine, nailing me to the wall, making it impossible to breathe, to move. He seemed hurt and sad. "You lied to me."

I racked my brain for anything I could have lied about. I would never hurt him, and I had no secrets except—

"Your parents." He clarified.

"No." I shook my head, desperate to find my voice. "No, you don't understand, I would never lie to you."

"But," Lex sighed. "It feels like a lie. Like betrayal, Gabs. It sure as hell equals a pretty large omission on your part. First about the food, next about your parents. Damn it, Gabs. Why didn't you tell me?"

"I was too embarrassed, and you guys had already done so much for me!" I clenched my fists. "And I didn't want help! I had it under control!"

"Under control?" Lex roared back. "Under control?"

"Yes!"

"You mean when you were pressured every day to dance at the club? Or how about when you almost got raped in the freaking parking lot! Was that having things under control?"

"I didn't ask you to save me!" I shouted.

"You didn't have to!" He matched my tone as he charged toward me. "Because I always will!" His voice laced with hurt. "Because that's what friends do, Gabs! They save each other. They hold your head above water when you're drowning. They give you the life vest and promise you everything will be okay! Are we at least that, Gabs?"

Tears clouded my vision. "You said we were never friends."

"Gabs—" Lex's voice cracked. "We're so much more and you know it."

I nodded, unable to trust my voice.

"I don't want this if I can't have all of you."

"What?" I jerked my head up. "What do you mean?"

"This." He pointed between us. "I need you to be all in . . . I need all of you, Gabs. Not just the parts you think I want."

I was terrified by the words coming out of his mouth, because I knew what they meant for me, for him. This wasn't just a fling, it wasn't just a onetime thing, a playbook training exercise.

It was me and Lex.

I could only stare at him. Was he sure he wanted this? "But—"

"I want the sickness." Lex's lips twitched as a heartbreaking smile flashed across his face, making me dizzy. "I want to bring you soup when you don't feel well. I want to give you pot scones."

I burst out laughing as tears cascaded down my face.

"I want your body, Gabs. Believe me, it's probably unhealthy the number of times I think of you naked. But, Gabs, I need this too." He pressed his hand against my chest. "I want it all. Or I'm out."

"You ask a lot for a villain."

"Hey, yesterday I was a hero. Can't I be both?"

"You already are," I whispered.

"Gabi." Lex pulled me into his arms. "I love you."

My heart dropped to my knees, then came flying back up into my chest, taking off in crazy cadence as words got caught in my throat. Finally, I found my voice. "I love you too."

Giddiness swept through me as my stomach erupted with butterflies, as if I'd been keeping this giant secret, maybe from myself and clearly from Lex and Ian. I loved him. I'd loved him a long time. It felt so good saying it out loud, as if the pieces I was holding so close to my chest finally broke free and found their home.

In his arms.

His lips twisted into a half-smile. "Of course you do. I'm awesome."

"You ruined our moment." I giggled as he picked me up into his arms and set me on the washing machine.

"Guess I'll have to create another one." He nipped my lips once, twice, then kissed me hard across the mouth. His tongue teased my lower lip until I whimpered in frustration.

His hands gripped my butt as he slid me closer to his body. "You're mine, Gabi. Always have been. Always will be."

"Yes," I agreed, rocking into him as he rained kisses down my neck. "Yes."

"What the HELL is this!" Ian's voice boomed from the door.

Lex's mouth froze on mine.

Our eyes locked.

And for the first time in my life, I saw legitimate fear in Lex's eyes as he slowly turned his head toward Ian. "Man, listen—"

"Listen!" Ian repeated. "You want me to listen?"

In a blur of yelling and obscenities, Ian was on top of Lex, punching the crap out of him while Lex took it.

"Ian, stop it!" I wailed. "Stop!"

"You bastard! I warned you!" Another punch to the jaw, while Lex still refused to defend himself. "You promised!"

"Ian, stop!" I tried prying him free, but he shook me off.

Blood poured from Lex's nose and maybe from his mouth—it was impossible to tell.

Crack, thump. Ian struck with a one-two motion. Bruises were already forming on Lex's cheeks, and a cut above his right eye smeared a trail of blood down his temple. *Crack.* Another hit sprayed blood across the top of the dryer.

My screams and pleas didn't faze him as my best friend kept hitting Lex until I was convinced the man who'd finally declared his love was going to pass out from blood loss.

Finally, my dad came charging in and pulled Ian free from a battered Lex.

I ran to Lex's side, tears blurring my vision. "Are you okay?"

"Can't feel my face," Lex muttered through a swollen bottom lip. "Isn't that a song?"

"We're done!" Ian screamed. "You hear me? We. Are. Done!"

He stalked out of the room.

The front door slammed.

And Lex Luthor, super villain, my hero, boyfriend, and the strongest guy I'd ever known, crumpled into my arms and didn't let go.

Since Ian had driven us, my mom had to drop us back off at the house. We could only hope Ian hadn't burned it down by then.

Lex couldn't see out of one eye, and his face was turning more purple by the minute. One cheek was so swollen I worried it was broken. Surely some of those cracks had been bones shattering. He hadn't said a word to me since the fight.

It was my fault.

I was the one who had pressured him to wait.

And now his face was broken. And quite possibly his heart.

I kept the tears in—a huge effort on my part, since it felt like someone had just died in my family and I hadn't been given enough time to grieve.

"Mija," my mom said from the front seat. "Just give Ian some time."

"Yeah," I croaked. "I will."

"And Lex." She reached back one of her hands. He squeezed it. "Take care of my girl."

"Always." He answered quickly, though his words were thick and a little slurred.

Once she drove off, we both stared at the house.

Unsure of what would greet us once we made it inside.

Lex reached for my hand just as I reached for his.

"He's not going to get over this." Tears clouded my vision as I looked up at Lex. "Is he?"

Lex's eyes were sad as he glanced down at me, not answering but choosing to kiss the top of my head instead.

We walked hand in hand into the house.

From the deathly silence inside, it was clear no one was home. The house was completely empty, but Ian's car was there.

A note sat on the counter beneath the walnut knife block. At least all the knives rested in their slots.

"*Went to Yakima. Airport taxi picked me up. Don't call*," I read, each word sounding like an explosion in the hushed kitchen.

"Shit." Lex wiped his face. "Isn't his sister in Yakima?"

I nodded dumbly. "They don't really get along anymore. The last time he was there was—"

"After Ian got injured," Lex finished.

I stared at the counter, at the note. "What do we do?"

"Well . . ." Lex wrapped an arm around me. "I think the only option we have is to give him space and, of course, take a lot of ibuprofen. Be honest, has the swelling gone down?"

I winced and then scrunched up my nose.

"Good thing I wasn't wearing my glasses."

"Yeah." I wrapped my arms around Lex's neck. "I'm sad, Lex."

He sighed, his forehead touching mine. "Me too."

"It's my fault," we said in unison.

"No way!" I smacked his chest. "I'm the one who wanted to wait."

"Right, but I'm the one who, in a moment of pure insanity, decided I was going to go after the girl that got away . . . even though I knew I could lose my best friend in the process."

"I'm not worth this," I admitted, shaking my head. "I'm not worth your friendship."

"And you think I'm worth you losing a family member?" Lex fired back. "Ian's a hothead. You know how he gets. Let's just wait it out."

"I think it would help if he knew . . ."

"Knew?"

"That I love you." I shrugged.

Lex's face fell as he pulled me into his arms. His mouth caressed mine with a soft kiss. "And the damsel fell for the villain. Write that, Disney."

I rolled my eyes, then finished it off with a yawn.

"Bed." Lex smacked me on the butt and stepped back. "Let's go."

Was he serious? He couldn't be serious. "Lex, as much as I love you, I can't have sex with you right now. I don't think I have the focus to pay attention to the manual."

"Manual," Lex said gruffly. "When have I ever made you use the manual?"

"True." What I needed was our banter, our joking. I needed to know that even after everything, we were still us, Lex and Gabi.

"And what type of guy sleeps with his girlfriend after she's been sobbing her eyes out over losing her best friend? Am I that bad of a person?"

"Do you really want me to answer that?" I teased, turning my back so he wouldn't see the fresh tears forming. "You're Lex." I shivered as he wrapped his arms around me from behind. "The world could come crashing down around you, and if I flashed boob—"

"Shh." Lex nipped my neck. "My sensitive ears send bad signals to my body when I hear trigger words."

"Any other words I should know about?"

"Gabi, don't make me talk dirty."

I squirmed as he kept kissing my neck and then untangled me from his arms. I slowly led him up the stairs and over to his bed. I lay down, waiting for him to follow.

Lex watched me, a playful smile crossing his features as he pulled off my shoes, pants, and shirt, then tucked me in, drawing the covers all the way up to my chin.

When he didn't join me, I frowned. "Where are you going?"

He sighed and pointed to his computer. "Crime doesn't fight itself, Sunshine."

I fell asleep with a smile on my face.

Even though my heart hurt.

Chapter Forty-Two

Lex

Ian finally showed up three days later. I had spent most of the evening finishing the new coding and then gone downstairs to hook up the coffee machine when my steps faltered.

Ian was sitting at the breakfast bar, reading the freaking newspaper and drinking coffee as if he hadn't just basically kicked both Gabi and me out of his life.

"Ian," I mumbled as I walked over to the coffeepot and poured a generous amount in my favorite Yoda mug.

"How long?" he said from behind the newspaper. I couldn't see his face, didn't need to see it to know he was pissed. "How long have you been sleeping with her?"

I was running on three hours of sleep.

Not the conversation I wanted to have, especially before my first sip of coffee.

"Does it really matter, Ian?"

"Yes." He slammed the newspaper down onto the table. "It matters. How. Long."

I did the mental calculations. "A month."

"A month!" he roared, jumping to his feet.

I calmly set down my mug. "Ian, I've had a thing for her since freshman year."

Holy shit, did he just stop breathing?

Hell. I killed my best friend.

Ian's left eye started a slow tick while I backed away to put space between us just in case he decided to slam me against the oven.

"Four years," he repeated. "So, what? You've been practicing with all those women since then?" Voice raised, he covered his face with his hands. "Lex, what the hell do you expect me to do with this?"

"Not kill me, for starters," I grumbled. "I'd like to live to have children someday."

Not the right thing to say, not at all.

"SHE'S PREGNANT?"

Damn me to hell. "No, you bastard, she's not pregnant." Though I'd be lying if I said the idea didn't make my heart flip a bit. Any child of ours would be . . . a complete and total hellion.

"Stop smiling," Ian barked.

I was smiling?

"Lex, you've stuffed your dick into some pretty bad situations. And now you're telling me you like my sister? You've been keeping it from me, and what's worse, you're inevitably going to break her heart. And you expect me to just stand by and do nothing? She's always been off-limits for this very reason! You wouldn't know commitment if it bit you in the ass!"

"Careful, kettle," I warned as anger tore through me. "You do realize that two months ago you were screwing anything that looked at you cross-eyed, right?"

"That's different!" Ian said defensively.

"How?"

"Blake wasn't your sister!"

"And if she were?"

He opened his mouth and closed it.

"Would it have stopped you?"

Again, silence. And he wasn't quite meeting my gaze.

We were at an impasse. I wasn't going to back down, and he refused to give me an inch or any slight acknowledgment that I could be right.

Footsteps sounded behind me and then Gabi appeared on my right, and her hand gripped mine. It was hard as hell not to give Ian a smug smirk followed by the finger. Hey, I never said I was completely mature!

It would push him over the edge he was oh so ready to push me off.

"Ian." Gabi's voice was hoarse. In an instant she released my hand and jumped into his arms. He held her tight.

And I watched.

Like I'd always done when they had a moment, but this time it was different. Before, it was like watching from the outside.

Now? Even though she was in his arms . . .

She was mine.

I felt her even when she was a few feet away.

I knew her taste.

Her smell.

What made her laugh.

What made her cry.

And I wasn't ever going to let her go, no matter what Ian might think. She was mine.

When he dropped her back to her feet and kissed her forehead, his gaze darted between the two of us as Gabi made her way into my arms.

"But—" He shook his head. "You hate each other."

"We still do," Gabi piped up. "Like last night, when he was working on your computer program . . . You know the one, right? The one you asked him to fix? He's been up three nights straight, only going to sleep after I crumbled melatonin in his coffee."

"Hey!" I barked. "I knew something was wrong with my vision!"

"You're fine." Gabi ignored me. "See? I still drug him, he still yells at me, and when I eat a donut, I feel his judgmental eyes."

I choked out a laugh. "Bullshit! I just wanted the donut, and you promised to share!"

"See?" Gabi spread her arms wide. "Still very dysfunctional. But it works for us."

"Damn right it works." I tugged her harder against me, swearing to never let go.

"Okay." Ian sighed and leaned back against the counter. "So help me God, if you break her heart, I will make your death look like an accident, Lex."

"Still friends?" I asked.

"That depends." Ian crossed his arms. "Do you love her?"

"Of course I do," I said quickly. "I wouldn't put our friendship through this if I didn't."

Ian looked ready to swallow his tongue. "I . . . thought that would be harder to get out of you."

"He told me he loved me right before you beat the crap out of him at my parents' house," Gabi said sweetly.

"Talk about a mood killer." I rubbed my still-sore jaw.

"You were . . ." Ian swallowed. "You were . . . fondling!"

"I don't even know what that means." I burst out laughing. "Really, man? Fondling is what you do in junior high when you don't know if you're touching a girl's breasts or her stomach."

Ian glared.

"No fondling." I held up my hands.

"Ian." Gabi stepped away from me. "Lex found out already, but I thought I'd tell you, um, about my parents—"

"I took care of it." Ian dismissed her with a quick shake of his head.

"What exactly did you do?"

Ian shrugged. "It wasn't me. It was my sister. I went to visit her in hell, and she talked some sense into me, gave me an idea, and I hauled ass back to Seattle to see if it would work."

"To see if what would work?" I asked, confused.

"We're getting too big. Gabi's not going to want to make out with random clients, and we can't work out of the house anymore. We're almost ready to graduate. It only made sense."

"What only made sense?" I had a bad feeling.

Ian smirked. "Ready for your field trip?"

CHAPTER FORTY-THREE

GABI

Ian told us both to hurry, which left me with no choice but to bust out the Uggs and hope that Lex and I didn't have a repeat of the fight of 2014 where he nearly set them on fire.

The minute I stepped out of my room, Lex stepped out of his.

A slow smirk spread across his face as he took in my attire. "Yoga pants, Uggs, and a sweatshirt. You pledging today or what?"

"Very funny." I shoved past him; he shoved me back. "Lex, I say this in the nicest way possible, but push me again and I'm literally putting my foot down so you trip and break your two front teeth."

"I've got teeth of steel."

"I wonder if that's why my mouth hurts. Learn to kiss." I winked and then took off running as he chased me down the hall.

"You can run! But you're wearing Uggs . . . They slow you down!"

Ian was waiting at the door as Lex and I stuttered to a stop, nearly stumbling over each other. Clearly, Lex was in a mood because he took that opportunity to pinch my butt.

"Stop it!" I smacked him in the chest. "I will hurt you!" I turned back to Ian.

He looked confused. "So the fighting . . ." He shook his head. "It's . . . still a thing?"

"Always." Lex shook his head. "Also, man, can you please address her shoe situation? She looks homeless."

"I am homeless!" I shouted.

"No, you live here." Ian smiled. "Across the hall from your boyfriend."

I beamed. I couldn't help it.

Ian rolled his eyes. "Okay, stop looking so happy."

We stepped outside together.

"A limo?" Lex frowned. "Wait, has that been here the whole time?"

Ian burst out laughing. "I honestly thought it would take hours to get you to admit you loved her. *Hours!* And then you go and handle it all like a man, ruining everything. You're supposed to be fighting your feelings, not planning your wedding! I thought you'd either bail or finally admit that you loved her, not threaten me." Ian rolled his eyes. "Don't get me wrong, I'm still mad as hell, but . . . if it's a match, it's a match, right?"

"Right." Lex breathed out a heavy sigh as his hand found mine. "Now, why is there a limo? You getting hitched?"

Ian shrugged. "Not now. Besides, I have news about Gabs's dad."

The driver opened the door. Blake was already sitting in the limo. I appreciated the fact that as a total tomboy she was wearing basically the same thing I was, minus the Uggs. Though she had on the ugliest rubber flip-flops I'd ever seen. Apparently Ian always hid them, but she found them every time. He'd finally given up.

"Hey!" Blake handed me a glass of champagne. It felt good to see her. During volleyball season it seemed like we were just passing ships. "That didn't take long."

"Yeah, well . . ." I scooted in next to her and drank from my glass. "Apparently Ian thought he was going to have to convince Lex of his feelings."

"But"—Lex barreled into the car and took a seat next to me—"I'm a fast learner, genius and all that, so I already knew I loved her."

Ian jumped in and slammed the door. "You guys ready?"

"Ready for what? And what does this have to do with my dad?" I asked.

"Lex and I will be in charge of hiring."

"Hiring?" Lex's eyebrows shot up. "Okay, what exactly are we hiring for?"

Ian grinned. "You'll see."

We drove a few miles until we hit downtown Seattle. We stopped near the Amazon campus and walked a block until we came face-to-face with a giant black skyscraper.

A sign in front said, "Office space available." And across the sign it said, "Sold."

"Ian?" Lex said. "Help me out."

"Facebook offered ten." Ian sighed. "Match.com offered twelve."

"For the building?" I guessed.

Ian turned. "Nope. For Wingmen Inc."

"Really?" Lex's eyes narrowed. "And as partner you didn't tell me?"

"Didn't have to." Ian sobered. "Hacking's your drug. Working for the man is the last thing you want for your life, especially since you have a good thing going. Microsoft can suck my ass."

They high-fived.

Men.

"So we're moving the business into this office?" I asked. "Isn't that really expensive?"

Both Lex and Ian grinned.

"What? What am I missing?"

"Sunshine . . ." Lex grabbed my hand. "Our app alone is worth more than eight million dollars, not including Wingmen Inc. and our software, if we expand."

"Eight," I repeated, "million?"

"We'll need to hire a team. Gabi's dad doesn't take shit from anyone." Ian looked between us. "And since Lex is still living, they clearly get along. I already texted him his starting salary and signing bonus." Ian swallowed. "Your mom called five minutes later, yelling in Spanish, and then she cried."

Tears filled my eyes. "Sounds like Mom."

"So . . ." Ian gripped Blake's hand, then brought it to his lips to kiss her knuckles. "What do you girls say? Work for us when you graduate?"

We both laughed.

"What?" Ian frowned.

"Can my signing bonus be Pirate's Booty?" I asked.

"Oooo, that's a good idea!" Blake agreed with an evil chuckle.

Ian rolled his eyes. "You'll have to take that up with HR."

"Damn HR, damn yellow tape!" I argued with a laugh while Lex pulled me in for a hug. "What do you think?"

"Me?" Lex's mouth found mine. "I think I want to buy you a car that can go more than one mile without dying. I think I want to be by your side until you kick me to the curb for being clingy. I've loved you for a long time . . . I'll continue to love you even longer."

My eyes filled with tears as Blake sighed heavily next to me.

But then fighting broke out as Blake smacked Ian. "You need to learn to say lines like that!"

"I'm romantic!" Ian argued. "Last week I bought you flowers!"

"I got stung by a bee in said flowers!"

"You scared it!"

Lex smiled against my mouth. "Make love and war?"

"Always more interesting that way."

"Let's go in." Ian smiled, leading us through the glass double doors. He snatched a few guest passes from the security booth in the lobby, and then we were riding the elevator.

To their offices.

"I can't believe you did it," Lex muttered. "I mean I can, but I can't."

"Yeah, well." Ian shared a look with all of us. "You guys can thank the sister . . . She's the one who said I needed to get my head out of my ass and stop feeling sorry for myself and be excited about the fact that my best friends had feelings for each other. It really does make the holidays so much easier."

I rolled my eyes. Typical Ian.

Blake looped her arm through his and laughed as he kissed her on the nose. She was super tall so it looked cute, whereas if Lex tried to kiss my nose I'd have to either be on the countertop or in his arms.

Blake and Ian weren't the perfect match either, but together, they made sense. Maybe not on paper, but in real life, there was no girl better suited for him.

And Lex? Well, Lex was the same way.

The elevators opened on the twelfth floor. A short hallway led into a large glass-encased lobby surrounded by lines of offices and then a set of cubicles in the middle.

"Wow." Lex squeezed my hand, then let go and started walking around. "It's perfect."

"Both corner offices are ours for the taking," Ian called out as Lex and I hurried down the hall toward the first corner office.

A leather couch was already inside, along with a random chair and a piece of paper on the floor.

"What do you think?" Lex asked without looking back at me.

"I think"—I nodded toward the couch—"that the brown couch has seen better days, but you may want to keep it."

"What?" Lex turned around. "Why?"

"Memories." I smirked, grabbing his hand and pulling him toward the couch, only stopping so that I could push him onto his back and straddle him. "It's the very first couch in your very first office . . . the very first couch you'll have sex on during the workday!"

"Gasp." Lex laughed. "I must be a complete and total man slut."

"Oh, you are. All the ladies think so, even that really old personal secretary you hired."

"I'm lost."

"Repeat after me: all of my secretaries will be old grandmas with charming smiles and ten grandchildren."

Lex burst out laughing, then tugged my mouth against his in a searing kiss before letting me go. "Sunshine, I could have Victoria's Secret supermodels working for me; hell, I'm pretty sure I was with one when—"

I glared.

"The point"—he kissed me again, smiling—"is they wouldn't be you. And it's always been you."

"Promise?" My voice was husky as I trailed tiny kisses down his neck.

"Yup, now move a little to the left. You know what the manual says. I have an equal opportunity neck; I need love on both sides, you know?"

I smacked him.

He shook his head. "Page five specifically states that if you slap me during foreplay, at least one of five dirty words must follow."

"I'm not calling your penis 'womb raider.'"

"Killjoy."

"I can't believe you actually gave a manual to girls before bed."

Lex tickled my sides and flipped me onto my back so that he was hovering over me. His gorgeous smile was illuminated by the light coming in from the windows behind him. "If you're not gonna do it right, why waste my time?"

"Hopeless," I fired back. "Good thing I never needed the manual."

"Nope." Lex shrugged. "Because you were always right. The perfect match."

"Aw," Ian said from the door. "You guys gonna break into songs from Disney? Because if you are, we can wait. Blake totally digs musicals."

"Let them have their moment!" Blake slugged Ian in the stomach.

He coughed out a curse and glared. "Must you be an athlete?"

"I've been lifting," she said proudly.

"No shit." He coughed again. "Lay off the roids."

She raised her arm again.

"Kidding! Geez!" He was still twice her size, but she was a strong girl, which Ian needed. "Alright, you lovebirds ready to go?"

"Nope." Lex tugged my body tighter against his. "Why talk when we can make out? Don't you have an office to go to?"

Ian frowned. "Yeah, but it's daylight."

We all fell silent.

"Right." Ian chuckled. "Right, Blake." He led her away from the office. "Have I ever told you that very vivid fantasy I had about a really sexy volleyball player naked on my desk?"

"You guys have serious problems." I laughed against Lex's mouth as he kissed me deeper, harder, his hands already tugging away my leggings, my Ugg boots trapping them in place.

"See!" Lex pointed. "The devil makes those boots!"

I rolled my eyes. "Lex, I'll take them off . . . but first . . . tell me something."

"Anything."

"In the playbook, the last page, it says 'And they lived . . .' What's that supposed to mean?"

"Sunshine, it means that the couple has to finish the story. They decide the ending."

"And ours?"

"Happily." He kissed the side of my mouth. "Ever." He kissed both eyelids. "After." He kissed my nose. "Now take off those damn boots."

Epilogue

Lex

10 months later

"Hot damn, I'd love to tap that," I said aloud as Gabi weaved her way through the large crowd. She was wearing a tight red dress and heels that went on for miles, and I was already envisioning her naked—wearing the heels, of course—in my bed. I gave her a nod of approval as she smiled at a board member and then finally stopped in front of me.

"Stop flirting with Stan," I said, huskiness lacing my voice.

"Stan golfs with my dad. He's seventy. He's on the board of directors because his wife says he gets depressed sitting in his big house."

"How hard for Stan, living in a mansion."

"Look who's talking," Gabi teased, pulling her bottom lip into her mouth, her white teeth biting down on the red lipstick.

"Damn it, don't look at me like that if you want me to behave."

"When have you ever behaved?"

She knew me so well.

"It's Christmas, you know," Gabi pointed out. "I may have a little . . . surprise for you back at the house."

"Aw, Sunshine, did you bake?"

She slugged me in the shoulder. "No, Mr. Vice President."

"I love it when you talk dirty. Last night when you called me 'sir' in bed, I nearly orga—"

"Ian!" Gabi choked out, interrupting me. "How's . . . life?"

He frowned. "You been drinking?"

"Loads," I answered for her, then wrapped my arm around her shoulders. "I better get the fiancée home. You know . . . how she . . . tires."

Gabi glared daggers at me. I ignored her. As per usual.

Ian shook his head. "I don't even want to know whatever the hell little sex play you guys have got going on right now. Have you seen Blake?"

"Eating." Gabi laughed. "She's been doing nothing but eating since she got here."

"She's eating for two!" Ian said defensively as Blake made her way over to us. At six months pregnant, she looked more rock star than usual. Almost like pregnancy was her superpower. Her skin was gorgeous, and her smile was electric. Ian did good with Blake.

"Sorry." Blake smiled sheepishly. "It's just, they have these amazing little bacon-wrapped pickles."

I made a gagging noise.

"You just wait!" She laughed, pointing her finger at Gabi.

I stiffened while Ian paled and shot me an accusing glare.

"Chill." Gabi rolled her eyes. "I'm not pregnant. Some of us still have a few credits left!"

Gabi's dad made his way toward our little group. "Ian, Lex, it's time."

I kissed Gabi on the head for good luck and followed Ian as we made our way to the stage.

The applause was deafening as we took front and center. My eyes locked on Gabi as I mouthed, "I love you."

Tears filled her eyes as she mouthed it back.

"It's been a great year," Ian started. "We've tripled our clientele and started selling the app overseas."

More cheering.

"Thanks to Lex, our resident tech guru, The Villain Bracelet 1.0 sold to Apple for fifty million dollars." I beamed. It was hard not to. After I'd won over Gabi, it hit me: why not have a type of bat signal that girls could send, whenever they were in bad situations, to request help? The bracelet had different settings for blind dates, bad dates, scary situations, walking home by themselves. Whenever a girl was doing any of those things, she could change the settings and press a simple alert if she was in trouble. It notified the police of her location and sent a text to her closest friend or family member. "Lex? A few words."

I stepped forward, my eyes gazing over the large crowd that had gathered for our celebration.

Years ago I would have lived for this type of attention and recognition.

But in that moment, all I cared about was sharing it with Gabi.

"I'm so proud to share this moment with my best friend and fiancée." She was both. "She's my everything. My partner in crime, my lover, the person I turn to for both business . . ." I barely kept myself from saying "pleasure" out loud—especially with her father looking at me from across the room. "I guess what I'm trying to say is: she's my home, my family, my world, and I'm so happy that she said yes."

People clapped, but I had eyes for her, only her.

Funny how we'd started out as enemies.

Turned into lovers.

Ended as best friends. And so much more.

"Thank you . . . and Ian?" I continued, "We did good, man. We did good."

Ian and I shook hands while cameras went off, and I went in search of Gabi. When I couldn't find her in the crowd I panicked, until something pinched my ass.

I turned and glared.

Gabi waved her fingers at me. "Ready to blow this party, Lex Luthor?"

"I'll ready the escape vehicle."

"Oooo . . ." She pulled me in for a kiss. "I love it when you're bad."

"I'm so bad I'll let you eat Pirate's Booty in bed." She shivered. "While I watch." My tongue caressed her outer ear as she burst out laughing.

"So, what's Lex Luthor's weakness? You never told me."

"I think that would be obvious." I shrugged, leading her out the door. "It's sassy-mouthed short girls who wear ugly-as-hell Uggs and shout my name."

"I shout your name a lot."

"I know."

"Lex! Do the dishes!" she yelled.

"Lex!" I joined in with my best falsetto. "Right, there! Oh, that feels so good, a little to the left."

People glanced curiously in our direction.

Gabi smacked me in the stomach. "Does a whore ever change its spots?"

"Let's hope not!" I picked her up, tossed her over my shoulder, and slapped her ass. "Let's go, future Mrs. Luthor."

"Hey!" she squealed. "Does that mean I get my own villain name?"

"We'll talk about it."

"Lex!"

"As in, oh look, I brought it to the table for discussion and the board voted no. Sorry, Sunshine."

"Lex!"

"You can drive the sidecar. And fetch my laundry. And when I'm feeling really generous, I'll let you touch my freeze gun."

"Lex Luthor doesn't have a freeze gun."

I chuckled suggestively. "But he does have a gun. You've felt it."

"You're gross."

"You love me!"

"I do." She giggled. "Clearly I've been corrupted by the Dark Side."

"It's better over here. Trust me."

"I do," she whispered. "I do."

Acknowledgments

I'm so thankful to God for allowing me to follow my dreams every single day . . . All glory and thanks always goes to him first. With that being said, most of these books wouldn't be possible without a huge team of people! Thank you so much to Katherine Tate, Liza Tice, Kristin Van Dyken, and Jill Sava for being a sounding board for much of this book. Melody, as always, you were such a joy to work with from start to finish, and you helped mold this product into something amazing! I love how you push me!

Erica, my agent, superwoman, thank you for believing in me and my writing process and, you know, fighting crime on my behalf. You're awesome.

The team at Skyscape, Courtney and all the publicity, you guys are rock stars. When we talked about the marketing for this concept, I'm pretty sure I went home and jumped up and down in excitement. Thank you so much for believing in me as an author and allowing me to write for you!

Danielle Sanchez and the Inkslinger team . . . thank you for all the work you put into each release!

Bloggers.

Oh man. Bloggers and reviewers. Again, I feel like I need to just start dedicating books to you guys. Thank you for all of your constant support, and thank you for reading my books, seriously. I can't thank you enough.

Rachel's New Rockin Readers, Jill, Becca, AHHH, and all of the many people in that group who make my job so much fun. Thank you for putting up with my craziness!

And Nate, thanks for not judging me when I ask you crazy questions about guys' psyches. I think this is why I LOVE writing from the guy's point of view!

As always you can connect with me on Facebook/Instagram/Twitter! To keep up on my new releases text MAFIA to 66866!

Hugs,

RVD

About the Author

Photo © 2014 Lauren Watson Perry, Perrywinkle Photography

A master of lighthearted love stories, author Rachel Van Dyken has seen her books appear on national bestseller lists including the *New York Times*, the *Wall Street Journal*, and *USA Today*. A devoted lover of Starbucks, Swedish Fish, and The Bachelor, Rachel lives in Idaho with her husband, son, and two boxers. Follow her writing journey at www.rachelvandykenauthor.com.